A Time of Acceptance

Book 3 in the Bovey Tracey Saga

A South Devon Town
During the Commonwealth
1651

Jim Marshall

Front cover image:
Painting of Oliver Cromwell
by Samuel Cooper, 1656

ISBN: 978-1-917129-69-5

*This is for my brother Norman.
Without him, my early life would have been
nigh on impossible. I miss him!*

FOREWORD

This is the third in the series. King Charles I is dead, executed in 1649 by order of the famous signed death warrant – that was to prove so disastrous for some people twelve years later.

Now, we are in 1651. Things remain relatively calm down in South Devon. Being far removed from the seat of power, the inhabitants simply concentrate on matters closest to their hearts – family, food, health.

Matters further north take on a different complexion as Prince Charles (already King Charles II of Scotland) makes one final and rather pathetic bid to stage a comeback.

Religious fanatics make an unwanted appearance, young people settle down. Life for the vast majority simply goes on.

CONTENTS

CHARACTERS
Real people in BOLD

In Bovey Tracey

Bakery	John Ramsey (41), Evelyn (39)
Smithy	Abel Smith (42), Faith (38)
	Simon Smith (19), Imelda (17)
	Jack (1)
Apothecary	James Ramsey (42), Avril (39)
	Nell Dawkins (9)
Smallhold	Gil Ramsey (21), Ella (20)
	Rosie (4), Jamie (2)
Tavern	Dick Allen (40), Sal (36)
Bookshop	Henri Bessant (45), Eloise (41)
	Gaston Bessant (22), Glory (21)
Hedger	Will Fletcher (37), Patience (34)
	May (14), Maud (12)
Church	**James Forbes** (vicar 37)
	Ralph Goodes (churchwarden 31)
	Sam Fewings (sexton 59)

The Parke Estate

Steward	Luke Barton (52), Grace (46)
Bailiff	Peter Cove (43), Laura (41)
	Harry Cove (21), Mary (19)
	Hob Slater (15)
Staff	Sam Garvey (24), Robert Hook (23)
Shepherd	Bernie Wheatcroft (15)

The Brimley Estate

Owner	Lady Violette Charlton (65)
Steward	Luke Farmer (25), Meg (21)
	Hal (13)
Gardeners	Rob Garside (33), Kit Warden (24)

Lustleigh
Reeve   Thomas Axelby (53), Francis (33),
               Lisa (28)

Exeter
Rougemont   Sir Horace Drew (deputy sheriff)
              Captain Lionel Brooke (27)
              Sergeant Paul Larkin (28)

Westminster
Parliament **John Bradshaw, Henry Ireton**
              Richard Ingoldsby
Army   **Oliver Cromwell, Thomas Fairfax**
              Sir George Monck
Agent   Matthew Kent (26)

Royalist volunteers
              Sir Lucien Pellow, Matt Crowley,
              Herbert Grindley, Seth Borthwick.

CHAPTER I

The small town of Bovey Tracey shimmered in the heat. The previous week had seen temperatures slowly rising until the workers in the fields – and there were many of them – took breaks every hour to find the relief of shade against the tall hedgerows. August of the year 1651 was being blessed by one and all as the crops grew and ripened. It had rained during June, sufficient to see the growth burgeoning. All that was needed was a continuation of the good weather until harvest. If that happened, there would be food aplenty to see them through the winter, and that was something that had not happened the previous year.

The first shop on the right above the mill was the apothecary. Its windows and doors were wide open to catch and funnel any breeze that might alleviate the heat within the building. James Ramsey, now in his forty-second year, mopped his brow for the umpteenth time as he strove to concentrate on his weekly 'examination' of his very young apprentice. He was seated at the table in the parlour that was situated immediately behind the shop itself.

In the shop, his wife Avril, also mopped her brow as she sliced a large bunch of mint into shreds, later to be pounded with other ingredients into a paste. She had devised a special tool for this purpose – a crescent-shaped knife with a handle at either end that she rocked backwards and forwards to shred the leaves. It had been made for her by Abel Smith – the town's blacksmith.

The third member of the household was nine years old. Nell Dawkins, adopted when she was four by James and Avril, was the very young apprentice undergoing her weekly 'examination'. Not that she was in the least bit intimidated by this weekly inquisition – she welcomed them as it gave her the opportunity to remind them and herself that she was indeed learning – and learning well.

"A patient comes into the shop and asks for something that will make him sleep as he finds it difficult to get the necessary rest. What would you prescribe?" James posed his penultimate question.

Nell pulled at her lower lip and frowned in concentration.

"Chamomile or Valerian," she answered after a few moments.

"Absolutely correct," James gave her a broad grin. "Now, is there anything else that might do the trick?"

"Well, yes. There is dwale," Nell admitted.

"And why are you not prescribing it?"

"Because it can kill as easily as it can cure," came the confident reply. "If the patient came again and wanted something more powerful, I would ask yours or Avril's advice. I would *never* sell it to someone just like that!"

"And how might it kill? What is in it that might be so deadly?"

Nell went into another silence as she sought in her memory for the answer. Suddenly, her bright blue eyes widened, and she gave a grin of satisfaction.

"Henbane, opium and wild lettuce – and sometimes belladonna."

"Well done!" James patted her hand. "Surgeons use it to put a patient to sleep before an amputation or similar operation. It is to be used only by those who know of its potency. Last question today. What is Betony used for?"

"Oh, that's easy. Helping digestion and ailments of the bowels."

"Enough for today, young lady. By the time you are fifteen, I shall propose you as my assistant. You will probably know more than me by that time!"

"Aye – and more than me, as well," came a voice from the shop. Avril had been following the 'examination' as she sliced, chopped and ground her ingredients. "Come and finish this paste for me whilst I take a rest from this infernal heat!"

Nell climbed down from her stool, smoothed out her immaculate white apron and went to take over from Avril. James motioned his wife out from the parlour and past the kitchen into the rear garden where herbs of many varieties were growing. He and Avril subsided onto a bench under the shade of a spreading apple tree.

"I never cease to be amazed at her thirst for knowledge," James grunted. "How many other children of her age could have absorbed so much – or even wanted to?"

"I can think of only one – Mary, now our schoolteacher," Avril admitted. "But think a bit further than her at fifteen. With that mass of golden curls and those lovely blue eyes, she will be pursued by every boy for miles around."

"Aye, that she will. I shall have to exercise a strong right arm to keep them at arm's length. But I also have the strongest suspicion that she will do that herself without any help from me."

"You have that right," Avril laughed. "She has the common sense of an adult already!"

* * *

"Will Cromwell ever be forgiven for his actions in Ireland?" Lady Violette Charlton asked. The disgusted expression on her old face suggested that, whatever anyone else may believe, she wouldn't ever forgive it.

Matthew Kent sat upright in his chair and faced the old lady.

"The actions he took were deemed necessary at the time," he stated firmly.

Lady Violette, owner of the small Brimley estate was a guest at the large hall at Parke House. She was, and always would be, a staunch and unwavering supporter of the monarchy. Kent, on the other hand, was a roving emissary for parliament. Inside his doublet was his warrant.

'Matthew Kent by this warrant is declared an agent of Parliament and is to be afforded every courtesy and assistance in his enquiries from whomsoever he deems it necessary to seek such information and that any person attempting to evade his questioning or to attempt any injury upon his person shall be deemed an enemy of The Commonwealth'. It was signed and sealed by no less a personage than John Bradshaw, the President of the Council of State.

Two other people were present at this meeting. Luke Barton, as Steward, represented his lord, Sir John Vickery – absent about his duties and interests at Westminster – and Peter Cove, Bailiff of the manor.

"But how many were massacred at Drogheda?" Barton asked. "The rumour for the past two years is that it was many thousands.

"You dismiss the many hundreds of Protestants who were massacred in the north of Ireland by Irish Catholics?" Kent countered.

"Utterly disproportionate!" Lady Violette growled. "Drogheda surrendered, or so I was informed. What need was there to inflict mass murder afterwards?"

"Ireton is holding the fort there," Cove added his thoughts. "But what need is there as Ireland is utterly subdued. What need for Cromwell to leave his son-in-law there?"

"So that Cromwell's presence is a constant threat against renewed uprising," Kent replied. "Believe me, it works!"

"Then how is that the Scots have managed to raise so many in support of Charles?"

"And to what effect?" Kent snorted. "David Leslie never learned his lesson when his army were utterly defeated at Dunbar – and that is not so far removed from Edinburgh. And now, or so rumour has it, he is again leading a Scottish Army with Charles Stewart at his side. They are reported well south of Lancaster at this time. If he or Stewart believe for one moment that the North of England will flock to his cause, they are woefully mistaken. They are seen merely as an invading army and the people of the North will have no truck with that – Charles Stewart notwithstanding!"

That caused three other heads to frown. Many believed that Charles Stewart should be crowned Charles II of England as well as he had already been declared as king of Scotland. However, many more in England were as committed to Parliament – as one had put it, 'we are in a time of quiet resignation – resigned to rule by Parliament'.

"One thing puzzled me at the time of his acceptance by Scotland," Lady Violette thought aloud. "How in the name of heaven did he reconcile his own beliefs with those of the ruling Covenanters in Scotland. For, had he been unable to reconcile himself, the Scots would have had none of him!"

"Indeed, that is so," Kent nodded. "But perhaps you mistake his beliefs as set in stone, Lady Violette. Perhaps he is as much a politician as an upholder of the Anglican creed. Perhaps he saw this as the only way to realise his ambition – using necessity as the mother of his invention.”

“Now you are being absurd!” Lady Violette snorted again. “Our uncrowned king would never stoop so low as to make a pact with the devil to achieve the throne of England!”

Barton nodded vigorously, signalling his total agreement. Peter Cove looked thoughtful.

“Sooner or later – and I suspect sooner – Cromwell and Parliament will bring this invasion to battle. Believe me, there will be only one inevitable outcome. Leslie and his Scots will be defeated, and Charles Stewart will be either dead, a prisoner, or fled abroad,” Kent stated.

That again was met with a period of silence. Lady Violette and Luke Barton were both anguished by Kent’s last statement, although Peter Cove silently agreed with the prognosis. Much as it pained him to admit it, he believed that Kent had it absolutely bang to rights. Being a bit of a diplomat, he attempted to change the subject.

“And what brings you here of all places?” he asked. “We were under the impression that you were based at Tiverton and into Cornwall.”

“Indeed, I am,” Kent admitted. “But mine is a sort of roving commission. I had business to attend to in Ashburton and, Parke being so close, thought it rude not to call in and reacquaint myself with this area. I have always been met with quiet toleration and politeness hereabouts.”

“I well remember saying to you when we first met two years past that we are not in the habit of shooting the messenger, no matter what the message,” Lady Violette laughed, also trying to lighten the mood of gloom.

“That, my lady, is just as well because I do indeed have another matter to bring to your attention. You may remember two years past that a small contingent of soldiers was stationed at Bovey Tracey. Well, if my information is correct, you may well have to host another of its kind in the near future – not, I hasten to add, that there is any specific reason for that. It is simply that small units are being stationed here, there and everywhere.”

"The previous chap, I believe his name was Larkins, was a great help to us on a few occasions. I for one would not mind if he were to be the one sent back," Cove nodded.

"It is more than likely," Kent replied. "His familiarity with your town and its neighbours would make him an obvious choice."

There came a discrete tap at the door. It opened to admit one of the young house servants.

"Er, my lady, master steward. Cook sent me to say that a cold collation is served in the dining room."

"That is most thoughtful," Lady Violette arose from her chair. "A cold collation with salads would be most welcome. It is far too hot for a stew or roast meats!"

* * *

About the same time, a totally different and far more boisterous dinner was taking place in a cottage two doors up from the apothecary. It was the home of Gil Ramsey, James' nephew. Gil and his wife Ella – the daughter of Abel and Faith Smith – were watching with amusement as their daughter Rosie attempted to put a spoonful of pottage into the tiny mouth of her brother Jamie.

"Come on, Jamie – it is lovely!" Rosie cajoled the little boy. Rosie, now well over four years old, had been adamant that she had wanted a sister and not a brother. Many tantrums had been experienced at the thought that Ella would *not* provide her with the longed-for sister. However, immediately after Jamie's birth two years since, Rosie had taken on the role of nursemaid, teacher, protector, and now feeder. Somehow or other, the role of senior sibling had suited her very nicely!

"No! Don't like!" Jamie yelled defiance as the spoon was edged further towards lips firmly shut against intrusion.

"I like it," Rosie said, emptying the spoon into her own mouth, rolling her eyes in apparent ecstasy. "Now, you try."

"No!"

"Then you go hungry until supper. I never heard such a fuss!" Rosie removed the bowl from the table.

That proved too much for Gil and Ella, who burst out laughing at the spectacle of their somewhat precocious daughter acting as the stern mistress. Rosie paused in the doorway.

"Why is that funny?" she demanded.

"It is almost the same conversation I used to have with you," Ella wiped tears of mirth from her eyes. "And now you know what I went through."

"I was always a good girl," Rosie shot back.

"You, my little angel, were and still are the most obstinate child I have ever known," Gil swooped on Rosie and picked her up. He tickled her until Rosie had to beg him to stop.

Gil put her down, thanked Ella for his dinner and went out to their large plot where he grew vegetables and salad crops for sale. Further down were the chickens – over forty of them now and earning more precious coins from eggs, and pullets that were destined for Simon Dingle, the town's butcher.

Rosie had returned to her indignant face.

"Mama – was I not a good girl?"

"Sometimes, you were a very good girl," Ella gave Rosie's curls a pat. "At other times, you were Jamie – defiant, wilful, and a holy terror."

"But I'm being good now!"

"Indeed, you are. Now, what are we going to do with this little fellow? He must be absolutely starving."

"Do you remember Mistress Green? She once told me that hunger is good for the soul. What's a soul, mama?"

Mercy Green had until some eighteen months previously, been the owner of the town bookshop. Her husband Hubert had died during a very severe outbreak of what was called the winter sickness – shivering and very high fever. It had carried off many of the town's small population, despite the best efforts of Avril, James and Mary Ramsey. Both Hubert and Mercy had been ultra-puritan; Mercy still was and had sold up to move to the Americas.

"A soul is supposed to be the part of you that lives on after you die," Ella hoped that would be an end to that conversation.

"But what part? Is it your brain?"

Ella was saved by the arrival of Maud Fletcher, now a quiet and thoughtful twelve-year-old, the elder daughter of Wilf Fletcher. Maud had looked after Rosie when Rosie had been very young. She now was in sole command of the chickens and the sale of eggs. She came in morning and afternoon from her home up at the top of the town, just before the smithy and the bakery.

"Hungry!" came an anguished yell from Jamie, now sitting in a corner of the parlour and chewing on a stump of log.

"Jamie wouldn't eat his pottage," Rosie explained.

"I remember another like that," Maud gave Ella a grin. "I used to give her a small heel of bread to keep her quiet."

Ella laughed and went to the kitchen shelf to get a small piece of crusty bread. Jamie seized on it with a whoop of pleasure. He then stuck out his tongue to his sister. Rosie pretended she had not noticed as both Ella and Maud went out for their afternoon's work – Ella to hoe the vegetables and Maud to feed the chickens and tend to any chicks who might have appeared. Rosie went over to Jamie, knelt by his side and gave him a cuddle. The two started playing with a ball of wool, Rosie now in the role of nursemaid. Peace settled once again on the cottage.

* * *

There was still a half hour to go before Mary dismissed the class for the day. She sat on her stool facing the thirteen children and, like most others in the south of England, mopped her brow. She regarded the piece of soggy linen with distaste. It was stifling inside the classroom despite doors open at front and rear and windows as wide as they would go. She looked up at thirteen expectant faces.

"We are going to finish today with reading out loud," she announced, knowing that this would be greeted by stifled groans. "Everybody, open your books at page fifteen and we shall start with Tommy at the back. Tommy, when you are ready, start reading, please."

Tommy, the son of a farmhand from the Heath, stood up and looked nervously at the page. He took a deep breath and started.

"SirBedeveredrewhisswordandraisedhisshield," he announced.

"Right, Tommy. I want you to stop and count the words you have just spoken."

Tommy, an eight-year-old with a mass of freckles, followed the words with his finger.

"Er, Nine, Miss Mary," he replied.

"Yes, nine. And you uttered them as if they were all one word. Now – slow down and start again."

"Sir Bedevere drew his sword and raised his shield."

"Much better. Carry on please."

"The dragon stood still and blew flames from his nose. The raised shield protected the knight from harm." Tommy paused and tried an old ploy to see if he could divert Mary's attention. "Please, Miss Mary, why would the shield protect him? If it was made of metal, it would have got red hot – like the iron Master Smith heats up in his forge. If it had been wood, it would have burned up."

"Clever lad," Mary grinned to herself. Abel Smith was the town blacksmith whose daughter Ella was married to her brother Gil. Abel was also next-door neighbour to her mother's and father's bakery. A hand shot up from a boy in the front row.

"Please, Miss, all the knights of the round table were protected by magic – so the flames from the dragon would not have hurt him."

Mary capitulated and decided to draw on their memories instead.

"And how do we know they were protected by magic?" she asked, wondering if any one of them could recall how that was reported to have happened.

That was met by silence, thirteen screwed up faces as memories were searched. It was Paul Goodes, the nine-year-old son of the verger, who raised an eventual hand.

"Please, Miss Mary; Merlin said they were protected when King Arthur waved Caliban over them one night."

"Yes, well remembered. Except that the sword was called Excalibur, not Caliban."

"Please, Miss – how does a sword become magic?" a girl from the middle row asked. Kat Gates was ten, and the daughter of the miller and his wife. Mary recognised this immediately as an attempt to further the distraction. She decided to forget the reading and show them how 'magic' was accomplished.

"I shall now show you some magic," she announced. She got up and fetched three cups from the back room, placed them upside down in a row on the desk before her. Under the middle one, she places a small pebble.

"Now," she continued as thirteen faces craned to see what she was up to. "I'm going to make the pebble disappear."

She shuffled the three cups around and around rapidly, making sure that the one with the pebble slid just far enough over the edge of the desk to let the stone fall into her lap. She continued to move the cups around.

"Who can tell me which cup the pebble is under?"

A chorus of shouted answers greeted this question. Mary looked at the class and grinned widely. One by one, she lifted the cups and set them to one side.

"There – I told you I could make it disappear by magic! Now, who believes that I have magical powers?"

Very slowly, thirteen hands were raised.

"You are all wrong," Mary announced, picking up the pebble from her lap and putting it on the table. "I let it fall out as I moved the cups around. I did it very fast so that you would not notice. So, you see, it was not magic at all. It was a trick. So, forget all about magic; it does not exist. What you were reading is a story written years ago by someone who wanted to tell a good tale. There are many books about Arthur – and they are all slightly different."

"But, Miss Mary, Jesus magicked the loaves and fishes!" Paul Goodes. "It's in the bible!"

"Yes, and what gave Jesus the power to do that?"

"He was the Son of God, so he could do *anything!*"

"And that certainly is *not* magic, is it? Jesus did it because He had the power. We cannot do it because we do not have the power. All we can do is to fool people by trickery. So, when the fair comes here again, look for the way that the man *could* be tricking you. He most certainly does not have magical powers. Right, bring your books up and put them on the shelf. Class is dismissed."

When the resulting stampede had died away, Mary sat back and again mopped perspiration from her forehead. Had she spoiled the children's belief in magic, she wondered? It was a rather lovely part of childhood – the sense of awe and wonderment. No, she told herself. These children were now old enough to be informed properly.

The school had been running for over eighteen months, thanks mainly to a massive donation from Lady Violette, who also provided much of the day-to-day running expenses. Mary, until she had been unanimously voted in as the schoolmistress, had been James' and Avril's apprentice – nearly a fully-fledged apothecary herself.

Just over a year ago, she had married Harry Cove, son of the Bailiff. They lived in some comfort at the large cottage on the Parke Estate where Harry was understudy to his father. There was never any doubt in anyone's mind, that Harry would take over the duties of Bailiff when his father retired.

She very thankfully closed and locked the school and walked slowly down the main street to the crossroads beyond the mill and the bridge over the river. At the crossroads, she went straight on for a few hundred yards, then turned in through the large estate gates. Had she turned left at the crossroads, she would have arrived at Newton Abbot, a larger town about five miles distant. Had she turned right, she would have climbed slowly uphill to the more distant Lustleigh and Moretonhampstead. Had she not turned into the estate, she would have climbed more steeply onto Dartmoor and ended up at Haytor, then much further, Widecombe.

Harry was coming out of the stables as she approached. He was leading his own horse and Mary's favourite large pony. Both were saddled and tacked.

"Good afternoon, beautiful wife," he grinned, putting a kiss on Mary's cheek. "Fancy a ride up onto the moor before supper? It will be cooler up there."

Mary returned the kiss. "Just let me change into my riding skirt and I shall be very happy to go somewhere cooler. That classroom resembles my parents' bread oven!"

In her split riding skirt, Mary joined Harry. They rode slowly up the steep incline until they emerged into open moorland. There, in the cooler air, they trotted past the twin granite outcrops that was Haytor, until they reached a point where the view was incredible. There, Harry lifted Mary down and they sat together on the large stone where months before, Harry had officially proposed to her.

"Regrets?" he asked.

"None spring to mind," she laughed, a faint breeze ruffling her hair – which she had uncovered as soon as she had been able.

CHAPTER II

Gone was Wednesday's and Thursday's scorching sun. In its place on the Saturday had come driving rain, flying in from the distant Atlantic and propelled by storm-forced winds. It was certainly not what the people required. Much more, they groaned, and the crops will be flattened and sodden. Those down on the coast in places such as the fishing port of Brixham, knew from experience that the rainstorm would be of short duration. Most others feared the worst; a poor harvest would be followed by a winter of near starvation. These fears were to prove groundless.

Wales was proving to be just as wet as Devon and Cornwall. In the wooded hills to the north of Abergavenny, close on a hundred men of all ages sat under large trees and cursed. The trees were in full leaf; this canopy directed the relentless rain down towards the peripheral small roots. Relatively dry oases existed around the trunks. The men had been moving around the Welsh/English border for months, never sure when they would be gathered into the much larger fold of the royalist army. All they knew was that this army was under the command of David Leslie, a Scottish general, who had among his entourage Charles Stewart – son of the executed Charles I. Charles had long before been declared King Charles II of Scotland. Despite severe defeats and drawbacks, Leslie had managed to forge a way down the west of England and was now reputedly somewhere north of the city of Worcester. The ultimate aim was to defeat the parliamentary forces and have Charles proclaimed king of England.

"Satan's armpits!" one old and gnarled man snarled. "This rain must have been sent by that bastard Cromwell himself!"

"Two days ago, you were cursing the heat of the sun," Matt Crowley grinned at him. The two were amongst a group of five sitting under the cover of a large elm tree. Matt had left his home in Bovey Tracey not long after his father, the town's carpenter, had died of the winter fever. Two things had spurred his departure. First was the burning desire for adventure. Second was his fierce loyalty to the king – although at that time England had no king.

Matt had joined up with a small group of disaffected young men in Dartington some many months before. This group had been directed to join a larger group north of Avonmouth. From there, they had followed the banks of the Severn until they were met by another group. Together, they had crossed the broad estuary into Wales – first to Chepstow and then by small leaps and bounds to where they now rested under the trees. Worcester was about sixty miles to their east. According to rumour, that was where they were heading to join up with the army.

The group was armed with a variety of weapons. Matt had somehow 'acquired' a short sword to add to his own dagger. Others had billhooks, pikes, long swords. A very few had pistols tucked into their belts, but with precious few round bullets and even less powder in covered horns. They had all been promised an issue of pistols when the army itself was formed. Matt raised his head.

"The rain is easing," he muttered, more in hope than in the expectation of a cessation.

"Mark my words," the older man growled. "It will be back! Puritan prayers are being answered every day we are held here and not fighting them as we should!"

"Have you not listened to one word our captain has said?" Matt said with a shrug. "We are merely being held here until the time is ripe for us to muster. He also said that there were many more groups just like us scattered hither and yon – all of us waiting for the summons. We *will* fight Cromwell when it is considered we are sufficient in number and in weapons."

"And what is meant to happen after the fight is over and Cromwell put to flight?" the older man was not going to be distracted from his outpouring of imagined pessimism. "I shall tell you what! Puritanism will be no more and, in its stead, will remain the age-long dispute between Protestants and Catholics. Hear me well, young stripling! We shall replace one fight with another – and so on until we are all submerged in fighting until we die!"

"Miserable old bugger!" growled a lad to Matt's left. "And which would you be? Catholic or Protestant? You certainly be no Puritan given the obscenities you utter from morning to night!"

"I be for the Protestant Church of England – always have been and always will be. I swear a lot because I see nothing good, simply things and matters that make me mad with anger."

"You're still a miserable old bugger!" the lad muttered.

"You have spoken of the end of Parliament," Matt prodded, wondering whether the older man could be provoked to make more predictions. "What if Cromwell defeats us?"

"Then prepare for a letting of blood the world has not yet seen!"

"You believe Cromwell and Parliament will massacre all who stand against them?"

"Just look what he did to those in Ireland who stood against him. Thousands slaughtered, even though they had surrendered in good faith. Again, mark my words – if we are defeated then England's Protestants and Catholics will be put to the sword in their many thousands."

"What? Even those Protestants who have adhered to Parliament? And many have."

"I see nothing but blood spilled across the land!"

"Then we had better not lose!" Matt grinned. He, and most others in the large group, envisaged nothing like the prognosis of that strange man. What they saw was either victory and a king restored to the throne, or defeat leading either to a messy death or an ignominious return to life under Parliament.

"See!" Matt laughed. "The rain is no more now than a dribble."

* * *

The following day, being Sunday, saw a large congregation inside the church of Saints Peter, Paul, and Thomas. The service was subtly altered, being mainly prayers and a homily. The parish was being served by an 'acceptable' reverend – acceptable to the more puritan leanings of the authorities. The long-time vicar had been relieved of his duties, probably due to his having been chaplain to Prince Charles. Nevertheless, the Reverend James Forbes attended the service, sitting right at the back. He could certainly not fault the homily – the celebrant had taken as his text a passage from the Book of Job – 'have you ever in your days commanded the morning light?' In other words, we are all powerless in the light of God's creation.

Avril and Mary, amongst a few others, would dearly have liked to debate this, but knew that it would be a fruitless exercise. Mary in particular knew that she had to tread very warily when teaching her schoolchildren!

It had become a sort of ritual that, on the third Sunday of each month, a very large group gathered at the tavern for Sunday dinner. That Sunday was no exception to the rule. The group comprised a numerous and varied 'expanded' family.

James and Avril, with Nell were the first to arrive at the far end of the large taproom where their special table had been made ready – in effect, five tables grouped together. James' brother John Ramsey, the town baker, with his wife Evelyn were next to arrive. Abel Smith, the blacksmith, his wife Faith, their son Simon and his wife Imelda followed, Imelda carrying their baby Jack, now just over one year old. They were followed by John's and Evelyn's son Gil with his wife Ella, the daughter of the Smiths. With them were Rosie and little Jamie. Last to arrive were Josiah and Alice Grubb, Imelda's parents. Josiah was the town's shoemaker and leatherworker. Seventeen people, all laughing and making jokes, settled themselves for their ritual monthly meal.

Sal Allen, wife of Dick the owner of the tavern, peeped out through the bead curtain that separated the taproom from the kitchens. Within that very large space, three cooks and an equal number of scullions laboured at dicing, cooking, peeling and spit-turning. The taproom would be bursting with over forty people soon enough.

"Glory, Zach," Sal called over her shoulder. "The Ramseys are all here. Go and serve ale and whatever they require."

Glory, still unmarried at the age of twenty-one despite being blessed with the face and figure of an angel, bustled over to the barrels and drew three large jugs of their best ale. Zachary, two years senior to his sister, drew a large pitcher of Gascony wine. All these were placed in the middle of the extended table.

Ella poured a measure of ale into two cups and added an equal amount of water, then placed them before Rosie and Jamie. Both these were sitting atop tall stools as the normal benches would have been too short for them to reach the tabletop.

Rosie immediately gulped down half of her drink. Despite it being what he was given at every meal at home, Jamie eyed the cup with suspicion. He pushed it away.

"No like!" he shouted.

Imelda who had been holding a smaller cup of exactly the same concoction to Jack's little mouth, gave the little boy a stern look.

"Jack is drinking his like a good boy," she said.

"Jamie is *not* a good boy!" Rosie declared. "Jamie never does what he is told."

"Do!" shouted a defiant Jamie.

"Enough of this, if you please," Ella regarded her two children with a mixture of love and exasperation. "Jamie – drink properly and stop making such a nuisance of yourself. Behave properly or you shall not get any dinner!"

"Don't want dinner!"

Abel Smith glanced at Ella and received a nod. He rose up to his great height and swooped on Jamie, lifting him high above his head. Jamie shrieked with delight as his head nearly touched a rafter.

"More?" Abel asked.

"Please, grandpapa."

"Then drink your drink, eat your dinner, and I'll hoist you up again."

"Yes, grandpapa."

"Now say sorry to your mother."

"Sorry, mama."

Abel Smith was held in some awe by the majority of the town. Not only was he the tallest for miles around, he was built like a mighty bull, with muscles bulging everywhere you looked. His son Simon was built on similar lines.

Ella gave her father a grin as he resumed his seat. Nothing like a huge grandfather to instil compliance, she muttered to herself. Gil and Ella had experimented with the new vegetable potato some two years previously. They had proved a huge success and had immediately been added to the tavern's menu. Sal had devised a method of serving them that met with universal approval. She washed and scrubbed them cut them in half, then roasted them in the fat dripping from the spitted and roasting meats.

The main course arrived soon after – lamb roasted with rosemary and mint, roasted potatoes, cabbage and turnips fried in butter. Silence descended on the taproom as forty hungry diners savoured the food. Even Jamie, his portion cut into small pieces, gobbled it down with relish.

At one point during the consumption of these treats, Simon nudged Imelda who in turn nudged Gil and Ella. They all looked fascinated at a small table nearer to the door where the Huguenot family were seated.

Henri Bessant, his wife Eloise and their son Gaston had bought the bookshop that had previously been owned by Hubert and Mercy Green. Hubert, like too many of the inhabitants, had died from the winter fever. Mercy, an ultra-puritan, had sold up and taken passage to new England, The Bessant family had proved hugely popular and had been absorbed into the town within weeks. Gaston, a young man only a couple of years older than Glory, had immediately caught the eye of that young woman. Gaston was tall and impossibly good looking. He also had impeccable manners and a lilting French accent that had Glory turning somersaults. Glory was attending to that table with what could only be described as unwarranted attention.

It was common knowledge that Gaston and Glory were greatly attracted to one another. It was also assumed that it would not be long before they declared their betrothal.

"That will be the last bit of work we get out of her for a while," Zachary grumbled aloud as he passed the big table. He was carrying a pile of empty platters and seemingly doing the work of five people.

"You'll soon be doing it all yourself by the look of things," Gil laughed.

"And what do you think I'm doing now?" Zachary snorted as he disappeared through the curtain.

"I still cannot believe that Glory is still unwed," Imelda muttered. "She is quite definitely the town beauty and has been for years past."

"You forget yourself, my angel," Simon gave his wife a grin. "You are a beauty beyond price!"

"If you believe that gets you away from the chores, you are sadly mistaken," Imelda snorted.

"And what chores would they be?" Faith asked. "Simon spends all day with his father in the forge and the rest of the time being waited on by you and me!"

Imelda was about to reply when the large table was joined by two more very latecomers – Lou Crowley and the little boy Felix. Lou was the widow of Peter Crowley, who had been the town's main carpenter; he also had died of the winter fever. Little Felix was a tiny boy who had been found abandoned in a tumbledown shed at the side of the River Bovey. As Lou's son had made off to join up with other royalists, Lou had been all alone and had jumped at the chance to 'adopt' the little chap. She had vacated the cottage and the workshop and now lived in the rooms above the schoolroom, paying a small rent by producing very high-quality woollen cloth on her small loom.

"And how are you and that little chap faring?" Evelyn enquired. The whole village had taken a great interest in the little fellow.

"We fare well, thank you," Lou answered with a broad smile. Evelyn was very happy to see that smile as it had taken Lou a long time to come to terms with the loss of husband and son. "Felix eats well, do you not, my poppet?"

Nobody had been able to fix a true date for the child's birth. The general consensus amongst the women was that he had been around three months when he had been discovered, wailing and abandoned. A short while later, the body of a young woman had been discovered not that far from the baby. It had been assumed that she had been the mother. The rest had remained a complete mystery.

Therefore, Felix was probably about two years and a month or so, toddling about and, in Lou's words, into everything. From the moment he had been able to speak, he had referred to Lou as 'mama'. Nobody had ever disabused him of that notion as it was agreed that he needed that certainty and stability.

Felix struggled free from Lou and made a beeline for Jamie. The two of them sat themselves down on the floor and started playing with a kitten, one of the brood that had appeared one evening, courtesy of the tavern's cat.

Ella looked at her little son and his new playmate.

"Those two will bear watching like a hawk," she announced to general agreement. "I have the horrid suspicion that they will get up to far worse pranks than we ever had from Hob!"

"Talk of the devil!" Abel broke in as the tavern door opened to admit the fifteen-year-old lad who the Bailiff and his wife had adopted when he had been orphaned as a baby. Hob had been known as the town's practical joker. He was messenger and general handyman for the Bailiff.

"Has anyone seen Master Bailiff?" he shouted. "There are two dead bodies in the field beyond the church."

* * *

The tavern erupted into shouted chaos. Who? Why? When?

As the hubbub died away, James said that nobody there had seen the Bailiff that day, that he and his family had not been at the church and had not appeared at the tavern.

"Master Fletcher found them just an hour past," Hob explained. Will Fletcher was the town's ditcher and hedger – responsible for making sure all drainage ditches were kept clear and that hedges along the roads were trimmed to allow clear passage. "He is standing guard until I can find Master Bailiff."

Coming down the main street from the church, the tavern was the first possible place Hob could reasonably have expected to find Peter Cove. He turned on his heels and pelted down the street towards the crossroads and the Parke estate.

Instead of going peaceably to their homes at the end of their dinner, the occupants of the tavern stayed exactly where they were, agog with the news and rife with speculation. They had heard of nobody missing – and local news spread like wildfire throughout that small town.

Not long after Hob had shot off, the door opened again and in strode Peter Cove, Bailiff. With him was his son Harry and Harry's wife Mary. Cove made immediately for Avril – who was acknowledged as the nearest thing the town had to a physician. She and Mary had coped between them with the dreadful outbreak of winter fever.

"I would deem it a favour if you would come with me to examine these two bodies," he said. "They are fully dressed and appear to be man and woman of middle years."

"Yes, of course," Avril got up and followed the Bailiff out of the tavern. With Harry and Mary, the four were followed at a

19

respectable distance by a host of diners. Hob was standing in the street a short way past the church, guarding the gate into the large field that had been let fallow the previous year.

The small procession made its way along the hedgerow on the left to a spot where Will Fletcher was standing. He moved aside to reveal two adult bodies laid side by side. Avril went to kneel at the side of the woman, whilst Mary did the same at the side of the man. They looked at one another and then started a preliminary examination. Each face was peaceful, eyes closed. Prising open an eyelid, Avril could find no blood spots that would have indicated strangulation. Mary did the same and both shook their heads. No marks either on the necks, ankles or wrists.

"Nothing so far," Avril said quietly. "We will need to have them moved so that we may examine them thoroughly."

"And no signs of a struggle," Peter Cove muttered, examining the tall grass that surrounded the two bodies. "Hob!" he yelled.

Hob galloped over. He had still never quite mastered the art of walking anywhere.

"Get down to the barn and summon Sam Garvey and Haddock. Grab mounts and get back here as quickly as you can."

Sam Garvey and Robert Hook (Haddock to everyone) were ex-parliamentary soldiers and expert trackers. They were employed at the estate. Hob again took off at breakneck speed.

Cove again turned to Avril and Mary. "Have you any indication how long they have lain here?"

"Stiffness is well advanced, so at least a whole day," Avril answered. "In this hot weather, it is hard to tell as the heat may well have delayed the onset of the rigor." She waved away a cluster of flies that wanted to settle on the exposed flesh. "The sooner we get them under cover and away from these flies the better!"

"And how is that they have yet to be discovered by the crows and rooks, not to mention the foxes?" Mary queried. "There is no sign on them of any predation!"

"This is getting to be some mystery," Cove stood hands on hips. "First of all, I want those two to scour the area for any sign of how they arrived here, and whether they were accompanied by anyone else. As soon as that is completed, we will move them into the south aisle of the church so they can be covered up and ready for your examination."

"I would expect that to be tomorrow after dinner at the earliest," Avril replied. "It will take that long at least for the stiffness to release the limbs."

A few minutes later, hooves clattered up the road and Hob and the two men came over to the Bailiff. Cove briefly explained what he needed. Sam Garvey and Robert Hook nodded their understanding, but first knelt at the feet of the bodies and removed one shoe from each. Then they stood up and started at the hedgerow, working up until they came to the western boundary of the field. Both came back with the shoes, which they carefully replaced on the stiff feet.

"Footprints exactly matching the shoes are in the lane beyond the top – there is a gap in the hedge allowing access to the lane. There are no other prints anywhere near them," Haddock announced. "It would seem they came down the lane together, came through the gap and walked down the field. The grasses would have recovered well by now, so no sign of them arriving at this spot."

"Came down the lane from which direction?" Cove asked.

"From eastwards, the lane goes to Teign Village."

Cove thought about that for a moment.

"And no sign of any third party?"

"None, Master Bailiff."

Hob was sent to fetch two large boards so that the bodies could be carried back to the church, where they were laid on trestles in the small south transept. The bodies were covered in clean sheets to await further examination.

Cove had asked all the people gathered in the street to look at the two faces. Nobody had recognised them. He would do the same with the remainder of the town. Then an idea struck him.

"Hob – Go and find Mistress Bessant and ask her to come here with her drawing materials." Eloise Bessant was an accomplished artist.

Later, Cove had two pieces of paper with charcoal sketches of the two faces. They were a very remarkable likeness to the bodies. He would need the drawings to show to those living further afield.

CHAPTER III

It had taken just one night for the news of the bodies to reach every house in Bovey Tracey, Parke Estate, and Brimley. It had spread even further afield to the outlying farms and hamlets. It was no surprise therefore, that Matthew Kent appeared at the church after his breakfast. Anything untoward in the area he saw as legitimately his to investigate.

Avril was there already, along with Bailiff Cove. Mary, otherwise engaged at the school, had said she would pop up later that morning when the children went for their dinner. Avril was examining the male body as Kent entered the church. The sheet had been pulled down to expose the body down as far as the navel.

Despite the amount of body open to examination, Avril was concentrating only on the head, and the lower part of the face in particular.

"Hmmmm," she muttered.

"You have found something?" Cove asked, as Kent peered over his shoulder.

"Yes – something that just *might* explain these two deaths. I have already done this examination on the woman, and I have found the same on this man. There are marks around the mouths – fading now after the amount of time that has passed. The insides of both mouths appear burned and there is the same smell coming from both of them. Without doing a lot more work, my initial thought is aconite – more usually called wolfsbane."

"But aconite is used on the skin, is it not?" Cove remarked.

"Indeed, it is, and *never* upon my recommendation or on James'. It is very dangerous. Taken internally in quantity, it can stop the heart in moments."

"How long would you and James need to be certain of this?"

"Oh, not long. We will have an answer for you in an hour or less."

"Then, if you really find it's aconite poisoning, I shall have to send a message to the sheriff. All suspicious deaths must be reported."

Leaving Avril to take whatever samples she required, and to cover the two bodies again, Peter Cove left the church. Kent followed him down the steps to the street.

"Well," he said, falling into step at the side of the tall bailiff. "You seem to have a deep mystery on your hands."

"Indeed, I do. What I must also do is to have those two trackers go over that field again with a very fine comb. If what Mistress Ramsey says is proved to be correct, then how did two people manage to walk down a lane, cross into a field, and then suddenly die side by side from monkshood poison? Either they were poisoned by a third party, or it was a suicide pact – and that I find very difficult to believe. Why would two people trek all the way from wherever, just to pick that particular spot in which to end their lives? Surely, if such was their intention, they would have done so in their own home!"

"I can certainly take your point – it seems unlikely to say the least. Look, may I offer you my services? Whilst you and your expert trackers scour the field and the lane again, why don't I ride back the way they seem to have come and enquire at every dwelling I come across – see if anyone is missing, or that anyone recognises their description?"

"I would be very grateful for any help that I can get – and I thank you most sincerely for the offer. You had better take with you the two drawings."

* * *

Sam Garvey and Richard Hook, collected by the bailiff along with young Hob, gathered as a foursome at the place where the bodies had been discovered.

"What we must do is to cover every square inch of the surrounding field, then the gap in the hedge – make sure that we have overlooked nothing. You two are the experts, so I suggest that I go with Garvey and you, Hob, go with Hook. You probably have the youngest and sharpest eyesight of all of us."

"In which case, Master Bailiff, may I suggest that I take the left towards the left hedge, and Haddock takes the right. We search every blade of grass between this site and the far hedge."

The slow and painstaking search commenced. Hob, absolutely thrilled at being a part of such important work, moved a short way to Hook's right and followed the tracker's example, looking to left and right before taking a small step forward.

It took the two sets of searchers over an hour to cover the distance to the top hedge and, by the time they were almost there, they had searched a wide tract about seventy yards long by twenty yards wide. It was just as they were all nearing that top hedge that Hob spotted something glinting in the sunlight."

"Something here, Master Bailiff," he almost shrieked in his excitement.

"Then do not move or touch anything. The rest of us must finish our search so that not a spot is missed."

In an agony of suspense, Hob hopped from foot to foot as he waited until the others had finished and had joined him.

"Right, lad. Show us," Cove commanded.

Hob pointed at a spot about a yard in front of him, a spot that was just inches from the top boundary hedge.

"Tis there I saw it glinting in the sun," he said.

Hook knelt down in the long grass and slowly reached forward, parting the stalks until he had uncovered what Hob had seen. There, at the base of the long grass was a brooch. It was face-uppermost and consisted of a large green stone surrounded by a golden setting. Hook picked it up and handed it behind him to the Bailiff. Then he reached forward again and handed back a golden cross on a thin, golden chain.

"That was concealed under the brooch," he reported. Garvey joined him and between them they minutely searched all around the place where the baubles had been.

"Not a sign of anyone having been anywhere near here," Garvey reported. "Not a print or even a disturbed blade of grass."

Cove looked up at the hedge. "According to what you found yesterday, they came along that lane and past this spot. If there is no sign of anyone having been this side, then the only way they could have got there is by being thrown from the lane over the hedge. Hob, stay right here and we shall go out into the lane to see whether there are any marks that prove or disprove that theory."

Hob waited until he heard their footsteps in the lane. "I'm right here," he called as they were about to pass his position.

There came a period of silence until Garvey spotted a couple of very faint prints in the tall verge.

"Man's footprints here," he said. "Very faint but identical to those in the middle of the lane."

Cove went to the other side of the lane and found a small stone about the size of the brooch.

"Toss that over the hedge and let's see where it lands."

Hob had the good sense to retreat a couple of paces. The stone arced over the hedge and fell not a foot from where the brooch and chain had been found.

"Almost spot on, Master Bailiff," he called.

On the way back to the Parke Estate, Cove and his helpers called into the butchers where Simon Dingle was busy separating legs of lamb into smaller joints.

"And what may I do for you, Master Bailiff?" he laid his cleaver to one side.

"A word with your good lady, if you please," Cove answered.

Stella Cove had been, before her marriage, daughter of a jeweller and silversmith in Ashburton. She came through to the shop, dusting flour from her hands. Cove placed the brooch, cross and chain on the counter.

"Can you tell me what these are, and possibly their worth?" Cove asked.

Stella picked up the brooch and moved outside into broad daylight. Then she came back for the cross and chain.

"There are of considerable worth," she stated. "I remember more than enough to say that the large stone is an emerald and that the metals are gold. At a rough estimate, both together are worth more than the average worker could earn in two or more years."

All four, plus the butcher, whistled at that statement. The average wage was somewhere about two shillings per day, or twenty-five pounds each year. If the two pieces were worth fifty pounds or more, then whoever had owned them was definitely someone of great wealth.

Simon Dingle asked the obvious question.

"Did they belong to the two people found in the field?"

"That we do not know," Cove answered. It was useless prevaricating as the news would be in every home within the hour. "They were not on the bodies, but in the field at some distance from where the two persons were found. Either they owned them and discarded them, or they had stolen them and threw them away, or they were nothing at all to do with them. I have not the slightest clue at the moment."

"I do not envy you the task – it seems like three mysteries all rolled into one!"

"I make it five mysteries at the very least," Cove grunted as they left the butcher's shop. Back at Parke, Cove locked the two pieces securely in the estate's strong box.

* * *

Avril and James did not get around to testing the tiny samples until after dinner as the shop was unusually busy with people wanting salves to use on sunburned skin. Even though the day was overcast, people had waited until they could bear the sting no longer; some even had well-formed blisters. Being quizzed, Nell had searched her memory before coming up with chamomile and/or calendula as being effective in reducing redness and rashes, as well as soothing burned patches.

Avril had used a small spatula to remove the small amounts of residue in the mouths of the two dead bodies. With Nell watching every move, James ground up a small amount of aconite that they kept, along with other dangerous things such as belladonna, in a locked cupboard. And then, using a long piece of scrubbed marble, the two started mixing the ground aconite with various liquids – ale, wine, water and some others from stoppered bottles. They stood back and regarded the array.

"First of all, let us try the original on a rat," James said, going to a cage outside the back door where they kept captured rodents. He donned thick gauntlets and brought one in to where Avril had smeared a tiny portion of the samples onto a piece of bread. The rat was fed into a small cage and the bread poked between the close bars.

Most highly noxious substances caused either vomiting, convulsions, or frantic movements. This caused none of them. Within ten minutes, the rat laid on its side panting and was dead in another two minutes.

"Well, we at least know that the two of them had aconite or something very similar in their systems," James observed, handing the cage for Nell to dispose of the carcass.

A half-hour later, the three had isolated two of their 'mixtures' as being a close match to the samples. Two more rats were brought in. One of them simply vomited up his piece of bread and whatever else had remained in its stomach. The other one did exactly as the first rat had done.

"Aconite and weak ale?" Nell had learned a lot that afternoon, watching the careful procedures.

"Unless there is another answer altogether, which I deem very unlikely," Avril was relieved to have her preliminary diagnosis confirmed. "Nell – would you like to convey the findings to Master Cove?"

Nell beamed at the prospect of being the one to convey such momentous news. She put a small bonnet over her curls and sped off, much as she had seen Hob do on many an occasion.

"Oho," Cove grunted as he received the news. "So, we are looking for someone who can mix aconite with weak ale! Perhaps they did it themselves!"

"But that is a terrible sin!" Nell couldn't help bursting out.

"Who knows what goes through the minds of people who are that desperate? Or those with evil murder in their thoughts?

* * *

The next morning, immediately having finished his breakfast of eggs, ham and fresh baked bread, Matthew Kent started off upon his quest. The two drawings he had put safely into a leather pouch that went into his small saddlebag. He first rode up to the lane behind the twenty-acre field, the field in which the bodies had been discovered. And then he set off along the lane in a north-easterly direction where the trackers had found the prints. For about a mile, he saw no signs of habitation either to left or right. And then he came to a crossroads that had him scratching his head. He knew enough of the area to disregard both left and right forks; left wound its way up onto the moor, whilst right led a very meandering path all the way to Newton Abbot. The more likely route was straight ahead where a small collection of dwellings was called Teign Village – probably from the River Teign that flowed not far past it.

Dismounting, he looped the reins over a post at the gate of the first cottage he encountered. His knock was answered by a small boy who had a piece of pie clutched in a fist and a mouth stuffed with a large bite.

"Da!" he yelled, treating Kent to a shower of crumbs. "Man at the door!"

A large man dressed in normal clothes covered by a brown apron with pockets full of tools came from the back parlour.

"Who are you and what is your business here?" the man growled. Kent was very used to receiving greetings like that. People up and down the entire country were on edge.

"Nothing untoward, I assure you," he gave a disarming smile. "I am on an errand for the Bailiff from Bovey Tracey. Two people have been found and I'm trying to discover who they might be."

"And what good is that? What did they look like?"

"I can show you precisely," Kent answered, holding out the two drawings.

"Never seen them before!" The man slammed the door in Kent's face.

"And a very good morning to you, too," Kent muttered.

With varying degrees of politeness, he received the same answer at every one of the ten cottages. He shrugged his shoulders, packed the drawings safely into the wallet and rode slowly further towards the river, leaving the little village behind.

"Hoi, mister!" came a muffled voice from the other side of the hedge on his left.

He made to pull the reins to stop when he got another muffled message.

"Don't stop or they'll know you're speaking to someone. I caught a look at those there faces. You'd better turn left at the river and go about two miles up that road. I think I know where they're from. Large house – stone at the bottom and timbers at the top, grey slates on the roof. You didn't get this from me!"

Kent was fairly certain that his informant was the little lad from the first house.

"Never heard a word!" he replied softly, then rode on at the same pace.

A little further on, he came to the river where his lane met a larger road going from left to right. He turned left and rode on until her had travelled what he calculated as a couple of miles. Rounding a shallow bend, he saw the house exactly as the lad had described. Once again, he dismounted and looped the reins over a gatepost. The walk up to a substantial house took him a few minutes. Mounting the two steps, he knocked at the large oak door.

Listening carefully, he was able to hear only one thing, a deafening silence. Not a shuffled footstep, a creaking door, nothing. He knocked louder and received the same response. He noticed a path leading around the house to the right. As he went, he peered into the front window, then into two more at the side. When he reached the back, he again found a window that revealed nothing. The back door was also locked and barred. The rear garden was well maintained, with rows of beans and peas, what looked like the tops of carrots, and another row of cabbages. All looked as if care and attention had been spent on its upkeep.

Retracing his steps, he was about to mount his horse when a pony and cart lumbered towards him down the road. Atop a small pile of hay was an old chap chewing on a straw. The old man raised his hand to an old hat perched atop a mass of white hair.

"Won't find them there, master," he said, pulling the pony to a stop. "They be gone to Exeter to see her mother – she be ailing."

"May I show you two drawings, to see if you recognise them?" Kent asked, removing the two pieces of paper from the wallet. The old man bent down and gave the drawings one look.

"Aye, that be Mistress Ann and Master Lucas. Why have you drawings of them?"

"I am on a mission for the Bovey Tracey Bailiff. Two bodies were found in a field there and I am trying to identify them."

That news seemed to stun the old chap.

"But they be gone to Exeter. Why were they at Bovey?"

"That is what we urgently need to discover. Can you tell me more about them?"

From the long speech that followed, it appeared that Ann and Lucas Dodds had lived in the large house for less than a year. They had arrived, they said, from Exeter. Local gossip had it that they had two grown-up children – a son working at the Exeter Guildhall as a clerk, and a daughter married to a jeweller in the same city. The two parents had not mixed socially with other residents hereabouts and were known to be a bit reclusive, although polite when spoken to. Kent thanked the old chap and made his slow way back to report his findings to Peter Cove.

"Lucas and Ann Dodds, eh?" Cove rubbed his chin. "Can't say I have ever heard those names before. It would seem that I have a journey to Exeter then."

"If you would like company, then I shall be happy to go with you," Kent offered. He was intrigued and did not want to miss out on the unravelling tale.

"Then may I propose that we start early on the morrow?"

Kent enjoyed a late dinner and spent the entire afternoon wandering about the field and the lane behind it. He discovered absolutely nothing.

CHAPTER IV

Not that far to the west of the city of Worcester was the medium-sized town of Leominster. To the north of that town were woods and open fields and, in one of those fields at the edge of an extensive wood, forty armed men were camped. They were but one group that were camped within a ten-mile radius. The particular group by the wood had marched a circuitous route from Abergavenny, taking four days to reach their new destination.

"It's Worcester, for sure," the same old chap was stating with as much certainty as ever since Matt had clapped eyes on him more than a week before.

"And what brings you to that conclusion, other than the fact that Worcester is the nearest city to where we are?" Matt asked, tongue in cheek. This drew chuckles from the three others who were sat with Matt and the sage around a smouldering fire.

"Stands to reason, or it would if you had the power of reason within that thick skull!" the older man growled. "Worcester has always held out for the king – the old one whose head was removed. They are sure to be as steadfast towards the one we want to put in his place."

"You could say that equally for many a city hereabouts – Hereford, Shrewsbury, for example. Even towns like Ledbury have never wavered," Matt's nearest companion laughed. "So, what makes Worcester special?"

"It is where Leslie is headed, along with his Scots!"

"And you are privy to this sensitive information?"

"I do not need to be privy, you dolt. I, alone it would seem amongst you thick-headed rabble, have the ability to reason things out. Therefore, I say that we are headed for Worcester. Before too long, we shall be facing that Cromwell and his army. You mark my words!"

Matt's neighbour, one Herbert Grindley, was not so easily put off. He was a tall and powerful young man who had joined that particular group after it had left the Bristol area.

"As we are but one group, and many others like ours are scattered around, it surely makes more sense that we be used severally, to harass and pick off Cromwell's lot – reduce their numbers well before any pitched battle. Otherwise, why are we not in one, large army?"

"Because, you long streak, that is not the way Leslie has ever proceeded. Up until now, he has gathered as many in one place as possible to force a decisive battle!"

"And that served him so well at Dunbar and other places!" Matt scoffed. "That tactic resulted in crushing defeats. No, I agree with Herb. It makes far more sense for us and the other groups to act independently so as to wreak as much harm as possible – appear by night, pick on, let us say, the baggage train, do as much damage as we may, then disappear again to do the same some nights later."

"Aye, any by so doing, slowly weaken that army," Herbert nodded. "That's sound tactics – not a pitched battle against an army that is whole and entire!"

"That's as maybe," came a voice from behind the small group. It was a well-known voice as the five scrambled to their feet. Sir Lucian Pellow had been given command of the group of forty. He was a man of middle years, small, thin, and as fast as a whippet.

"Er, just thinking aloud, sir," Herbert said deferentially.

"And not bad thinking, at that!" Pellow grunted. "However, tis not for the likes of you, or even me come to that, to outthink our commanders. It is our duty to do as bid. Whether that be to confront Cromwell en-masse, or to harry bits and pieces, or even to pack up and go home, it is all the same. We do as bid!"

"If I may make so bold, sir – may I make a wager that I am right – that we are ordered to Worcester to confront Cromwell in a pitched battle?" The older man would not be silenced.

"You most certainly may make so bold, Borthwick. And I shall have none of it as my suspicions match yours!" Pellow laughed.

Seb Borthwick gave a small bow to his commander and leered at the others as much as to say, 'I told you so!'

"And now perhaps I shall join you in eating whatever that thing is that you are roasting above the flames," Pellow sat down and gestured the other five to follow suit.

"'Tis but a small buck we found in the woods. It appeared to have been abandoned as it was limping on only three legs," Herb admitted, not looking at his commander in the eye.

"Aye, limping because it had been caught in a trap and then poached," Pellow grinned.

Using sharpened daggers, each member of the group sliced off portions of the roasted buck and started chewing, nobody disturbing what was for them a veritable feast.

Matt was the first to break the silence as the carcass, much reduced, continued to spit and cook.

"Sir, may I ask a question? Is that army of Cromwell's as deadly as others say?"

Pellow leaned back on his elbows and considered how best to answer that.

"Deadly, yes they are. And let me tell you why. They are trained and organised in such a way as has never yet been seen. Each man in each little unit, in each company, in each regiment, knows exactly what to do and how to do it. They work as one man, devising tactics as circumstances demand. Cromwell is as able a commander as it is possible to be. There is only one way in which his army may *ever* be beaten and that is by overwhelming numbers – numbers that are able to absorb hideous losses and *still* press on until their advantage is unbeatable."

"And, sir, if I may ask again, shall we have such numbers?"

"That, young man, is our fondest wish. We shall not know until it is either too late, or we are victorious."

"Will there not be some parley before the clash?" Herbert asked.

"Cromwell is a man of very few words!" came the reply. "So, no – I sincerely doubt such an exchange will take place."

Pellow stood up and motioned the others to stay sitting.

"That buck, however obtained, was excellent," he said, turned on his heel and went to confront another small group.

"And who amongst you is going to take my wager?" Borthwick demanded.

"After what Sir Lucien has just said, I shall not, thank you," Matt grunted. "Even though I still believe Herb has the right tactic, I fear that we shall not be skirmishing after all."

* * *

The heat of the previous days had abated somewhat, a fact for which Mary in her classroom was truly thankful. She had just finished a small demonstration on her chalkboard and was about to quiz her pupils.

"Now – we have three columns. The first is for the pounds, the second for the shillings, the third for the pennies," she managed to get out before being aware of a forest of hands raised. She picked one at random.

"Tad, you have a question?"

"Aye, Miss Mary. If they are pounds, shillings and pennies, why are they not P, S, and P? You have labelled the columns, L, S, and D."

Mary gave a sigh and saw there was no escape from a long and, probably to her pupils, a bewildering explanation. Just telling them that it was 'how it had always been', would not suffice.

"The S is certainly for the shillings. Tad, how many shillings are there in a pound?"

The small lad's face screwed up into a fierce scowl of concentration.

"Er, twenty, Miss Mary."

"And how many pennies make up a shilling?"

That was far easier. "Twelve," came the immediate response.

"Let us first deal with the problem of D standing for pennies. You will remember from last week when I was telling you about the Romans? Well, they left England over a thousand years ago. Their word for one of their coins was denarius. Somehow or other, that letter D has stayed with us ever since, making one penny being entered under that column."

Tad remained standing. "What is a farthing, then?" he asked.

"Right – one half-penny is a half-penny, as you all must already know. The farthing is one quarter of a penny – a fourth of a penny – hence the shortened name of farthing – a 'fourthing'."

Tad, curiosity satisfied, sat down again. Mary was just about to enter the more complicated explanation of the L standing for Pound, when the bell rang from the back room. Lou Crowley, as a part of her agreement with Mary, acted as timekeeper. Every day, she would descend the stairs and ring the bell for end of morning school, and then again in late afternoon for the end of day.

"We shall continue this afternoon, when I shall set you all a task that will be new to you. Class dismissed."

All the children scampered off home for their dinner. Mary walked down the street and into the Parke estate, where she lived with Harry Cove at the Bailiff's large cottage. Dinner was ready by the time she arrived, set out on the large table in the parlour.

"My father is away to Exeter," Harry explained. "Making further enquiries about the two bodies. It seems that they were living near Teign Village and had children in the city."

"And any more news about the manner of their death?" Mary asked, having swallowed a spoonful of fish soup.

Laura Cove looked up from her soup. "No – Avril and James determined that aconite was responsible. What is still unknown is how it was administered. Either they took it themselves in some dreadful pact, or they were fed it under duress."

"Either way is horrible to contemplate," Mary shivered.

"But it simply has to be one or the other," Harry grimaced.

Harry had raised no objections to the fact that the children still referred to their teacher, and his wife, as 'Miss Mary', although she would more correctly be addressed as 'Mistress Cove'. Somehow or other, it was accepted by one and all that a schoolmistress should be a Miss somebody or other!

"It is correct that Master Kent accompanied him?" Mary asked.

"Aye – he has taken a great interest in this mystery. I suppose, as Parliament's roving agent, he deems it his business," Harry answered. "Believe it or not, I quite like the man."

"Oh, many do," Laura Cove nodded. "And, before I am subjected to a forest of raised eyebrows, it has nothing to do with his looks. It is all to do with his manner and politeness."

"Aye, mother, we believe you," Harry grinned.

"Oh, tush and piffle!" Laura grinned back. "Mary would agree with me, wouldn't you, Mary?"

"Oh indeed I would," Mary nodded. "Admittedly, he is a fine looking man, but his manner is faultless."

"Dear God, both of you have a shine for the fellow!" Harry laughed aloud.

"Tis just as well that Glory has accepted Gaston as her betrothed, or she would become a contender for Master Kent's affections!" Mary added.

"That is one very good match," Laura nodded. "Gaston has impeccable manners and is a handsome young man, whilst Glory needs to put her flirting days behind her. She is quite stunning to look at and has never wanted for male attention. Gaston will have his work cut out keeping her eyes fixed on him."

Mary then changed the subject and told them about the wrestling bout she was having with the children concerning the pounds, shillings, and pence.

"I sincerely hope that they have forgotten all about the L standing for pounds. That would take me the better part of the afternoon explaining why we adopted something from the French of all people!"

"But many of our English words derive from old French," Harry objected. "Given that Norman French was the language of the conquerors, it would be a miracle if some did not still exist!"

"And that Norman French was the language of the court for centuries afterwards!" Laura added.

Not for the first time, Mary was exceedingly glad that she had married into a family that could converse and argue with knowledge behind their thoughts. She had been with James and Avril for many years, learning the apothecary's business and had got used to listening to those two very knowledgeable people conversing together. Her own education had expanded tenfold in that time.

"But that would inevitably lead to them pestering me for the story of the Conquest – not to say its aftermath! I have a timetable of lessons to which I must adhere if I am to get anywhere with them.”

“And what is on that timetable for the afternoon?”

“Ah! Something they will initially detest; but something I sincerely hope they will come to relish. I am going to make them write down their thoughts on the book they have all been reading aloud. I want them to write their honest opinions. That will cause them to think, and to think constructively.”

Mary’s fears were realised when, resuming her place at the front of the class, she set them to the task. Some groaned, whilst others stared blankly at her. Only one or two grabbed pens and started to write. Tad was one of those who gazed at her wide-eyed in blank amazement. But then, to Mary’s joy, he replaced an expression of blankness with one of frowning concentration. Then he started to write.

*　*　*

Had Matthew Kent been privy to the comments about him at the Cove’s table, he would have been both slightly embarrassed and amused. He and Peter Cove had arrived at the guildhall well before dinner, which they had eaten at a neighbouring tavern.

Their first task was to enquire whether a young man of the name Dodds worked there. The harassed senior clerk who they accosted, threw down his pen and simply pointed to the end of the large room where three young men sitting on tall stools laboured at ledgers.

“Thank you, but which one is he?” Cove probed.

“The one with the black hair,” came the reply.

“Then we must have words with him. We have news that will come as a great shock.”

“He cannot be spared from his duties. It will have to wait until the working day is finished!”

“We bring news for him that will render him unfit to concentrate on his work for some time!”

“Then it is doubly important that he not be disturbed until work is finished!”

“Where may I find the Sheriff?” Cove asked. “He needs be told the same information.”

"Where may you find the Sheriff? He is far away in Barnstaple. You will have to make do with the deputy!"

"And where may *he* be found?" Cove persisted.

"I have not the slightest idea. Now go away and leave me to my very important work!"

Kent nudged Cove and gave him a wink. He fished inside his inner pocket and drew out his warrant. He laid it over the paper on the man's desk.

"Read that, then get off your backside and conduct us to the deputy – wherever that may be!" he ordered.

The man read the warrant, opened and closed his mouth a few times, then swallowed.

"Oh! Um! Er! Yes, Certainly!" He slid off his stool and set off at a brisk pace, up a wide staircase and along a corroder. He knocked at a door and entered.

"Two *gentlemen* to see you, Sir Horace," he turned and fled.

Kent again offered the warrant to the balding man sitting behind a large desk that was covered in papers and scrolls. The man rose, handed the warrant back and waved them to chairs.

"And how may a country bumpkin of a deputy sheriff assist one from parliament?" he asked, his voice betraying both annoyance and resignation at the same time.

"Matthew Kent. This gentleman is Peter Cove, Bailiff for Bovey Tracey. I will leave it to Master Cove to explain why we are here."

"Sir Horace," Cove began. "We have two unexplained deaths, both the subject of poisoning by aconite." He went on to explain where they were found and the condition of the bodies. "We have since discovered that they are Lucas and Ann Dodds, living in a large house no more than three miles from the town."

At the name, Sir Horace sat up a lot straighter in his chair. "Dodds, you say? I seem to recall a young clerk of that name working in the writing office."

"We are reliably informed that this young man is their son. That is why we are here, trying to discover all that we may about his parents. Their deaths are extremely mysterious."

"Mysterious? I'll say they are mysterious! I shall send down for the young man, and you may certainly question him in my presence. I am now as intrigued as you are."

"Does the name Dodds mean anything to you other than it being the name of a guildhall employee?"

"Yes, but not that recently. I seem to remember the name being associated with some religious sect or other – but that was at least a year past, perhaps even longer ago than that."

He rang a bell and informed the servant who appeared as if by magic that young Dodds was to be brought immediately to the office. It all went quiet for a while until a knock sounded and in came Master Dodds, a tall and thin young man who bore some facial resemblance to the dead man.

"Come here and sit. This gentleman has news for you," Sir Horace beckoned him forward.

The young man peered at Cove and then gave a smile of recognition.

"Master Bailiff, what brings you here? I recognise you from my old home."

Cove cleared his throat, not in the least looking forward to what he was about to divulge.

"A few days back, two bodies were discovered in the large field behind our town church," he said, hoping to get to the crux of the matter with as little delay as possible. "Our investigations suggest that they are the bodies of Lucas and Ann Dodds."

The young man's face paled as the news sank in. "But I had a letter from them only last week saying that they were planning a visit to Exeter to see both me and my sister!"

The drawings were produced. Very reluctantly, the young man agreed that they were indeed his parents. He paused for a moment.

"You say that they were found in a field. Why should that be? Who put them there? How did they come to die?"

"We have discovered also that they were both the subject of poisoning by aconite – some residue was found in both mouths. However, there was no sign whatsoever of any other person being present around the site where the bodies were found – almost fifty yards from the top hedge and twenty from the left hedge. Expert trackers could find no trace whatsoever except for the footprints of both your parents in the lane at the top of the field."

The young man whose name was Ethan, closed his eyes.

"I can imagine the field, although I left home some three years ago to take up my present post. The lane goes through Teign Village to the river, and our house is then up some distance on the left."

"Can you think of anyone who might wish your parents harm?"

"No – certainly not. They were very private people and would not have antagonised anyone deliberately."

"Please forgive my asking the next question, but I must do so. Can you think of any reason why your mother and father would plan to end their own lives – together, and in that particular place?"

The young man again closed his eyes and went silent for a few moments.

"They mentioned some years past that it was one of the rules. My sister and I never understood what rules were being referred to, nor who had written those rules."

"Did they belong to any particular religious sect?"

"Aye, they did, and it was one both Ellen and I wanted no part of. Now and again, strange folk would arrive at the house. All would go out into the garden and start performing strange rituals, dancing, swaying, and wailing quietly. When I asked one day what it was all about, I was told that it was harmless and not to bother my head with it."

"You say strange folk. In what way strange?"

"Well, both men and women were dressed head to foot in robes of dark green – no belts, no ornaments of any kind – and they were always solemn-faced, never spoke either to Ellen or to me."

"And you have no notion what this sect may be?"

"No, none whatsoever. Now, if I may be excused, I must hurry to my sister and break this news."

"I would deem it a favour if you would allow us all to accompany you. There are questions that we need ask of her."

"Sir, may I at least have a short time with her before you pose those questions?"

"You certainly may. It would be unseemly for us to disrupt what is surely going to be a painful interview."

The four men left the guildhall and walked down the street to where another street bisected it. At the corner was the shop of a jeweller. Ethan went to the door and went inside, leaving the other three to wait for a suitable time to elapse before they entered. However, it was not long before Ethan came out again.

"I have told her as much as I know. She is taking the news better than I had feared she might. My brother-in-law is away at present, so the shop is being looked after by his journeyman. Please, come through and I will introduce you."

Ellen, the sister, was a year older than her brother. She was sat before an empty fireplace, the weather being far too warm for its use. She made to rise as the imposing figure of Sir Horace Drew entered, but he laid a hand on her shoulder.

"Nay, mistress – you have no need to rise. These two gentlemen are from Bovey Tracey. Master Cove, the Bailiff, and Master Kent, a Parliamentary Agent. I take it that your brother has appraised you already of the circumstances of your bereavement."

"Aye, sir – he has. My mother and father were found dead in the middle of a large field – poisoned and alone. Please, how can this be?"

"With your permission, sir?" Cove looked at the deputy sheriff, who nodded his agreement. Cove took a chair and faced the young woman.

"Your brother happened to mention that your parents were sometimes visited by people who were dressed in plain robes. Did you ever witness such an occurrence?"

Clearly trying to compose herself, the young woman took several deep breaths before answering.

"On many more than one occasion," she stated. "I came here three years ago when I married, but before that I was with my parents at their home. The visits were quite regular, perhaps once every month. Three, sometimes four, people would arrive on horseback dressed in ordinary clothes. Once they had been welcomed into the house, they and mother and father would don long robes and repair to the back of the garden where they performed some strange ritual that consisted of steps as if in a slow dance, never touching one another, then chanting quietly and wailing softly. I found it all very disturbing but had been told from an early age that it was none of my affair. They never once answered any questions I put to them, simply told it was none of my affair. I soon gave up what I knew to be a fruitless quest. I have absolutely no idea who these persons were."

"Were they the same people every time?"

"No, they were not – and that made me wonder all the more. Over the years, I suppose twenty or slightly more different persons made up the visiting groups."

"One final question. Do you remember any of the words that were chanted?"

"One word stuck in my mind as it was repeated over and over. It sounded like 'remissionem'. But I have no idea whether it was precisely that word, or what it meant."

"I believe that we have taken up too much of your time, so we will leave you and your brother to comfort one another. Fear not, Master Dodds, I shall speak to the clerk in charge of your office. You have leave of absence for the rest of this week – and at no loss of salary."

"For that, sir, I thank you. Ellen and I have a lot to discuss. I may ask for help in arranging for their funeral."

"I shall be at your service whenever you need it," Cove added as the three men took their leave. They walked back together in silence, pausing only at the main office.

"Young Master Dodds has my permission to take paid leave of absence for the rest of this week," Sir Horace addressed the chief clerk.

That person stood deferentially but immediately raised objections.

"But what of the important work that will be left undone – sir?"

"Arrange that others see to its completion. If not, then do it yourself! The young man has had the most awful experience and I fully expect that he will be treated properly and with due kindness. If not, I shall enquire the reason."

Sir Horace Drew stood with his thumbs hooked into his belt as once again the three men stood at the main doors.

"Your stay here gentlemen, will have to be extended. Meet me here again, mounted, at ten in the morning and we shall ride a short distance to where I have an idea I may find someone who is, I truly believe, able to begin unravelling this business."

* * *

That evening saw yet another large gathering at the tavern. It was Ella's birthday and she had just turned twenty. Naturally, every member of that vastly extended family was included. Brom the bakery came John and Evelyn Ramsey; from the smithy came Abel, Faith, Simon, Imelda, and little Jack Smith. From the apothecary came James and Avril Ramsey, plus young Nell Dawkins. From the shoemakers came Josiah and Alice Grubb, Imelda's parents. Lastly, from the smallholding, came Gil, Ella herself, with Rosie and Jamie. Abel caught Ella, his daughter, and swung her up towards the roof.

"A day of joy to you," he grinned as he set her down again.

"Thank you, papa. Gil has already made a great fuss of me."

"And rightly so," Abel boomed. "He is turning out to be a fair husband for our little girl."

"Not such a little girl any longer, papa. I have borne two children already and who knows how many more we shall be blessed with."

The enormous blacksmith swung a friendly punch at his son's equally massive shoulder.

"Hear that, Simon? You sister has *two* children! You mother and I look forward to our fourth grandchild."

Simon, the punch hardly registering, grinned at his father. "Patience, papa! Imelda is still struggling with little Jack!"

"Indeed, I am," Imelda joined them. "He is the sweetest child – sometimes. But at others, can be fretful and somewhat wilful."

"Wilful, you say?" Ella spoke up from the head of the table where her seat had been garlanded. "Try coping with Jamie if you want an example of wilfulness. Indeed, without Rosie's eagle eye, I would be unable to get any work done at all."

"Not that long ago," Gil laughed, "you were levelling that same wilfulness at Rosie."

"Having a young brother has brought out what I never expected to find – care and thoughtfulness."

"Bollocks!" came an angry and very juvenile shout from beneath the table.

Gill, smothering a massive grin, dived underneath and hauled out a squealing Jamie.

"Where on earth did you hear such a word?" Ella was set to administer a smack on his bottom.

"Dada said it this morning when he hit his thumb!" came the defiant reply.

The whole tavern dissolved into gales of laughter. Gil stood with a struggling little boy in his arms and went a deep red.

"Aye, I did – and it hurt!" he said defiantly.

"Your father would never have said such a word, would you, John?" Evelyn remonstrated.

"Indeed, I would not!" John Ramsey stated firmly.

"I heard what you said grandpapa, when you dropped that loaf," Rosie butted in. "And it was not that word!"

"And what would it have been?" James, John's brother probed mischievously.

"Grandpapa said, 'Satan's buttocks'," Rosie replied. "And then he kicked the loaf into the street. Satan is supposed to be a serpent – and serpents do not have buttocks!"

Once again, the entire placed rocked with gales of laughter. John in his turn, went bright red.

"Before this happy day turns into a festival of profanity, may I suggest we all raise our glasses to Ella – and then let us all sit and enjoy the feast," Faith demanded.

The toast over, and a happy Ella seated amongst her garlands, the food started arriving. And then peace descended, the happy voices stilled as knives sliced and spoons spooned – apart from one rather unsettled little boy.

"Don't like," Jamie pushed his small platter away from him. Sitting atop a pile of cushions, he regarded a small pile of vegetables with disgust. "Want egg!"

Having their own large flock of hens, he was used to eggs in every conceivable manner of presentation. His favourite of all was hard-boiled.

As Glory was taking an evening off to be with Gaston and his parents, Zachary was looking after the large party, helped by one of the scullery maids. He came to stand behind Jamie, reached past him with a hard-boiled egg on a small saucer.

"You like these though, don't you?" he enquired.

Jamie made a grab for the egg but was thwarted when Zachary moved the saucer out of his reach. Jamie looked up at the tall young man and out came his lower lip, ready to make his feelings known.

"I'm going to cut the egg into four bits," Zachary said. "You eat one large spoon of vegetables and I'll give you a bit of the egg. Is that to your liking?"

The word 'no' was hovering on the lad's lips until he took another look at the quartered egg. He dug a reluctant spoon into the peas, diced carrots and turnips in gravy. This was transferred to a small mouth, chewed and swallowed hastily.

"Yuk! Don't like!"

The portion of egg seemed to restore his better nature – and so the pile of vegetables slowly diminished.

"How would you like to adopt a little boy?" Ella asked.

"No thank you, I've enough trouble as it is with Glory hardly ever present. Then, when she is, she spends most of her time regarding herself in the mirror!"

Jamie had the last word as the first course came to an end. He gave a resounding burp, then looked around expecting a burst of laughter. Instead, at a stern look from Ella, everyone studiously ignored him. Jamie scowled at everyone. He had been aiming for another distraction and was furious that he didn't get one.

CHAPTER V

Cove and Kent had spent a comfortable night in a tavern not three doors from the guildhall. Their talk over supper had been full of questions unanswered. Why was the deputy sheriff in the guildhall and not in the castle offices? Where was he going to take them the next day? Obviously to someone he believed could throw more light on the problem. Why was the deputy sheriff taking such an inordinate interest in the case? What to make of the daughter's tale of multiple people visiting the Dodds – and what the hell was the meaning of all this strange ritual?

They ate a very leisurely breakfast the next morning and were waiting with their horses outside the guildhall just before ten o'clock. Promptly at the stroke of ten, Sir Horace came riding to meet them.

"Good morning, gentlemen. Mount up and we shall set off on a ride of no more than two miles."

And that was the sum total of the speech they had with him until they arrived at the destination. Travelling roughly east, they passed through the village of Heavitree and stopped at a row of small cottages about a further half-mile onwards. And then Sir Horace broke his silence.

"In this cottage, gentlemen, is a person who I am confident can throw a bright light on these strange happenings. I shall not say what are my thoughts as I would wish them to come straight from one who's knowledge is far greater than mine."

They looped the reins over a small gatepost and followed Sir Horace up to the door of the first of the cottages. His knock was answered after a longish gap.

"Horace, you young rascal! Welcome. Come away in and I shall treat you to my finest brew!"

Standing in the doorway was a very tall, thin and slightly emaciated figure of a very old man. Dressed simply in a black robe, his lean features were topped by the remnants of a white tonsure.

"Ned, forgive this unannounced visit, but I have brought these gentlemen to witness first-hand the knowledge you have stored in that mighty cranium for so many years!"

Sir Horace followed the stooping figure into a small parlour in which, despite the heat of the outside day, a fire was crackling merrily in the grate. The old man waved everyone to chairs, taking his at the fireside.

Sir Horace introduced the two and then let them know whose house they were visiting.

"Gentlemen, let me introduce my uncle – Canon Ned Rigby. For years, he was in charge of the library and scriptorium of the cathedral. What he does not know about religious and quasi-religious goings on is probably not worth knowing. Ned, these gentlemen are from Bovey Tracey – well, Master Cove is the bailiff there. Master Kent has some warrant from parliament. Perhaps, Master Cove, you would relate all that is known of your mystery?"

Before Cove could start, the old chap clapped his hands. A door at the rear of the parlour opened and a dwarf-like figure scuttled in.

"You reverence summoned me?" he squeaked.

"Aye, Gruff – I summoned you. Pray bring in a large pitcher of that brew we perfected yesterday, and four pewter mugs."

"Certainly, your reverence," the diminutive figure scuttled away.

"Gruff and I amuse ourselves perfecting the brewing of good ale. It passes very pleasantly the few days that the Good Lord allows me to enjoy."

The ale, when sampled, was even better than they had expected, and all were happy to shower compliments on the old canon and his assistant.

"And now, Master Cove, regale me with your story."

He listened attentively as Cove related the finding of the bodies, their condition and location, the information gleaned from both the son and daughter. At the end of this long recitation, Canon Rigby looked over at his nephew and nodded.

"I had thought this all dead and buried many years since," he said very quietly. "My nephew sitting beside you has brought you to me as I suspect he has a notion what this be all about. So now, you will have to listen to an old man's reminiscences."

He paused and quaffed from his mug.

"During my many years in the scriptorium and the library, I indulged myself almost from day one in the study of old parchments and manuscripts that are stored there. These range widely from cathedral and diocesan matters to liturgy, canon law, and ceremonial. Also, there are many that deal with heresies and sects that never conformed to the accepted norms. Now, these range back some hundreds of years, and it is only my deep study of Latin that enabled me to make sense of some of them. Back in the early reign of the eighth Henry, all was peace and harmony. The church bowed before Rome, as did the king and almost the entire population. However, there were a few exceptions. One of them caused me to pay it time and interest. I appeared that there was a sect that slowly grew in the counties of Devon and Somerset. It never, or so I truly believe, grew to more than a hundred or so misguided individuals. It seems to have originated from the teachings of an obscure, retired priest who was called Ignatius Plumb. He had retired to a hut from his parish that was never named, but which I suspect to have been towards Exmoor. The main thrust of his argument was that Almighty God, having created man, saw that his creation was less than perfect. After all, the Book of Genesis hardly casts his first creations in a good light, does it? Plumb went on to expand this to encompass all of mankind – that original sin can *never* be expunged, that mankind is inherently wicked and that it is the absolute duty of every man, woman and child to beg forgiveness throughout the whole of their lives. He titled his sect 'The Vale of Sorrow'. And it is this that I suspect your two people adhered to. I honestly believed it to be gone until you mentioned two things to me. One was the wearing of the dark green robes, totally unadorned. The second was the constantly repeated word 'remissionem'. That is a Latin word that means 'forgiveness'. It appeared in the Latin Mass of the Roman Church, closely followed by the word 'peccatorum' – the forgiveness of sins. Plumb insisted that the word be chanted repeatedly, accompanied by wailing and beating of breasts. That is what I think is at the back of all this."

Sir Horace looked at his uncle and nodded. "I did wonder," he said. "I well remember the stories you used to relate to us when we were all much younger."

Kent was the first to raise a question.

"It certainly would accord with the observations of the son and daughter," he was deep in thought. "But how may that then tie in with the deaths that we discovered?"

"That is the appalling continuation of Plumb's teachings," the Canon replied. "He taught that, should any adherent to his teachings reach a point in their lives when they realised that their pleadings were not to God's liking, then the person was considered by God to be unworthy of any further part in his creation – and had an obligation to end his or her life as totally without purpose."

"Dear Lord – that is against every teaching of the church – be it the old Roman Church, our English one, or even the Puritan teachings. Taking one's own life is the ultimate sin!" Cove almost gasped.

"Indeed, it is," Canon Rigby nodded. "And that was what made the sect so abhorrent to most people."

Kent had been deep in thought.

"Then this Vale of Sorrow could not have died out with the demise of its original adherents. Either it has been smouldering away undetected for many years, or someone has found it and given it a wicked resurrection."

"Exactly my thoughts," Canon Rigby agreed. "And I fear the former of your options – that it has indeed been alive in tiny pockets and is only now come to light with these deaths. Plumb himself died before the old Roman Church authorities could haul him before their court. It was believed at the time that there was no natural explanation for his death. He may well have practised what he preached!"

"Then the very first thing we must do when we return is to organise a very thorough search for these visitors to the Dodds' home," Sir Horace declared. "How we may go about it is going to be a problem. But at the very least, we have some solution to the two deaths, repugnant though that explanation may be."

"My duty is clear," Kent stood up. "I must immediately return to Westminster and relay these findings to the authorities. Surely, the religious beliefs of both parliament and the English Church must coincide and must be reconciled to root out this heresy!"

"And, in the meantime, assure those to whom you report that every effort will be made to find and arrest those who are complicit in this evil," Sir Horace stated.

Thanking the old Canon, the three returned to Exeter, Kent to collect his things and start the journey to Westminster, Cove to return to Bovey Tracey, and Sir Horace to sit in his office and ponder how he might even start the search.

* * *

Two days after the meeting with Canon Rigby, the last Saturday of August left behind the heat of the preceding weeks and returned to overcast skies and a fairly strong westerly wind. These same weather conditions existed far to the north of Bovey Tracey.

Sir Lucien Pellow had received his orders some few days previously and had followed them to the letter. He had led his troop on a long march eastwards in the direction of the city of Worcester. Late that Saturday afternoon, they had arrived at their destination, a large open space just to the north of the cathedral.

They had crossed the river Severn with the cathedral just to their south, then had joined three more troops who were all camped in that great open space to the east of the river. Pellow left his troop to join the other commanders for a briefing, promising to let them all know what the plan was when he returned.

"There – what did I say?" Borthwick could hardly conceal his smugness.

Nobody chose to rise to the bait. They had their work cut out erecting their small tents, shedding their equipment and getting a small fire ready. They had barely started to eat their meagre rations when their commander returned and drew everyone about him.

"We in this position are the northernmost group," he started to scratch out a plan with a stick on the ground. He drew a slightly wiggly line. "This is the river that we crossed, and here we are. To the south-east of us are three more groups of regiments. They are all grouped just to the east of the cathedral. King Charles is with David Leslie, the Earls of Derby, Shrewsbury and Cleveland, in the commandery that is between two of the regimental groupings. Then, to the south of us, and on the other side of the river, are three more regimental groupings. Therefore, we have the entire city under our control – and also the crossing of the river. Altogether, we have about sixteen thousand in number, the bulk of them Scottish. There seems little point in changing the disposition of our forces unless we are brought to battle. Should that happen, then any group could be moved as circumstances dictate. Now, I suggest that you all get as much rest as you can. Our scouts are out far and wide, so we should get ample warning if parliament moves its army towards us."

Back in their small tent, Matt Crowley, Herb Grindley and Seb Borthwick mulled things over.

"Sixteen thousand is not that large a force," Grindley muttered. "The Scots cannot have had much success recruiting to our cause as they moved southwards!"

"Cannot matter," Borthwick retaliated. "We hold all the strategic points about the city. We command the river crossings and have good views south and east from where parliament's forces are bound to approach."

Matt had nothing to add to any of this. He was both terrified and wildly excited at the prospect of action. In that, he was just one of thousands either scared stiff or eager to fight.

* * *

Some miles to the south-east of Worcester, another talk was taking place. Oliver Cromwell was conferring with John Lambert, one of his commanders. They were being briefed by one of their forward scouts.

"How many did you say?" Lambert seemed amazed at what he had just been told.

"Certainly much less than twenty thousand, sir," the man replied. "Our agents in the city have been most assiduous and have plotted seven defensive positions dotted around the city. I have indicated their positions on the map. I have put the best figures against each one of them – and they amount to somewhere in the region on fifteen to sixteen thousand.”

For only the third time that month, Cromwell allowed a tiny smile to alter his normally stern features. He rubbed his hands together, thanked the man and dismissed him.

“Well John – think we can manage?” he asked.

“Might be a close-run thing,” Lambert grinned. “Sixteen thousand in seven defensive positions against our measly twenty-eight thousand highly trained and disciplined men. Might take us as long as two hours!”

* * *

That same evening, Peter Cove met with Luke Barton, the steward, James and Avril Ramsey, and Mary. He thought it only right that they learned what he had learned.

“Vale of Sorrow? Never heard of them,” Barton grunted. “Sound like a lot of madmen!”

“According to the daughter, there were just as many mad women as men,” Cove informed them. “It would most definitely account for a suicide pact between the two of them. How in the name of Heaven can people be so misguided?”

“I believe, all too easily,” Mary added her thoughts. “Think of the Infidels who hurled themselves against our crusaders – never a thought for their own lives – just as madly keen to have their lives ended with a promise of an instant place in paradise. One has only to turn such belief on its head to see that others could be just as easily swayed. One ends his life in what he sees as glorious victory, the other ends his life in what he sees as abject failure.”

“I sometimes wonder whether you should be teaching philosophy at a university rather than teaching small children to read and write,” James laughed.

“I know which I would rather be doing,” Mary shrugged. “Watching the little faces as things slowly become apparent, as their understanding deepens, is the best reward I can think of.”

“Further to your example, Mary,” Avril was frowning. “Could it not also explain the willingness of those same crusaders to hurl themselves against the Infidels, with the promise of an eternal place in heaven – as vouchsafed by various Popes?"

"But the two are hardly the same," James argued. "Infidels and Crusaders were both willing to die trying to achieve something. These Vale of Sorrow characters are admitting that they have *failed* to achieve anything at all!"

"Anyway, whatever the philosophical rights and wrongs, my task is to endeavour to locate other members of this weird sect – and they simply must exist hereabouts."

"Then may I wish you every success in that endeavour," Barton gave the Bailiff a pat on the shoulder. "You are going to have to have the Devil's own luck."

"I may have to call upon his services before much longer," Peter Cove sighed. "But before it comes to that, is there anyone here in the town who may fit the bill?"

"Mercy Green would have certainly been at the head of my list, but she is now probably on her knees somewhere in the New World," Barton gave a laugh.

"She would not have been on mine," James argued. "She was far too committed to the ultra-Puritan way of life. She would have seen suicide as a mortal offence to God!"

"It would be useless consulting Dick or Sal Allen up at the tavern," Mary commented. "The sort of person we are looking for would hardly visit it!"

The talk ranged all the way down the town, nearly everyone being dismissed as being far removed from the character of the two dead people.

"Just a thought," Luke Barton was musing aloud. "Who is that strange fellow up at Lustleigh – the Reeve."

"Thomas Axelby?" Cove nodded slowly. "I would agree that he is somewhat strange. I have never had any sort of conversation with him. Whenever I am anywhere near there, all I receive is a nod of acknowledgement."

"I have spoken to his daughter," Avril commented. "I believe she is called Lisa and is always very soberly dressed all in black. She came to consult me some months past on a personal matter. She is indeed a very strange one – it took me a long time to prise from her the nature of her complaint. She must be nearing thirty years and, as far as I am aware, has never shown any interest in marrying. Even when I had discovered her problem, she spoke hardly at all. She seemed to me to be desperately sad."

"Thomas also has a son," Cove added. "I think he is called Francis. He is older than his sister and also dresses as she does – black from head to toe. What he does, and where he does it, I have no idea. But from all I hear, he is as withdrawn as Lisa. Yes, perhaps that family would bear a little investigation."

"Is not Thomas a widower?" Barton queried.

"Aye – his wife died many years past. Thomas has lived in his cottage from the day he was born – took over the post of Reeve when his own father died, and that must have been at least twenty years back."

"The other people of the village must have been content to vote Thomas as Reeve in succession to his father," James said. "But when that happened, his children would still have been less than ten years of age. I wonder what a friendly villager might tell us of those times?"

"I have just the person in mind," Cove smiled for the first time that evening. "In Brimley is the young steward – a chap named Luke Farmer. He is married to Meg, and she is the daughter of Laxton Groves, the woodcutter. I do believe that Groves has been in the village all his life as well. I shall visit Brimley in the morning and see what I may learn."

And on that slightly hopeful note, the meeting broke up. Mary, who was already at home, went to find Harry her husband to relate all she had heard. Barton simply went to the next large cottage on the estate. James and Avril walked back to their cottage in the town, both of them mulling over what they had learned. It was all most disturbing.

CHAPTER VI

The first thing that Peter Cove did on the Sunday was to call at the tavern to appraise Kent of his intention to visit Brimley, and to ask if Kent would like to accompany him.

"I take it you have some purpose in mind other than partaking of Lady Violette's wine cellar," Kent grinned.

"I am that transparent?" Cove grinned back. "Aye, I most certainly have. There is a young woman there who can hopefully supply some information concerning people who live in her birth village. There is just a faint possibility that two of them could fit into the mould of our two suicides. As I say, it is merely a possibility, but one that I cannot ignore."

"Then give me ten minutes and I shall join you – even though I may be forced to sample more of the good Lady's most excellent wines!"

The first thing they had to do when they arrived at Brimley was to announce themselves to Lady Violette. Not to do so would have been extremely rude. They were soon sitting in the magnificent hall, each with a glass of very excellent Bordeaux. Cove took it upon himself to explain the reason for the visit, plus what they had learned about the two people who had killed themselves.

"That is shocking!" was that Lady's response. "Believe it or not, I am old enough to have a vague recollection of this Vale of Sorrow. Living in London, one became aware of every story and rumour within a few days of its happening – no matter where in this country it occurred. The matter was short-lived as everyone believed it had been eradicated. Seemingly not, if what you say is happening now!"

"We would be most grateful if we were able to question someone in your employ, my lady," Cove presented the reason for the visit.

"Surely you do not suspect anyone here of such profanity?"

"Most certainly not! But she might well have some information about people in Lustleigh that could prove enlightening."

"Then you must be referring to young Meg. She lived there until she married my new steward. I shall send for her."

Meg arrived some minutes later, tears streaming down her face.

"There is absolutely no need for tears, Meg," Lady Violette was quick to reassure her. "These gentlemen simply want to ask you about some people in your old village."

Meg grinned. "These tears are not of apprehension, my lady. They are tears resulting from many minutes chopping onions!"

Meg was waved to a small chair, where she sat and looked expectantly at the two men.

"Meg," Cove started. "You have heard about the two bodies which were found. It has since come to light that they took their own lives – and there is little doubt on that score. They belonged to a religious sect that approves of this – in fact, encourages it."

"But that is wickedness!" Meg gasped.

"Indeed, it is utter wickedness," Cove nodded. "Now, what we have to ask you must not be repeated under any circumstances. In your village are two people we are interested in – Francis and Lisa Axelby. We would be very glad if you would tell us your thoughts on them."

"Oh, Dear Lord! Do you suspect that they are of the same beliefs?"

"At this moment, no. But we have been told that their behaviour is not as normal young people. How do you remember them?"

"Exactly as that – not as normal young people, although they both be older that I am. They were almost always in one another's company – and that is *not* usual for a brother and sister. The rest of the village wondered if there was something *unnatural* in their association – if you get my meaning."

Cove and Kent exchanged a look, almost as if to say that that possibility had not even occurred to them – but indeed, might explain things.

"Just one further question, Meg – how do they both earn their living?"

Meg seemed far more at ease answering the question.

"I do not believe that Lisa ever did any paid work. She spent most of her time either in the home or with her brother in the woods. Francis did work as a bodger – and that is a very lonely occupation!"

"Please say nothing at all to anyone about this conversation. We will visit Lustleigh and make some further enquiries. They may very well be innocent of anything untoward, and it would be wrong to spread unfounded rumours."

Lady Violette gave Meg a nod of dismissal.

"Should anyone enquire, you may tell them that I have been asking you about dinner today. These two gentlemen will stay – I insist. So, what are you serving?"

"I have the remains of that haunch of venison, my lady. I intended to serve it with a wine and berry sauce, plus a variety of vegetables."

"And very delicious it sounds!"

When Meg had gone out with a final little curtsey to her mistress, Lady Violette turned again to her visitors.

"Delving further into that strange pair will call for subtlety," she smiled. "I am intrigued by this whole business. Is it too much to ask that you keep an old and inquisitive woman informed?"

"My Lady, we would never dream of keeping you from our investigation. Far from it – we would value whatever thoughts you might have upon the matter."

The venison in its sauce was just as good as they had all imagined.

* * *

Back in his office, Peter Cove went to the strong box and withdrew the brooch and the cross on its chain. He sat at his desk simply staring at them as if to demand of them where they had come from, who had owned them, and why had they been left close to the bodies? Had the two actually owned them? And if so, why had they taken them off and placed them near themselves before ending their lives? If they were *not* the owners, then how had they acquired them?

57

And that opened up another possibility. If they had *not* owned them and were not responsible for their placement, that meant that someone else had placed them there and had managed to leave no trace of their ever having been there. Cove put his head in his hand and knew it would start aching before long.

No! his head screamed at him. Do *not* complicate matters more than they are already! Start again from scratch. Point one – the brooch and cross were discovered near the dead bodies, fact! There was not the slightest sign of anyone else having been anywhere near the bodies, fact as vouchsafed by two very expert trackers. Therefore (or ergo, as he had heard Mary say), the items were indeed placed there by the two people who had died close to them.

Now think further on from that, he urged himself. He was interrupted by Hob who knocked on the door in his usual manner – as if he intended to demolish it. The young lad skidded to a halt in front of the desk.

"Master Bailiff – catastrophe!" he managed to blurt out.

Knowing Hob's leaning towards the over-dramatic, Cove gave the lad a stern look.

"And what can be so catastrophic that it causes you to utter only one word? You usually utter dozens!"

"Shepherd is in the courtyard, Master Bailiff. Says five ewes have been stolen!"

Cove leaned back in his chair and closed his eyes.

"Hob, answer me this. To whom does the shepherd report?"

"Master Steward," came the prompt reply.

"Then, in the name of all that is holy and sacred, why the bloody hell are you bothering me with this?"

"Because Master Steward be gone for the day to Ashburton!"

Cove uttered a long sigh and rose to put the jewels back into the strong box. Making sure that the box was securely locked, he went out to the main courtyard where an equally young Bernie Wheatcroft stood, mashing his old hat between his hands. Losing sheep was serious!

Cove turned to Hob. "Go and fetch either Garvey or Hook – does not matter which." He then turned to the young shepherd. Bernie had been appointed to take the place of a predecessor who had been arrested on a charge of rape and had been shot trying to escape.

"Tell me what has happened," he ordered.

"Sorry, Master Bailiff – t'were nothing of my fault! I went to sleep last night with all sheep fully accounted. My dog sleeps by my side and never woke me until sunrise. T'was when I went to the sheep again that I saw five were missing – all good ewes that would lamb for certain come the spring."

Sam Garvey trotted up to the Bailiff, followed by Hob – never intending to miss out on anything remotely exciting.

"Take us to the field and show me where the sheep were when you left them last night."

The field in question was just a little further up the lane from where the young shepherd had his hut. A Devon stone wall separated the two fields, the hut being set against it on the lower field side. Peering over the wall, Cove was able to see a flock of ewes contentedly munching away at the grass not twenty yards into the top field.

"So, you were asleep all night in the hut and your dog was by your side?"

"Aye, Master Bailiff. Lug would have woken me the second he heard anything amiss – and he did not."

"Where in that field were the sheep when you checked them before going to bed?"

"That's the odd thing, they were even closer to this wall than they are now. How can five be missing when Lug did not sense anything?"

Peter Cove had the very uneasy feeling that his life was spiralling downwards into a pit of mysteries. Luckily, he thought, I can hand this one over to Luke Barton when he returns – it is his problem and not mine. But in the meantime, he had to do something!

"Sam, go with young Bernie and see what you may find out."

Garvey and young Wheatcroft clambered over the wall, Lug leaping after them.

"Master Bailiff?" Cove heard a querulous Hob behind him. "That dog Lug came here not that long past – he is not Bernie's as his old dog was past working."

"Then where did Lug come from?"

"That I do not know, Master Bailiff. All I know is that Bernie has had him for some months now and has trained him to his ways."

It was not long before Garvey came back, a dispirited Bernie trailing in his wake. Garvey perched on the top of the wall whilst Lug leaped over again and made immediately for the hut, where he sat down facing outwards.

"Up in yonder corner is the gate. On t'other side be the lane and there be tracks of a cart leading upwards. Outside the gate are tracks where the cart had been turned around. Do you want me to follow those tracks, sir?"

"Aye, I most assuredly do. I shall accompany you. Let us see where they may lead. How large a cart would you say?"

"Of medium size, there be tracks also for one horse, so not a very large cart."

"On second thoughts then – Hob, go back and bring my horse and one for Sam. Hurry, as there could be rain to wash out the tracks!"

Needing no second bidding, Hob tore off down the field. Cove joined Sam Garvey on the wall. Bernie went to his remaining sheep – still over one hundred in number, and again counted them. "No more missing, Master Bailiff," he shouted.

"Where did Lug come from?" Cove shouted back.

"Master Steward brought him to me, must be back in March this year. He said that he had bought Lug from a chap in Chudleigh Knighton. Lug has been a very good dog ever since."

"Well, those tracks go nowhere near Chudleigh Knighton," Garvey grunted. "They point in the opposite direction."

Bernie, his task of counting completed, came to stand nervously by the wall. The sheep had disappeared whilst he had been in charge, and he feared recrimination.

"How may the five sheep be recognised?" Cove asked. "I see no markings on any of the others!"

"They *are* marked, Master Bailiff – although tis not easy to spot. They be Jacobs with short horns. There is a small notch cut on every one of them – about half-way down the right horn."

"So, were we to find three sheep similarly marked, there would be no question that they be the ones taken?"

"No question at all, sir."

"Unless the thieving bastard has marked his own flock in a similar manner," Garvey grunted.

There came the sound of hooves pattering up the lane. Garvey and Cove made their way to where Hob, astride the spare horse, was leading Cove's own chestnut.

"Hob – go back to Parke and make sure that Master Steward is made aware of what we are doing as soon as he returns. Sam – lead on and track this bloody cart."

The lane meandered left and right, the tracks easy to follow. Cove reckoned as they climbed slowly, that they would end up either at Becky Falls or even further at Manaton. By then, they would be well onto the moor. Garvey led, although a child of five could have followed those tracks.

And suddenly, the lane changed from soft going to rocky, the lane being of granite crushed by centuries of travelling feet and hooves. Garvey trotted ahead, looking intently at the ground before him, also to the left and the right. About a mile and a half into the granite path, he stopped and slid down to the ground.

"There, to the left is a smaller track. The same prints go along there. That horse has a slight nick in its left fore shoe. We must be just about level with Becky now."

He mounted up again and led off along this much smaller track. Rounding a bend, he could hear distinctly the sound of water cascading down over rocks. They were indeed very close to the waterfall. The tracks led him onwards until, rounding another bend, he halted.

"Manaton be just up yonder," he said, pointing to where a thin spiral of smoke could be seen. Someone up there had a fire going.

"Far too late in the day for baking bread," Cove muttered. "Must be a cooking fire."

Once again, the track turned to stony gravel. But well before they reached the source of the smoke, Garvey pointed to a patch of grass surrounded by gorse bushes.

"Cart stopped here, Master Bailiff," Garvey said, sliding down from his saddle for a closer look. "Lots of prints – horse, one man, cartwheels and some sheep droppings."

"Then, they were unloaded here. Now, where did they go?"

"That will take me some time," Garvey stated. "First, I shall find out where that cart went."

Cove minded the horses as Garvey followed faint traces in the short grass. He was gone about an hour, and Cove was getting very impatient.

"Two large huts over yonder rise," Garvey reported when he at last returned. The cart and the horse are there, but no sign of any man."

"Did anyone spot you?"

Garvey refrained from snorting. He was an expert at remaining unseen!

"Nay, Master Bailiff – not a soul spotted me."

"Then we can do no more today. On the morrow, Master Steward will come here with you and some of the men. Those sheep are hereabouts, and they *will* be found!"

* * *

Lady Violette made one of her rare visits to the little school on the Monday, a day of strong winds and the threat of rain. She arrived well before the children, hoping to have a word with her protégé Mary before lessons commenced. She sat perched on the edge of Mary's desk.

"And how are things progressing?" she asked.

Mary paused before answering. She was always very careful how she phrased her comments to Lady Violette in case they sounded like a plea for extra funds. The old lady had taken it upon herself to make up any deficit in the day-to-day running expenses, having previously, almost single-handedly, financed the opening of the establishment.

"To be frank my lady, things are progressing far better than I could ever have hoped. At least seven of the children are well advanced in their reading and writing. Some are even showing an interest in their arithmetic! And that is something I would have thought impossible."

"And what about any other subjects? I hear that some of the children press you for explanations that are, to put it delicately, more the matter for a vicar."

"I have to admit that I encourage all the children to raise questions that are bothering them. Some days ago, I was asked how it was that the magician at the summer fair was able to make things disappear. I showed them that it was naught but trickery, and that there was no magic involved. And then came the inevitable question – how did Jesus make enough food for the five thousand out of a few loaves and fishes. Was that just trickery as well, as it seemed to the lad that it was magic."

"Aye – I can see that would call for a very careful answer," Violette smiled. "And how did you manage it?"

"The only way that I could. I told them all that Jesus, being the Son of God, had the same powers that His Father had. That He could do anything that He saw was necessary – and that was *not* magic, but the power that nobody on this earth could ever possess."

"And did that answer suffice?"

"Aye, I do believe it did. Well, all except for one young girl. I saw her still frowning when class was dismissed. I do believe that I have a deep thinker in this school!"

"Then that is as much as anyone could ask. This world needs people who think – far more than it needs people who follow blindly anything they are told. Not that I am advocating heresy! Far from it. I believe you are one such, are you not? It is the main reason why I strongly supported your employment as teacher."

"I will be ever thankful that you did, my lady. I love being a part of their young lives, watching understanding dawn on their faces. But there is one matter that I must bring to your attention. I shall have to beg leave of absence in about seven months from now."

Lady Violette slipped from the desk, despite her advanced years, and went to Mary to embrace her in a warm hug.

"And is that impossibly handsome young husband of yours aware of this?"

"It is my intention to tell him this very evening. I had to be doubly sure myself. The only other to know is Avril – and I consulted her only yesterday. She is sworn to secrecy!"

"As am I! Never worry for an instant that your position here would be in jeopardy. You are invaluable to this school. I shall make what arrangements are necessary nearer the time. Now – are you content with your new condition?"

"I have to admit that I have never been more content. I feel as if I should be dancing in the street and singing."

"Then may the Lord bless you and keep you safe."

The timing was impeccable. The door opened and in came the usual avalanche of small children. There came a chorus of 'Good morning, My Lady. Good morning, Miss Mary'.

Mary beamed at her assembled class, and then ruined their good humour by setting them sums of addition and subtraction. Lady Violette smiled to herself and left.

* * *

There was absolutely no way that Hob was going to miss out on the search up on the moor. Even at fifteen years of age, he was still the rather excitable young lad he had been ever since the Coves had 'adopted' him as a very young boy. Matthew Kent was similarly not going to be left out of the search.

Consequently, ten people gathered on the lane that led up to the point where the small track veered off towards the two huts. Peter Cove had both Sam Garvey and Robert Hook with him. Kent was astride his horse. Others from the village had been pressed to join in the search. Young Gil Ramsey was there with his giant brother-in-law, Simon Smith. Gil had brought a stave and Simon had a huge club hanging from a loop on his belt. Henry Hoggs, son of the town saddler stood beside Gaston Bessant – both armed with staves. Luke Barton the Parke steward, sat astride his horse. He had been seething angry when he had learned of the theft of the sheep and was hell-bent on retrieving them. Finally, there was Hob, on the outskirts of the group and pretending he was not really there.

When the group had reached the point where the smaller group had halted the previous day, Barton – whose responsibility it was – motioned for absolute quiet. His first job was to tell Hob to stay where he was and to mind the horses. Hob's face dropped in dismay at the thought of not being 'in at the kill'. But orders were orders. He gathered the reins and led the horses to a patch of scrubby grass.

Garvey and Hook were told to scout ahead and report back. The two huddled together and held a whispered conversation. Then Sam Garvey went off to the left whilst Robert Hook sidled off to the right. Within seconds they had completely disappeared. The others found a place where they could sit and wait. They waited for about an hour and were getting a trifle restless when, causing them to start in surprise, Robert Hook appeared as if from nowhere. He sat down in the middle of the group and started reporting very quietly.

"Sam's watching from cover – no chance they will see him. The two huts are definitely occupied. The left one houses the horse, cart, and bales of hay. The right-hand one seems to be the home for three men. One is pottering about, chopping wood. The other two took a bit of finding. They are about a half-mile beyond the huts on a large open patch of rough grass. They are tending a quite large flock of sheep. We think they number about fifty. They have no dog with them – nor did we see sign of one back at the huts. Believe me, if there had been one, we would have found it."

"Then here is what we do," Luke Barton decided. "The first thing to do is to take the one man – and take him silently, so that the others have no idea they are minus a man."

He detailed Hook to lead Henry Hoggs – who was very handy in a fight – and bring the man back to them, unconscious would do nicely!

The two were back about thirty minutes later, a small individual over Henry's shoulder. The man was dumped unceremoniously on the ground, then bound hand and foot and gagged with a rag. He looked to be in his forties and was unrecognised by anyone.

"Never even knew we were there," Hook chuckled. "I tapped him on the shoulder and Henry slugged him – didn't even bother using his club. Couldn't have been easier!"

"Then, all we have to do is to grab those other two and gather all those sheep together and get them down to our fields," Luke Barton gave a satisfied nod. "Hob – grab one of those pieces of rope we brought and secure this chap to that boulder. You can keep an eye on him whilst we go and deal with the others."

Hob was disgusted that he was not to witness the final act of the drama, especially as Simon was going to take part. However, he knew far better than to disobey his masters, so he put a rope around the man's bound wrists and secured him to a large granite boulder, then stood back as the man was showing signs of recovery.

"You bloody well let me loose, you stripling, or I'll finish you!" he snarled, managing to shift the gag and eyeing his young captor with loathing.

Hob didn't even bother with a reply. Instead, he went to the bailiff's horse and drew out the short sword from its scabbard. He walked slowly towards his captive, making huge slashing motions with the sword.

"Nurr – Nah – Nurr – Nah!" he grunted with each slash. The bound man cowered back against the boulder.

"You keep away from me – you're bloody mad, a half-wit!" he whimpered.

Hob turned away to hide a huge grin. He knew he would have little trouble from the man.

Meanwhile, the others had followed Hook as he made his silent way to where Sam Garvey was crouched behind the remains of a stone wall.

"The two are working without a dog – which serves us very well," Sam said quietly. "May I suggest that half go all the way around to cut off their escape?"

"Good thinking," Barton nodded. He looked around. "Hook, you take Gil, Simon and Gaston with you. Get around to the far end of the field under cover and don't show yourselves until we make our move from here."

"Follow me," Hook whispered to his three. He went to the far left of the wall and then disappeared into a hollow. In a further fifteen minutes, the group of four were at the far end of the field, ready to intercept anyone fleeing. He cupped his hands around his mouth and emitted the warbling sound of a collared dove. From a distance, he received another in reply.

"They know we're ready," He whispered.

Peering through a bunch of gorse, the four watched as the others showed themselves, walking purposefully towards the flock and the two men. It took a few moments for their presence to be noticed. One of the men, a rather scrawny chap, made a wild dash for the right side of the field. Cove, who was extremely nimble on his feet, set off in pursuit and hurled himself at the man, bringing him down to the ground. The other man, seeing his way blocked, turned to Hook's end of the field and started running to make his own escape.

This man was large, with wide shoulders and a face snarling with rage. He drew out a large knife as he ran. Simon stood up in plain view and unhooked the large cudgel from his belt. Calmly, he climbed over the low wall and waited for his attacker to come to him. Gil, Gaston and Hook watched as Simon waited until the man was no more than ten yards from him, dropped to the ground and rolled sideways, taking a mighty swipe with the cudgel as the man hurtled on. Each of the three watchers heard a sickening crack as the man let out a bellow of pain and simply dropped to the ground, writhing in agony. Simon stood up and placed a very large boot on the wrist that was still holding the knife.

"Let go, or I shall break your hand as well as your leg!" he said quietly.

Gaston reached the two of them first, bent down and removed the knife from the squashed hand. He stuck it in his belt and grinned at the young giant.

"That was very well done," he remarked.

"Aye," Hook nodded. "I will have to remember that one!"

"No good asking if the man can walk," Gil laughed. "So – mister, whoever you are, start crawling down the field and join your other thieving mate!"

That exercise took quite a while, the others waiting patiently for the group to join them. Harry Hoggs was sitting on the captured man's legs, whilst Garvey had both knees on the shoulders.

"Well, Master Bailiff, you seem to have the legal authority here," Kent remarked to nobody in particular.

"Aye, I suppose I do at that," Cove replied. "So, let's do this all properly and legal. Master Steward," he turned to the man he had known all his life, and usually referred to hm as Luke. "Can you identify any of these sheep as belonging to the estate?"

Barton had been examining the sheep nearest to him, ignoring all those not Jacobs.

"Certainly, these two bear the mark of our sheep," he replied. "I have no doubt that the other three are here as well."

Cove asked Simon and Hook to go and fetch the third man from Hob's care.

"You get me away from that lunatic," the man snarled. "He be well mazed!"

Hob waved the sword and uttered his unintelligible grunts, giving the two a broad wink. Simon and Haddock burst out laughing, grabbed the man and frog-marched him to join the rest.

"So," Cove continued. "Master Steward, you have identified sheep as having been stolen from the estate. Do you charge these three with their theft?"

Not to be outdone in formality, Luke Barton gave a broad grin. "Aye, Master Bailiff, that I most solemnly do."

"Then I arrest you on a charge of sheep-stealing. You will be taken back to the estate and kept under lock and key until I devise a means of getting you into a proper prison. You with the damaged leg – you will have your arms bound behind you and hoisted upon a horse. You others will be similarly bound and will walk. Do not even think of attempting escape. You have already seen what happens!"

The three were trussed up. Cove had the injured man lifted onto the saddle of his own horse. He turned to Garvey and Hook.

"Stay with the sheep and, if you are able, start them on the walk down to the shepherd. He will identify ours and may be able to identify the owners of the rest."

Hob led the other horses and brought up the rear of the column. The two ambulant thieves were surrounded by the men, with the injured man slightly in front. Suddenly, without warning, the injured man dug his good heel into the side of his mount and the horse, obedient to the slightest touch, broke into a canter. Cove emitted a piercing whistle and shouted, '*Caspar, UP!*"

The horse, who had been with Cove for over seven years, obeyed instantly, skidded to a halt and reared up, causing the injured man to slide unceremoniously over its rear end and land with a bump on the track. Caspar trotted back to Peter Cove and was rewarded with a pat. The man laid on the track and groaned. He was in a far worse state than when he had started the ride. He was again hauled up into the saddle, as the group proceeded again, almost as if nothing had happened.

Arrived back at the estate, the three were locked securely into a small cellar. Sometime later, when everyone had gone back to their jobs and homes, Bernie came to report to the steward.

"All five safe within the fold again, Master Steward," he reported. "I recognise the mark of a flock up by Lustleigh – fifteen of them. The others have marks, but I do not recognise them."

Kent, Barton and Cove then had a conference. The three had somehow to be transported to Exeter and formally charged before the Sheriff. That would take a few days to organise. In the meantime, the three would be fed and watered, but not too generously. Word would be sent to other, nearby sheep owners.

* * *

True to her word, Mary went straight home after school ended. She found Harry chatting to Garvey about something or other, made an excuse and grabbed his hand. She led him up to their bedroom, sat him down on the bed and took his hand, looking him in the eye to see how her news was received.

"Harry, I've something very important to tell you," she began.

Harry, sensing something in her facial expression, pre-empted her.

"Are you with child?" he asked. "Because, if that be so, then you see before you the happiest man in Christendom."

"You are pleased?" Mary faltered.

"Pleased? My sweet wife, I am delighted beyond measure."

He stood up and grabbed her to him and showered her face with kisses.

"Does that answer your question?" he broke away breathlessly.

"Aye, I suppose it will have to do," Mary grinned. "Shall we tell everyone this evening?"

They somehow managed to get Peter and Laura Cove to visit the bakery after supper, where Mary and Harry announced their news.

"May the heavens be blessed – that will make three grandchildren," John Ramsey grabbed his daughter for a hug.

Inevitably, the whole of Bovey Tracey had the news by breakfast the next day. The school children all cheered as they arrived. Many found some excuse to visit and offer their good wishes. Mary felt that her life was complete; Harry almost danced about the estate, receiving slaps on the back from the men and kisses on the cheek from the women.

"Tis almost as if I had invented the system," he grinned to his mother.

CHAPTER VII

The second day of September started with a light shower that quickly petered out, leaving the troops to the north of the city or Worcester in better humour than when dawn had broken. Captain Lucien Pellow returned at ten in the morning and again drew his troop around him.

"Here is the latest information that I have managed to unearth," he squatted down and, with the aid of a stick, started to draw upon the flattened soil. He first drew another wiggly line to represent the river Severn. Around a curve on its eastern bank he drew another shape. "This is the city of Worcester, and we are just to its north. We are part of the centre group of three, all commanded by David Leslie. We are the centre of the three, and we are all of foot. To our right and left are the other two groups – all cavalry. To the east of the city are five more large groups, three of foot and two of horse. The king is with one of the cavalry groups, whilst the Duke of Hamilton is with the other. Now, well to the south of the city are another three very large groups of foot. We number in total some fourteen thousand."

"All very well," Herb Grindley muttered to Matt and Seb Borthwick. "But where's bloody Cromwell?"

"And all of our lot are predominantly Scots!" Borthwick muttered back.

"Our positions are ringed to the east and south by parliament," Pellow continued. "Most of them are to the south and east, but there are also some directly south, menacing our three large contingents. We in the north, are the most lightly threatened. That probably means that we will be called upon to reinforce the king and the duke – if that becomes necessary."

Matt had listened with close attention and could picture in his mind the various dispositions. He also had noted that there were no parliamentary forces at all to their west – although their own position was covered westwards by the river.

"The enemy have artillery pieces ranged against the duke and the king – so presumably, that is where the first major thrust may be expected. The best information we have is that there are large groups of parliamentary musketeers ranged against our southern forces. That is the situation as it stands today. I recommend that each and every one of you attends first to his weapons. Second, ally yourselves with your neighbours – get to know them so that you may recognise where each of you should be. Third, make sure that you consume your rations – a hungry soldier is an inefficient soldier. Fourth, and last, make your peace with Almighty God – for as sure as anything, some of you will be making His acquaintance fairly soon."

And on that somewhat sobering note, Pellow went to meet again with his fellow troop commanders. Borthwick stood hands on hips and all around him knew that they were in for another famous prediction. He did not disappoint.

"There will be no fighting until the morrow," he stated bluntly. "Makes no sense as we are all sizing up the other and have not anywhere near enough intelligence to plan final tactics. Mark my words, fighting will start early and will be swift and brutal!"

As it turned out, this was Borthwick's final prediction. He would not be alive to know that he had got it very nearly correct!

As afternoon turned to nightfall, Pellow returned to his troop. He deliberately kept one bit of information from his soldiers – as did all the other local commanders. The Scots and the few English mustered to the king's support numbered at most, fourteen thousand. Against them were ranged some twenty-eight to thirty thousand parliamentarians – and many of them were units of the New Model Army. Pellow did not sleep at all that night.

In a tent, to the south-east of the city, Cromwell slept very well indeed.

* * *

That afternoon, as work for the day was coming to a close and people were starting to relish the thought of supper, Gil and Ella sat around their parlour table with young May Fletcher. May, now nearly fourteen, had been the 'chicken and egg girl' ever since Nell had gone back to James and Avril Ramsey to be their apprentice apothecary. Nell had replaced Mary in that job when she had married Harry and had taken on the task of schoolmistress.

Rosie and Jamie were amusing themselves with a small kitten that had somehow or other insinuated itself into the house. The argument over what to name the kitten had raged over three whole days. In exasperation, Ella had finally had enough and had named the kitten Benjamin – that being the first male name that had entered her head. As it was far removed from any of the children's suggestions, it had been accepted – albeit with bad grace on Rosie's part.

For some months that year, either Gil or Ella had taken their surplus vegetables to the weekly market in Newton Abbot, some five miles to the south. The bulk of their produce was sold to the people of Bovey Tracey – especially to Dick and Sal Allen at the tavern. However, there was always a surplus that would have been wasted had there not been a ready outlet for it in the neighbouring town.

"I truly believe that the time has come for us to offer eggs as well as vegetables at the market," Ella stated – not for the first time. Naturally, May was very keen that this happened, as she relished the thought of a weekly outing to the much larger town and its attractions, prominent amongst which was the son of the market manager!

Gil, normally far more impetuous than Ella, had been slow to come to agreement with the plan. Now, he seemed more than keen.

"Why just eggs?" he queried, "why not pullets as well? After all, how many hens have we now?"

"Ninety-seven – at least when I counted them this morning," May replied.

"What we must be aware of is that, with winter not far away, egg laying will diminish. Therefore, we should not deplete our hens too severely or egg sales will fall," Ella warned.

"Aye, tis a fine balance," Gil nodded. "Why do we not start with just five and see where that leads us. After all, there might already be a sufficiency of supply in Newton."

As is still the case, most locals referred to the towns as Bovey and Newton, rather than the elongated Bovey Tracey and Newton Abbot.

"If May is to go to market, I want to come too!" came a voice from the far corner, proving that Rosie had been following the conversation with wagging ears.

"You, my little hellion, shall stay here and mind your brother!" Ella said firmly.

"Not fair!" screeched an affronted Rosie.

"Tis, so!" came from little Jamie, seizing on any opportunity to disagree with his older sister.

"That is more than enough," Ella replied. "Anymore nonsense and the pair of you go to bed minus supper!"

"What is for supper, mama?" Rosie wanted reassurance that the bribe was worth the chance.

"We shall have bacon with eggs and bread, then coddled apples with honey."

That turned the tide immediately. Such a supper was well worth immediate compliance.

Turning back to the main topic, Ella continued. "We shall not know how many eggs we shall take this next market day until the day itself dawns. But - were you to hazard a guess, May – how many would you think?"

May furrowed her otherwise smooth brow and thought.

"I would estimate four dozen at the very least – unless all the hens decide to withdraw their labour!"

"Then, with five pullets, it will be worth the effort," Gil nodded. "Now – how do we transport the pullets?"

As was common with many small communities, there was a pooling of resources in the small town. Four families owned a small cart and horse – the bakers, who were Gil's parents – the Dingles, the butchers - the Gates – the millers, and Gil and Ella – the smallholders. Gil and Ella shared the cart on market days with the butchers.

"One thing be for certain," Ella grinned, "It shall not be made by my papa and brother. Such a contrivance would need four oxen to pull it!"

"Aye," Gil laughed, "something made of iron by those two would rival the keep of a castle! Something light, such as a crate made of hurdles, would be ideal. I shall go to Trusham and get those two hurdle makers to construct something suitable."

Much to Rosie's great relief, that seemed to end the discussion. Not too long after that, the supper arrived, along with the coddled apples in honey. A very satisfied little girl curled up into her bed that night.

"Somehow, I shall get to market," she whispered a confidence into her pillow.

* * *

That same evening, Luke Barton, Peter Cove, and Matthew Kent resumed yet another subject – how to discover the identity of those members of the Vale of Tears.

"Tis imperative that we find them – as they are the only ones to know how, when, and why those two ended their lives. The matter cannot be left as it stands!" Cove insisted.

"Pardon me if I assume the role of Devil's advocate," Kent turned an apologetic face to the other two. "What harm will it do to leave matters as they are – and simply let the two children in Exeter bury their parents – and then let the matter rest?"

"Tell me, Master Kent, would such a solution satisfy you?" Luke Barton gave him a wry smile.

"It most assuredly would not!" Kent stated. "However, it is surely worth asking the question – is it worth the time and effort delving into this Vale of Tears when other matters need your attention? Master Bailiff has a town to supervise, whilst Master Steward has an estate to run and manage."

"That is indeed a good question – and both of us are hard pressed as it is, what with sheep thieves, the end of harvest, repairs to assess and manage," Barton agreed.

"Then, gentlemen, let me offer my services. You have both read my warrant and observed the signature thereupon. I have license to enquire into any and all matters that impinge upon the good order of the country. The taking of one's own life is a matter for the church. The matter of condoning – nay, even encouraging such action – is the worst heresy. It is also a matter that is of grave concern. I am more than willing to take on such investigation. I shall, of course, keep you both fully informed of any progress I may make – should I be able to pry such information from this secretive coven!"

Barton and Cove exchanged glances. "We readily accept that offer. And may we both wish you every success. I'm sure that we both feel that you may well need the Devil's own luck – seeing as how you will be dealing with what would appear to be the Devil's own business. Tis sure as pennies that it is not God's business!"

"And one task falls to me," Cove grunted. "I shall ride to Totnes and see the Constable so that a few of his men may come to collect our sheep thieves and take them, with a written report, to the Sheriff at Exeter."

* * *

That evening also saw another meeting. This time at Brimley. Harry took Mary to see Lady Violette. There was no way he was allowing his wife to travel in the glom by herself – certainly not in her condition. Mary was highly amused to see the care and lavish attention with which he treated her. Despite continually telling him that pregnancy was not an illness, not debilitating, not weakening in any way, shape or form – nevertheless, he was constantly dancing attendance, plumping cushions, getting her to sit with her feet up. Mary had given up and had accepted his ministrations, sure that they would not last – at least until he saw her going about her daily life as usual.

Lady Violette looked up from her monthly perusal of the school accounts ledger.

"You are as thrifty with my money as ever," she said, peering over her small spectacles that she now had to use for close work. "Despite my assurances to the contrary, you seem to think that every penny you spend brings me closer to penury. You devotion to my purse is admirable. It is also unnecessary. I have repeatedly assured you that you may spend whatever you believe to be needed."

"Lady Violette, I am always conscious of the fact that I am spending your money, and not mine. I would be just as careful with my own – more so in fact, as I have little to spend."

75

"Are you telling me that your very handsome husband keeps you short of necessary funds?" the old lady gave Harry a conspiratorial wink.

"Indeed not!" Mary riposted. "Harry is the very soul of generosity. Should I ever ask, he would give me his last penny."

"I know he would, my dear. I was just making merry at your seriousness. Now – and I want the absolute truth – what is truly *needed* by the school?"

Mary thought for a moment.

"One thing immediately springs to mind," she said, "an up-to-date map of Europe. So many things have happened, are happening, that are of concern to us here in England that I need not only to speak of them to the children, but also to show them where these happenings take place – and their geographical connection to us here on our island."

"Broadening minds? I most heartily agree with that! Let us be honest, most of the children at the school have never ventured further afield than the next town or village. Some indeed, have never left Bovey!"

"In that respect, Lady Violette," Harry admitted, "I have never been further that Exeter to the east, Brixham to the south, and Bodmin to the far west."

"So, where might one expect to find such a map?"

"There is said to be a cartographer in Exeter. His shop is close by Rougemont, or so I have been informed. That Master Kent told me of it when last I spoke to him."

"Then make your enquiries and purchase whatever you deem necessary – and do *not* consider the price. Broadened and educated minds are priceless!"

CHAPTER VIII

The morning of the third of September brought grey skies but mercifully little or no rain. Now and again, a fitful sun played hide and seek with the low clouds, promising much, but delivering little.

Just to the north of the city of Worcester, the three large contingents under the Scot David Leslie, stood to at just after eight o'clock. Already, to the east and certainly audible, came the sounds of musket fire. Quite obviously, the main royalist groups to the east of the city were coming under fire. At any moment, Matt Crowley and his comrades expected messengers to come galloping from the east with requests to come to reinforce the king's regiments.

One arrived hot and breathless on a sweating mount, but from the south where he reported that the royalist troops were under heavy attack. But seemingly, there was no request for them to go south and help out in that quarter.

By mid-morning, Leslie had still not received any request to move either east or south. Messengers arrived in a steady stream well before noon. Seemingly, from what little information managed to dribble down to the rank and file, the royalists in the east had attempted a mass sortie towards the parliamentary forces but had been driven back. Numbers of losses on both sides, from the rumours that filtered down, ranged anywhere between one hundred and five thousand. On which side, it was not made clear.

What was absolutely certain to the members of Sir Lucien Pellow's troop was that the sounds of battle were getting slowly and inexorably closer. Matt and his closest mate, Herbert Grindley, were in the rearmost rank of their troop. Sebastian Borthwick, just in front of them, was still giving anyone who would listen his analysis of the situation.

"The king will most certainly be massing for another sortie to the east. He has seen what happened at the last attempt and will not make the same mistakes again. This time, he will break through and will encircle Cromwell, then head south to assist those down below the town. Classical manoeuvre that has been practised for many a year!"

"And that bastard Cromwell is not aware of it?" one grizzled man growled. "He outnumbers us, and we are outgunned. Why we are not running to assist the king is a mystery!"

"Tis not only a mystery," another added, "tis a fookin' disgrace!"

Sir Lucien, well aware of the sentiments boiling within his troop, Issued a strong warning.

"You will all remain exactly where you are, ready to fight when ordered – and only when and where ordered!"

For the next hour, no such order was received.

* * *

Having received the agreement of the other 'shareholders', Gil set off that morning driving the cart to Trusham. He and Ella had agreed that the sooner they increased their sales with eggs and a few pullets the better. The six-mile journey took just over one hour, the horse enjoying the fact that he was pulling an empty cart. The weather down in Devon was much more pleasant than that in the north around Worcester – Gil basked in early autumn sunshine and whistled tunelessly to himself.

Michael Brown and Hugh Ratcliffe were hard at work when Gil eventually pulled up outside their cottage. The two were a highly unlikely pair – Brown an ex-royalist sergeant and Ratcliffe an ex-parliamentary tracker. The two had been thrown together after the hideous slaughter at Torrington back in 1646. Both had been injured and had found real friendship on their journey back south when they were sufficiently recovered. Brown had taken over his old family cottage and he and Ratcliffe had started what was to be a very successful business manufacturing hurdles.

They both recognised Gil immediately as they were constant visitors to Bovey Tracey, the Parke estate and most neighbouring villages. When Gil had explained his requirement, they both stood hands on hips and grinned.

"Should be the work of an hour at most," Michael Brown stated.

"Less than an hour for me!" Ratcliffe laughed. "How many chickens do you want housed in the thing?"

"Twill never be more than ten – at least not for many a long month," Gil replied.

"Then a simple hurdle cage with a door – say five feet in length by two in width – that should do the trick," Ratcliffe muttered.

"Why do you not take an ale at the tavern whilst we cobble the thing together?" Brown suggested. "By the time you have finished your second mug, we should be just about done."

"I seem to recall the potency of the ale in this tavern," Gil laughed. "Two mugs and I shall sleep all the way back home. Luckily, this horse knows the way!"

He led the horse and cart to the tavern, unhitched the cob from the shafts and led it to the small trough. Then he went inside and ordered a mug of ale.

Meanwhile, the two hurdle makers set to and within minutes had constructed the frame of the cage from straight ash sticks. Then, going to the long trough where they kept split hazel soaking, they wove the bottom, top, and three sides. Brown made the other end from similar materials and then attached it to the open end of the cage with two leather hinges. It had taken them just under the hour to complete the work.

Gil had been watching them from the tavern, peering now and again through the front window. When he saw the two stand back to admire their work, he stood, went to harness horse to cart and walked back.

"That is exactly what is needed," he said, admiring the finished cage. "Now – how much do I owe you for it?"

"In coin - not a farthing," Brown gave him a large grin. "When we next come through Bovey, we would welcome a pullet for our table!"

"Given the excellence of the work, you shall have a brace," Gil grinned back. "My sincere thanks for a job well done."

The cage was loaded onto the cart and Gil set off back home with a cheerful wave to the two old soldiers. He knew that Ella and May would be very pleased with the result of his morning.

* * *

Peter Cove left Parke at about the same time as Gil left to travel to Trusham. However, on his horse, he trotted and cantered the seventeen miles to Totnes in just two hours. He also relished the warm sun. His journey took him via the village of Staverton – where he crossed the river Dart – then onwards via Dartington. He climbed the hill to the small castle where he found the Constable.

"Sheep stealers? Scum! Worry not, Master bailiff! I shall have them collected and shall hang the bastards myself!" the crusty old Constable growled. He was short, rotund, and obviously in a poor mood.

"Should they not stand trial first?" Cove ventured.

"Trial? Bollocks to trial first! Do you have written statements of their guilt?"

"Indeed, I do," Cove nodded. "From myself, the Parke Steward and a Parliamentary agent by the name of Matthew Kent."

"Kent? Know the fella! Made himself comfortable in the castle some time past. Holds a signed warrant. Good enough for me. They'll hang the moment my men bring them here. Now – come and take a glass of wine with me and a bite of dinner before you return. I shall send five of my men with you to collect the thieving buggers!"

After a hearty dinner of trout baked in almonds, mounds of buttered vegetables, and a raisin tart – not to mention two glasses of excellent burgundy – Cove set off back to Bovey with five hard looking soldiers, all mounted on wiry ponies that looked capable of a full day's march without the need for rest.

"Hand the statements to my sergeant," the Constable's parting words followed the party as they left the castle precincts. "Must keep the records straight!"

"Aye," grinned the sergeant, "records must be kept – even for thieving bastards like sheep thieves!"

And that is now the difference between the old and the new regimes, Cove thought to himself. Out with the old and in with the new efficient way of doing things. Records kept and all things in order. But he still nursed doubts as to the legality of summary execution on the mere whim of a castle Constable!

* * *

May was busy after dinner, making sure that the small water troughs were filled and that there was more than enough seed to see the large flock of hens through the night. She also had to separate Trumpet from the other cockerel – the two were having yet another argument as to who was the greater. Nell had christened the original cock Trumpet because of his strident call.

She was just emerging from the main hen shed when she became aware of a tousled head poking above the back fence. Beyond that enclosure was the Heath where, five years previously, the royalists had been routed.

"Hob – what be you doing there?" the fourteen-year-old girl asked, dusting soil and seeds from her pinafore.

She was rewarded with a broad grin. "What be I doing? I be watching a pretty maid, that's what I be doing!"

"Then you be wasting your time, young Hob. Go and watch my sister Maud. She be older than me and capable of boxing your ears. I do not have the time!"

"But you be prettier than Maud," Hob tried a winsome smile instead of a broad grin.

May, who knew that not to be the case, was nevertheless quite pleased to hear it said.

"No, I b'aint. Now go away and bother some other unfortunate soul."

"I will go away if you say you will walk with me after Sunday service."

"And why would I want to do something as daft as that?"

"Because you believe me to be the most handsome lad – and would be happy to be in my company!"

"You have a conceit as large as your head! But I shall think on it. Now – go away!"

May, not totally unaccustomed to receive attention from lads in the town, was just a trifle pleased that Hob had sought her out. Hob was regarded with fondness and admiration in the town. An orphan since just after his birth, he had been taken in by Peter and Laura Cove and had benefited from a safe and secure home. He was also a joker and just might not be taken too seriously!

May went into the kitchen to wash her hands. Ella was there preparing supper, being pestered by Rosie and Jamie for the edges cut from a pie.

"May I ask you a question?" May said, somewhat shyly. "Hob has asked me to walk with him come Sunday. Ought I to say yes? Or ought I to say no?"

Ella regarded the young girl with a smile. She had long wondered when May would start to cast off the manners of a young maid. She took May and sat her down before the parlour fire.

"Let us examine this in a logical way – as I am sure Mary would advise. "First – do you like Hob?"

"Oh, everyone likes Hob," May laughed. "There is nothing to dislike about Hob!"

"Then let me put it this way. Would you like Hob to kiss you?"

May blushed a deep pink. "I had never thought of Hob in that manner," she replied.

"Oh, come on, May! You are fourteen – hardly a little girl any longer. Gil kissed me when I were but twelve – and I liked it very much."

"Well, of course I have thought about it. I know Maud has been kissed by lots of the lads. But I have never allowed such a liberty."

"That still does not answer my question. Let us say that you meet Hob this coming Sunday and he takes your hand and walks with you along a quiet lane. Then he stops and gives you a soft kiss. What would you do?"

May burst into tears. "I do not know!" she wailed. "I believe I would be frozen to the spot, not knowing whether to respond or to run a mile from him."

"You came to me for advice, so I shall give it. Hob is a merry lad, but one I would trust with my life. He would not seek to take any advantage of such a situation. My advice is to say yes to him. You really need to come to terms with your emotions – and I'm sure you will be content with the result."

"But what if he *does* seek to take advantage of me?"

"Believe me, he will not. He knows full well that Master Bailiff would take the skin off his back – not to mention what your own papa would do! Apart from those dire consequences, Hob is too trustworthy to put you in any peril!"

May tried to compose herself, wiping her eyes on her sleeve. She would agree to the walk - but was still fearful that she was putting herself at some risk.

* * *

The afternoon was well advanced as Matt stood patiently in the rear rank beside his mate Herbert Grindley. They, with large contingents of the royalist cavalry to their left and right, had remained where they were in Pitchcroft Meadow, to the north of the city of Worcester. They were all absolutely astounded that no order came for them to advance, to come to the aid of other royalist forces who were fiercely engaged to the east and south of the city.

The main noises of battle came from the east of the city where bridges were contested, the initiative going first one way, then the other. Musketry fire was heard almost continuously, along with the occasional roar of cannon. Now and again, massed, bloodcurdling screams could be heard – but to the men waiting, it was not clear from which mouths those screams emanated. They could only stand and hope it was from parliamentary throats.

Throughout that long afternoon, riders came and went, reporting to David Leslie and his second in command. However, the more junior commanders were kept in ignorance of whatever messages were sent and received – unlike earlier in the day when Sir Lucien Pellow had been appraised and had then passed on this intelligence to his troop.

"What the hell is happening?" Matt said quietly to Herb. "Unless I get some information soon, I shall start shouting. Why are we not being told what is going on?"

"Oh, that is simplicity itself!" came from the rank in front. Inevitably, Borthwick had an opinion. "The king is winning glory and does not need our help."

"Either that, or we are being spared a massacre!" Herb countered. "We all know that we are hopelessly outnumbered. Why else would Leslie hold us back?"

"Again, mark my words," Borthwick shot back. "We shall see parliamentary soldiers fleeing in our direction very soon – and that is why we are here, to add to their misery!"

The sun slowly sank down over the hills to the west and, as it did so, many figures on foot and on horse appeared from the eastern side of the city.

"See – what did I say," Borthwick laughed. "Here they come – and right into our waiting arms."

However, the numbers advancing on them grew in number until a very large host was drawn up facing Leslie's position. Far from fleeing a defeat, the parliamentary forces looked in fine fettle and were obviously poised for a mass attack. It did not take more than a few minutes for the size of the opposition to register in the minds of Pellow and his troop.

"Oh, bloody hell!" Matt gulped. "We are the ones to be massacred if we stay here!"

"Then let us not stay here," Herb grunted and began to shuffle backwards.

Glancing to left and right, Matt did the same until the pair of them were some yards behind the rearmost rank. Then the two of them simply turned around and fled northwards. They did not stop running until they had reached the supposed safety of a stand of trees. They both stopped and hid, looking back to the position they had abandoned. It was s scene of absolute carnage, parliamentary soldiers hacking their way mercilessly through Leslie's forces. Many turned and ran towards the trees but were simply cut down. One managed to gallop as far as the trees, but simply sagged from his saddle and collapsed on the ground not ten feet from where the two were hiding.

Herb, summoning courage that he had always doubted he possessed, crept unseen to the fallen figure. It was obviously from his dress some junior commander, and he was dead. Herb slithered back into hiding, clutching a bulging purse of money.

"He won't be needing it," he said to Matt. "We need to use these trees as cover as we head away from here."

Having both recovered from their headlong dash, the two went to the top end of the stand of trees and set off at a fast pace for the security of a much larger wood to the north. Sounds of battle were fading as they scuttled into the safety of the close-packed trees.

Finding a small clearing, they stopped and collapsed panting under a large beech tree. Herb fished the heavy purse from his belt and opened it.

"We can buy our escape for many a mile with this lot," he whistled. He showed Matt the open purse. Inside was a pile of gold coins.

"But we are going in exactly the wrong direction if I need to return to my home," Matt groaned. "Going north, I am getting further and further away."

"South or east means running straight into Cromwell's bloodthirsty lot. West be Wales. North is our only hope for the time being," Grindley retorted.

Matt knew that he was right but had another thought.

"Most of the king's troops were Scots – and north is the way they will run!"

"Aye, that thought came to me as well," Herb nodded. "So, we keep a close eye out and avoid everyone. But first, we have to shed the appearance of soldiers."

They left their swords, lances, belts and any other signs of soldiery all bundled beneath a large bush, then set off again to the north. They walked all night, eating the remains of their meagre rations and drinking from the many streams that they crossed. They managed to remain unobserved simply by crossing fields, traversing hills and woods. By the time the sun arose to the east, they were again well secreted in a small wood. Slightly below them, and to their east, was a small town. Herb, who had memorised the maps, stated that he believed that it was Stourbridge – so they had walked at least twenty miles. Finding a well secluded spot in the wood, they fell into an exhausted sleep.

Well behind them, bands of escaping Scots were being rounded up and taken prisoner back to Worcester where Cromwell and his generals were thanking God for their victory. The parliamentary forces had lost a mere two hundred soldiers, whilst the king's army had lost nearly three thousand, with another ten thousand taken prisoner. It had been a stunning and complete victory!

CHAPTER IX

Peter Cove was in the middle of his breakfast when there came a thunderous knocking at the door. Hob, who had just finished his, looked at the Bailiff, then at Laura, then at Harry and Mary. All of them looked back at him with broad grins. Hob sighed and went to answer the summons. He was back a few moments later.

"Master Bailiff, four soldiers from the Constable in Totnes – come to collect those sheep thieves."

Cove stood up. "Hob – go to the office and fetch those two statements that are on my desk. I'll go and speak to the soldiers."

He went out to find four mounted soldiers and a mule pulling a large cart. The biggest of the soldiers dismounted and knuckled a salute.

"Mornin' Master Bailiff. Come to collect three piles of shit for hanging," he growled.

Peter Cove was *still* not happy with the fact that the three were about to be carted off for summary execution, without the right of a proper trial. What he needed, and had done for some time, was the advice of someone well versed in the law. There was a lawyer in private practice in Newton Abbot, but he couldn't keep riding over there every time he needed clarification.

"They're locked in a cellar," he nodded to the burly soldier. "If you come with me, then they're all yours."

"Not for long, they won't be!" the huge face split into a fierce grin.

A short time later, the three were trussed and loaded into the cart. Cove handed the statements to the big soldier, who again knuckled a polite salute, pocketed the statements, then led the procession down to the estate gates. Two of his soldiers rode at each side of the cart, whilst the fourth rode just behind, sword unsheathed and ready over his shoulder. Cove gave a sigh and went back indoors.

"Harry – I'm busy today. Would you ride to the shepherd and help with identifying the owners of those he does not yet know?"

"Aye, father," Harry rose and gave Mary a kiss on her cheek. "I shall see you at supper. Don't teach those children anything too controversial!"

"As if I would," Mary laughed. "Today I shall concentrate solely on the mysteries of addition and subtraction, perhaps with a little history thrown in. I need to get to Exeter to get that map that Lady Violette has promised. May I borrow your deputy on Saturday?"

"Why do not we all go for a ride to Exeter," Laura exclaimed. "I need to replenish my stock of fruit preserves before the winter sets in."

Mary, now with a docile pony of her own, made her way to the school as Harry set off for the shepherd and the search for the missing owners.

"Nay, Master Harry, nothing new since yesterday," young Bernie Wheatcroft said as Harry dismounted in the large field. His horse immediately moved a few paces and started cropping the lush grass.

"So, we have our five back, those that belong to the farmer up in Lustleigh, and the seven you identified as belonging to that chap down at the far end of the Heath. How many does that leave us to find?"

"Fifteen – and they all bear the same mark – a mark that nobody hereabouts seems to recognise. The Lustleigh farmer and the man from the Heath are coming this morning to collect their sheep. So, I have to be here to see that the right sheep – and only the right sheep, are collected."

"Then I shall have to ride hither and yon whilst you stay here. Let me see that mark again so that I can relate it to whoever I meet."

The mark was on the left horn of each and every one of the fifteen – but they were not Jacob sheep. They were a breed similar in all but colour. The mark was made up of two notches in the form of an arrowhead.

"Do you know what breed they be – for they certainly are not Jacobs?" Harry asked.

Bernie scratched his head and was about to say that he did not know, when a farmer arrived on a large cart.

"Come to collect my sheep," he said. "I'm from Lustleigh and you found them for me not far from where they were taken."

"Aye, we have them safe and sound," Harry replied, going to shake hands with the farmer who he recognised from meeting him months before at the town fair.

It took the farmer and Bernie little time to load the sheep into the cart. He was about to drive off when Harry had a thought.

"Before you go, do you know what breed those are?" he pointed to the group of fifteen that Bernie had managed to segregate.

"Aye – thems Dorset Downs! Dunno who owns them though."

"Then all I hope is that I do not have to ride to Dorset to find the owner!" Harry grunted.

"Nobody for miles around has them, that I do know," the farmer assured him. "You'll spend more time and money finding the owner than they will be worth. My advice is to spread the word and keep them with yours until someone comes to claim them. It may well be that nobody will."

Harry waved the farmer goodbye as the cart trundled out of the gate, then turned to young Bernie.

"Are you able to take on these extra sheep – now that we know what they are?"

"Aye, I can manage. But first, I need to see whether they are in lamb. If they be, then I shall have to ask for help come lambing time – tis only four months away."

"I shall have to tell Master Luke – his will be the responsibility."

"One further matter," Bernie grinned. "Ewes will come into season next year – and we do not have a Dorset Downs tup!"

"That *is* a problem," Harry agreed. "You shall have to talk the matter through with Master Steward."

"Wonder what lambs would be like if we let our own tups loose on them?" Bernie laughed. "Could be a right mish-mash!"

"Might get four-horned sheep!" Harry laughed in turn. "But I've seen sheep with four horns before. Look mighty weird!"

* * *

Gil and Ella were busy pulling carrots ready for washing and selling. Their barrow was already half full.

"Why do we not sell the carrot tops as well?" Ella asked. "I have used them in pottage before now and they tasted very good."

"Aye – that is a good idea. But we will have to wash them as well. Perhaps we could bundle them up in lots of a pound or two pounds. How much would we charge for them?"

"I have not the slightest idea," Ella shrugged. "They would be something new, so perhaps half the price for other green vegetables? After all, we sell turnip tops!"

Gill did not reply immediately, so Ella looked over at him to see what had distracted his attention. Gil was grinning and nodded towards the hen coop that was some distance away towards the heath. Ella followed his glance and smiled.

May was at the far fence and talking to Hob.

Hob had spent the early morning wondering whether he had the courage to go back and ask May if she had come to a decision. Eventually, summoning his normal good cheer, he set off and approached the fence. Peering over the top, he saw May emerging from the large coop with a basket brim full of eggs. Showing remarkable restraint, he allowed May to set the basket down before making his presence known. He knew that, had he called out, May might have been startled and dropped the basket – thereby ruining whatever chance he might have.

May looked up and saw the tousled head poking over the fence. She went over and gave him a good morning.

"Good day to you, May. Pardon me for interrupting your work, but I wondered if you had given thought to my proposal?"

"I do not recall receiving any proposal, Hob. After all, we are still a bit young for such!"

Hob went bright red until he saw the grin spreading over May's face. He gave a big grin back.

"Nay – not that sort of proposal," he laughed. "My proposal for you to come walking with me after Sunday service."

May was not going to let him off that lightly. "Then you dash my hopes for an early marriage!" she chuckled. "I have given that *request* some serious thought and would be very pleased to accept the idea of a pleasant walk with you."

Hob gaped for a second, hardly believing his luck.

"I shall wait for you at the church gate when the service is over. I promise that I shall be a perfect escort for you."

"My dada will be mighty pleased to hear that," May said in all seriousness. Will Fletcher was not known for his acceptance of any harm to his family.

"Honestly, May – I shall treat you with the greatest respect – I promise." And with that, he galloped back to the estate office, whistling happily.

* * *

The morning of the fifth of September found Matt and Herb Grindley again sheltering in a wood. They had spent the previous night as they had the night after the battle – walking northwards and avoiding all roads and settlements. Once again, they had not been spotted. Many times, they had heard distant shouts and galloping hooves. They guessed that the fleeing Scotsmen were still being pursued. Just before the first light of day, they had skirted the town of Wolverhampton to their east – keeping under as deep cover as they could find.

In front of them as they peered through the trees was a road that looked as if it went from east to west. Unbeknown to them, it was the road from Walsall to Telford. But, to proceed further north, they had to cross it. Greatly daring, Herb had taken a few pennies with him and had bought pies from a baker's shop that was just opening. Making sure he was not followed, he wound his way back through the wood to where Matt was getting a bit jumpy.

"Fresh pies," he grinned, handing two to Matt. They found a secluded spot between large bushes and chomped their way through this minor feast.

"That village I went to is called Codsall, and this is Codsall Wood," Herb reported. "Not that the name means anything to me. I told the baker that we were walking to Telford to find work as our last job in Wolverhampton had ended. By the way, we are stone cutters."

"Then I hope that our skills are never asked for – as I have none!" Matt grunted.

"Just to our right is a track that leads north. I suggest that we finish our meal, creep down to the road under cover and scoot across when there is nobody in sight. Then we can follow that track a bit further north before we take a chance and start off westwards. Then, when we have gone some miles that way, we could think about heading south again. We have more than enough coin to get us to the south of Spain!"

Matt was not too sure that this was the best plan. But, as he had no better idea to offer, nodded. The two sat quietly and munched their way through the meat pies before standing up and preparing to move yet again.

"What we most need is sleep," Matt grumbled. "Let us cross this damned road and find somewhere we can sleep the day through. Walking at night has served us well so far."

About an hour later they were again sheltering in deep cover – they were getting very good at finding safe spots. It had taken them some minutes before they had been certain they could scoot across the road without being seen. They had immediately gone to the side of the lane and had kept either behind hedgerows or trees until they both came to an abrupt stop. Immediately to their front was a high wall that stretched as far as they were able to see to both right and left.

"Now what?" Matt snorted. "This has to be the boundary of some large estate – so we dare not climb over it."

"Stay here out of sight and I'll creep along the wall to where the lane meets it. There must be a gate of some sort."

"And what bloody good will a gate do us?" Matt groused. "We cannot go through it, or we shall be spotted in seconds – or pounced upon by dogs!"

"Yes, I am fully aware of that," Herb said patiently as if he was talking to a wayward child. "But there may be some sign that tells us where we are. Do not worry, I shall not be seen!"

Without waiting for any response, he crept silently along the wall. After a few yards, the wall curved away from him, so he slid into the trees to follow it around to where he could see a pair of large gates. He crept a bit further along , crawling from one tree bole to the next, until he could see the gates properly, and not at an obtuse angle. He peered through the gates and saw the gable end of a very large house at the end of a drive. Across the lane, he glimpsed the top of a massive oak tree. At the far side of the gate was an inscription. He had seen enough and started crawling ever so carefully back to where the wall gave him cover again.

"Well?" Matt raised an eyebrow.

"One bloody great house down the end of a drive. Gates shut as you might imagine. There is an inscription to the wall on the far side of the gates. It says, 'Boscobel House'."

"Then we either stay here under cover until nightfall, or we follow this wall away from the gates and try to get to the next village to buy more food. We have more than enough water in our bottles, thanks to that stream we crossed a while back."

Herb Grindley frowned in thought for a moment. "Look – we have been very successful so far lying up by day and walking by night. Why do we not keep to this pattern until we are many miles away from danger?"

"In Wales, you mean? And what makes you think we are not in danger over the border?"

"We would only have to be in Wales until we are south of Worcester – then we can cross back into Gloucestershire and make our way to Bristol."

Matt was too tired to argue. As Herb had said, the method had stood them well thus far. The two moved back into the trees and found a safe spot where they could sleep.

* * *

The steward himself heard the soft knocking at the door. He peered out through a window and could see two figures lurking at the door to the back parlour. Not wishing to invite strangers into the house in the evening gloom, he hurried to the main hall where the master of the house was sitting by the side of a fire reading a bible.

"Master, there are two men knocking at the rear doors. Should I admit them?"

"No, you most assuredly should not. Fetch those two large servants and get them armed. Then we will all four go and answer the knock."

Some minutes later, the steward threw back the bolts on the rear door and opened it a crack. The two figures crept closer. The master of the house and his two servants could see at once that the two visitors posed no threat – no pistols in hand or hands on sword hilts. The taller of the two stood on the threshold, a somewhat bedraggled figure in torn clothes. He swept off his hat.

"We seek a place of safety," he announced quietly. "My colleague, Colonel Careless and I have spent all day hiding in that large oak tree and anything you can offer would be a blessing!"

It took a few more seconds for the four to realise who was speaking. Then, as one, they bent their knees.

"Your Majesty is most welcome. If you could suffer the constraints of our priest's hole, we will ensure that you remain safe until you are ready to leave. But first, I must ensure that you and the good Colonel are properly fed."

Totally unbeknown to Matt and Herb, the king they had *almost* fought for, spent an uncomfortable night in a priest's hole. The inhabitants of Boscobel House were *recusants*, Catholics who refused to obey the laws of the English Protestant faith. The search for him went on around the countryside of Staffordshire, all to no avail. King Charles II carried on his journey, disguised as a servant to a travelling lady.

The two did as they had previously – they awoke an hour after the king had arrived at Boscobel House – totally unaware of the momentous happenings so close to them. Five days later, they were in Builth Wells, having skirted Shrewsbury first of all. They still posed as itinerant labourers, buying food at bakers and taverns when they considered they were far enough away from danger.

They intended to start going south and east, to cross the broad River Severn at Chepstow, and then make their way to Bristol, where they could simply merge into the crowd.

CHAPTER X

The deliberately low-key Sunday service ended with everyone exchanging the sign of peace – which a very few *still* referred to as the *Pax Vobiscum.* They were careful to keep that invocation to themselves!

Hob, dressed in his Sunday best, shoes gleaming with polish, stood nervously at the gate, having been the first to leave the church. Would his luck hold? Would May change her mind at the last minute? Many in the small town would have been astounded had they been able to witness the inner turmoil – Hob was always cheeky, a Jack the Lad. He had even surprised himself. Surely, he reasoned, May must be somewhat special if she could wring such a change in him?

James, Avril and Nell passed him as he stood on one leg by the gate. Nell gave him a conspiratorial grin and whispered, 'good luck'. Quite obviously, his assignation was common knowledge!

John the baker and his family passed him. Gil and Ella were at the rear of this group, Rosie skipping along holding Ella's hand, and Jamie was being carried on Gil's shoulders. Ella gave Hob a wink as she passed him. Not for the first time that day, Hob blushed furiously. Where the hell was May?

Finally, after many other family groups had passed him by, out came the Fletchers – Will, the town's ditcher and hedger, his wife Patience, and their two daughters May and Maud. May peeled off from the group and came to Hob's side. Hob's eyes were rivetted on her father. Will looked a bit stern and raised one finger to the lad. Hob, recognising this as the direst of warnings, swallowed and gave a polite nod – 'yes, he would behave as the perfect gentleman'.

Maud gave him a saucy grin whilst her mother bestowed a smile. Hob even went so far as to offer May a slight bow! He held out his left arm in the correct gesture as May, also obeying strict protocol, laid her right hand gently on top. In a deafening silence, Hob led the way up the street and along the road that led towards the village of Chudleigh Knighton. As soon as they had turned the first bend, May, took off her hand from Hob's arm and took his hand in hers.

"There – that's better!" she grinned – then broke into a skipping step that Hob immediately followed. They proceeded along the road like a couple of five-year-olds, laughing and giggling.

"If my dada could see us now, he would order me home immediately," May remarked. "Tis just as well he cannot see!"

"Surely he does not expect you to act like an old maiden lady?" Hob replied, looking a bit puzzled. "You are fourteen years of age, and I am but one year older!"

"Believe me, Hob, that is *exactly* how he expects me to act. Honestly, it makes me cross at times, the way he keeps Maud and me on such a tight rein. If I tell you something, Hob, will you promise on your life not to tell anyone else?"

"Anything you tell me, May, I shall keep secret – I promise."

"Then – let me tell you this. I am fourteen as you know. My loving parents were married just six and a half months before the day I was born. So, how can my dada be so hypocritical? He '*knew*' my mama before they made their vows. And, before you get any ideas, that is *not* an invitation for you to act in a similar manner!"

As everyone knew, Hob was a brutally honest lad.

"Oh my!" he said quietly. "If I now say that such a thought never entered my head, that would be insulting to you – and I would never do that. So, to respond in a truthful manner, I shall admit that such a thought has occurred to me as you are very pretty. But I also know that it would not be right and might well anger you if I tried. So, I shall not try – as I said that I would respect you. And I do respect you."

"But do you *like* me?" May had stopped and stood facing him.

"May, I like you very much indeed. May I also tell you what is my dearest wish?"

"If you say that your dearest wish is to savour one of Master Ramsey's mutton pies, I shall stamp on your foot!"

"Tempting as the pie is, my dearest wish at this moment is to kiss you."

"Then we had better seek a more private location, as kissing in the middle of the road is hardly the best of behaviour!"

Hob gaped at her. "Does that mean you have no objection?"

"I can think of many objections, but nary a one that I am prepared to listen to!"

Seeing a gate further down the road, the went hand-in-hand to the seclusion of a high hedge. Some time later, as they stood apart after a long and quite tender kiss, Hob faced May.

"I could come to love you very much, May Fletcher," he said.

And that is what I hoped you would say, May thought to herself. I do believe I could come to love this young man very much too! Long gone were her worries about what she would feel like if and when Hob kissed her. She felt wonderful.

* * *

Matthew Kent awoke on the morning of the 12th September, nine days after the battle had been fought at Worcester. News of the final defeat of the king and his Scots army had filtered down to the south-west only a day after the royalist cause had been finally and irretrievably lost. Kent had wondered for a few days how this news made him feel. On the one hand, he was glad that the fighting had ended, but on the other hand, he had some sympathy for those who had been caught up in what had from the outset been a hopeless cause. Admittedly, the old king had enjoyed a few successes at first, but after that it had all been downhill, culminating in the trial and execution of the king.

Like many in the country, he was glad beyond measure that the autocratic rule had been brought to an end. As had the seeming threat of a king increasingly under the influence of his Catholic queen. But – to chop off the head of an anointed king?

Kent looked out of the small window in his upstairs room at the tavern in Bovey Tracey. The sun was just beginning to raise a cheerful face, promising a day of late warmth. Like everyone else outside the major cities, he was profoundly grateful for the weather being so kind – the harvests had been plentiful, safely gathered in, and stored away for the bitter weather that was sure to be hard on the heels of a benign autumn.

He arose and poured the ewer of water into the large washbowl, immersed his face in it and contemplated the need for a trim of hair and beard. No – another few days would suffice. Fully dressed, he descended to the main taproom where his breakfast was already laid out. He said a cheery 'good day' to Sal Allen, as that invariably happy landlady ladled spiced oatmeal into his bowl. Glory glided past, still seemingly in a daydream after her betrothal to Gaston Bessant. Soon, she would be married and gone to live with the bookseller's family. Zachary, Glory's younger brother, also came by – stomped in his case. He now had both his and Glory's duties to perform!

Kent was half-way through his bowl of oatmeal when he became aware of hoofbeats approaching up the slight hill from the crossroads. Dick Allen, the landlord, came bustling through, summoning the tavern's ostler as he went.

The horses came to a stop at the tavern and words were spoken. More hoofbeats signalled the removal of the horses to the stables, and the main door opened to reveal Dick Allen and four other figures. Kent did a double-take.

"By all that is holy!" he exclaimed. "Can this really be Sergeant Larkin?" He stood up and went to the tall figure with hand outstretched.

"By all that is holy!" the tall figure responded, pumping the outstretched hand. "Tis Master Kent. But this be not Sergeant Larkin – tis Lieutenant Larkin. And this be not Trooper Tamplin, but Sergeant Tamplin. You will recall Troopers Dellow and Young?"

"Indeed, I do – and my congratulations on the promotions. But what in the name of heaven brings you back here again?"

"Same as before, I suppose," Larkin grinned. "Keeping a weather eye on things in general. Also, I hear that you have bumped into a weird lot calling themselves The Vale of Sorrow."

"Yes, to my own personal sorrow, I have." Kent went on to relate all he knew so far – the two bodies, the jewellery, the two possible people in Lustleigh and the surrounding mystery.

By the end of that long narration, the four soldiers were sitting and enjoying once again the superior ale brewed by Sal.

"You, my wonderous landlady, have not lost the knack!" Larkin raised his mug to Sal, who beamed with pleasure.

"Back to your problem," Larkin turned again to Kent. "The name of this group is not unknown in Westminster. As far as I am aware, they are a highly secretive lot, emerging every so often with bodies around the countryside – and all completely unexplained suicides."

"I had a long chat with a Canon Rigby in Exeter some time ago," Kent went on. "He told me that the group exists solely for the purpose of pleading forgiveness for original sin – the harder they pray day and night, the more likely it is that Almighty God will hear their supplication and offer that forgiveness. How this forgiveness may manifest itself is unclear – to say the least! However, if members feel they are not even worthy to continue their supplication, they are encouraged to sacrifice themselves."

"That simply has to be the worst heresy of our time!" Larkin said, open-mouthed. "I was certainly not aware that this was their creed. I knew they were a secretive and somewhat heretical bunch, but that is horrendous. How sure is this Canon of his facts?"

"He seemed to me to be in complete earnest," Kent replied.

"Would you require our help in trying to trace any local adherents?"

"Strange to relate, I already have three who need to answer some questions. Thomas Axelby of Lustleigh – a widower, and his two grown children, Francis and Lisa have been pointed out to me as being 'strange' in their beliefs and habits."

"I would dearly like to come along with you when you question this family," Larkins growled. "Surely, it would not hurt to have armed soldiers to add weight to the interrogation?"

"Indeed, it would not hurt at all. I would be most grateful for the company," Kent agreed.

* * *

Harry and Mary had arrived at the cartographers in Exeter by eleven o'clock that morning, having ridden on a pair of chestnut mares that were similar in appearance they could have been twins. The two had enjoyed the ride and had turned it into a series of races, alternating with sedate walking and trotting. The shop smelled exactly as Mary had imagined it, old inks and parchment competing with the tobacco from the old shop owner's pipe.

"This one is probably the very best for your purposes," the old chap wheezed, taking a roll of parchment from a leather tube. He spread it out on the large table, using various objects to anchor the corners. The map was as comprehensive as was known – showing the Americas on the left, all the way to distant Cathay on the right. Each country was spelled out in beautifully created lettering, some countries being coloured in green, some in a light brown.

"What is the significance of the colouring?" Mary asked. The old man looked up at her and spread his hands wide.

"I have never been able to discover the answer to that," he grunted. "See those in green – Spain, Greece, parts of Muscovy? If you can discern what joins them, then I will eat my hat!"

"You hat is safe," Mary laughed, "for I cannot for the life of me see what they may have in common. But I agree that this is just what I would have dreamed of for display to my children."

Harry had been peering closely at the bottom right-hand corner. "There is a date, presumably when it was created. MDLVIII – is that not 1558?"

Mary peered at in in turn. "Me fecit MDLXIII – I made this in 1558. Have you ever been able to decipher the signature that follows?"

"No, and more's the pity!" the old man grunted. "I have spent many hours on this one map – on the significance of the colours, the date and the signature. The only one that speaks loudly is the year."

"Aye – the year of Bloody Mary's death and the coming of Elizabeth to the throne," Mary nodded. "This map, if indeed the date be correct, was made nearly one hundred years past. So much has happened since then!"

"Aye – Bess reigned, the Spaniards were sent packing, Jamie came from Scotland, his son lost his head, and *his* son is now in France – whilst we are governed by a parliament!"

"Nevertheless, if the price be suitable, this is the map that I would want," Mary could not take her eyes from the large parchment spread out on the table.

Later, at a nearby tavern, Harry and Mary ate a late dinner, the leather tube safely held between Harry's knees at the old trestle table.

"Happy?" he asked, looking at his wife's smiling face opposite him.

"In all things, happy!" Mary grinned. "With my map, with my school, but most of all with the husband I chose and the child of ours that now grows within."

"And you did have the luxury of choice," Harry pointed out. "So many young maids have no such choice."

Mary's gaze seemed far distant. "One day, and I know not when, *all* maids shall have the choice. Tis so very wrong that they do not!"

* * *

The next day was market day in Newton Abbot. Gil and Ella were up as the sun rose, getting their produce loaded onto the cart. May was not far behind them, packing eggs into baskets, and three pullets into the newly made cage. They all ate a very early breakfast, then, with Ella, Rosie and Jamie waving them off, set out for the short journey.

Perched together on the driving board, Gil was using the opportunity to find out May's feelings for young Hob. He went about it in a roundabout manner.

"I trust that young Hob treated you with all due respect," he probed.

"Oh, indeed he did. I should not have remained with him else."

"And what are your feelings for the young rapscallion?"

"They are what they always were – I have always liked Hob. But now, those feelings are just a little deeper than just liking."

"And how may that have come about?" Gil turned a grinning face towards the young girl.

May had the grace to blush. "It was when we kissed," she admitted. "Boys have kissed me before, but it was always because of some dare put upon them by their friends. This was different. Hob *wanted* to kiss me – and I wanted him to. So, it was different."

"Twas exactly the same with Ella and me – that first real kiss sealed our fates for once and all. After it, I knew there would never be another in my life."

"I wonder if it shall be the same for Hob and me? We have had only one walk together, but I want to be with him, and I know he wants my company. My dada has a strong liking for Hob, so there shall be no problem there. Maud keeps on teasing me, but I shall ignore her!"

"That is what sisters do," Gil laughed. "Mary used to tease me about Ella – but there she now is married to Harry and a child on the way. No more teasing now!"

Later that day, back in the cottage, Gil and May recounted their experience at their first market. Gil was ecstatic.

"Seventeen shillings and two pence," he said, rattling a well-filled purse.

"And a further nine shillings and seven pence from eggs and pullets," May was just as elated.

"Great merciful heavens," Ella laughed. "Riches beyond measure. When shall we have enough produce to repeat this miracle?"

"It would be well were we to repeat the business nearer to the coming winter. Folks will want to lay in stocks in fear of snow or very cold weather. Perhaps we should aim for November – and again in January?"

"Exactly my thoughts," Ella nodded. "Folks never have enough stocked by!"

CHAPTER XI

It had taken ten days for Matt and Herb Grindley to reach the border town of Chepstow, ten days of rain, sun, endless walking. Having arrived at the town, they determined that they would rest up for two days, perhaps find a cobbler and either have their boots repaired or buy new ones.

Thanks to the purloined purse taken from the officer's dead body, they still had most of the money remaining – and it was this more than anything else that prompted them to take a well-deserved break. They had developed a subterfuge – Herb kept the purse secreted inside his blouse, every morning handing Matt a few coins to spend on what they needed – thus, showing no abundant riches to anyone.

Sitting on a bench outside a pie shop, they savoured the crisp pastry and the succulent mutton and onion filling. They had eaten well since leaving the area around Boscobel House, still blissfully unaware of what had taken place there. It was still not decided which route they would take when they left Chepstow.

"One thing at least is certain," Matt grinned, "we have to cross the river, or we shall be in Wales until the day we die."

"Why do we not seek a boat, rather than going miles out of our way to find a bridge?" Herb suggested. "Surely, there must be small boats aplenty that would oblige for the right price."

"Have you noted how wide the river is?" Matt argued. "I suggest that we walk further into Wales – say as far as Cardiff where there will be boats regularly going between there and the Somerset shore. Burnham would be as good a place to aim for."

"And from there, where?" Herb wanted to know. Matt was the West Country lad and had far more knowledge of the entire area than his friend.

"Bridgewater first, then Taunton, on to Cullompton and then skirt around Exeter. By the time we get there, I shall be within a day's walk of my home."

"But why do we have to miss out Exeter?" Herb wanted to know.

"Because there will be a large garrison there and there could well be some within who will recognise me. Having come all this way, I have no intention of being apprehended as a king's man. No – we miss Exeter out and head around it for Bovey. Once there, we can spin some story of us simply going off to seek work for the months we have been away – perhaps as far as Kent. For certain, nowhere near Worcester!"

"That be all well and good for you," Herb grunted. "My home is many a week's journey from even here. Not that I've a home to go back to in truth. My old man married again before I left, and I have no wish to reside anywhere near that harridan!"

"Can she be really that bad?" Matt laughed.

"You do not know the half of it," Herb growled. "She has my father utterly bewitched. She has the face of a beautiful angel and a figure to match. It is when she opens her pretty mouth that it all changes. Venom and poison erupt that would put a serpent to shame. Nothing be good enough, nothing be clean enough, never enough coin for her bloody ladyship to squander. And the old fool simply smiles and goes out to earn more! No – there is no way on this Good Lord's earth that I will return there."

"As I have told you many times, my father, before he died was a carpenter – and a very good one. He was teaching me well until the winter fever took him – may he rest in peace. I still have some skill, so mayhap we could start up the business again. My poor mother would have had to sell the place and I have no notion where she may be now. I hope that she is still thereabouts, but I am not sure. I owe her a full explanation as I have treated her shamefully. But until we get there, I have only that hope to spur me on."

"Then that will be you settled – or hopefully. But I have no carpentry skills. My father was teaching me his business when I left – driven away by that evil witch!"

"You have never said what skill you learned," Matt prompted.

"My father was the village brewer of ales. I remember more than enough of that to make my way."

"There is no call for another brewer of ales in Bovey – Mistress Allen at the tavern is renowned far and wide as a genius in that skill."

"I also learned some of the art of the cooper," Herb added, almost as an afterthought.

Matt went into one of his periods of thought. Herb knew him well enough by that time to let him be, to let his mind wander hither and yon. Sometimes the result was a good enough thought; sometimes it led absolutely nowhere.

Pies eaten, the two stood up and started walking yet again. By unspoken consent, they set out for Cardiff where, in that large port, they would be bound to get passage across the channel to the Somerset shore. They had gone almost a mile before Matt broke his silence.

"What is involved in the work of a cooper?" he asked.

"Oh, simple enough," Herb answered. "First there are the top and bottom – made from good oak. Then there are the staves – also fashioned in oak and of equal shapes. Finally, there be the hoops of iron."

"It cannot be that simple!" Matt objected.

"Nay – you are correct there," Herb grinned. "The staves have to be to a set pattern and steamed to shape. Then the hoops have to be of three sizes – top and bottom, larger for a quarter way up and a quarter way down – then the largest one for the middle. Tis all done to a set of patterns that are never the same cooper to cooper."

"And have you the skill to create these patterns?"

"Aye – I believe I do."

"Then I definitely have the skill to fashion the oak. What we would need is a small cottage in which to live, a workplace to fashion the oak, a cabinet to steam the staves, and enough tools to make a start. Master Abel would provide the hoops – and he is a master smith."

"You make it all sound far too easy!" Herb grunted. "I am willing to wager we find a dozen pitfalls along the way!"

"That is a wager you would win," Matt acknowledged. "But think of this – what else may we do to earn ourselves a living? Pitfalls are things to be overcome. I say we use all our time on this journey to think it through properly."

"Oh, I agree that we must needs think hard about it and how it may be achieved. But I'm still of the opinion that one of those pitfalls will be deep enough to sink the plan!"

"Then let me think of this plan and you spend your time thinking of another!" Matt responded. "I'm willing to wager in my turn that you cannot come up with one that is better!"

"Then the plan is that we each think of a plan – you think of this plan whilst I devise yet another plan," Herb guffawed at the idea.

"I see a sign painted in gold letters," Matt retorted. "Crowley and Grindley – Coopers to His Majesty the King."

"There be no king, you idiot!" Herb snorted.

* * *

Matthew Kent and Paul Larkin arrived at the village of Lustleigh in mid-morning, and made straight for the Axelby home. Naturally, the father was not there – about his business in the woods. But both son and daughter were home, sitting outside under a shady tree reading their bibles. They looked up in annoyance as the two men approached, having tethered their horses by the gate.

Kent had decided on a full-on approach, no discreet questioning, but straight to the point. He stood before the brother and sister, hands on hips.

"It has been brought to my notice that you, and possibly your father, are members of a sect that calls itself the Vale of Sorrow," he stated it as a fact. "That sect is heretical, unlawful - and I am here to take you in for formal questioning."

"And by what authority to do presume to take us in?" the man asked, standing up and facing up to Kent.

"By this authority!" Kent answered, displaying his signed warrant.

"We recognise no such authority -so be on your way!" came the rejoinder.

"You do not recognise the authority of your own parliament? That in itself could be regarded as a treasonable statement. I would advise you not to make matters worse for yourselves."

"And what if I and my sister decline to be taken," Francis Axelby squared up to Kent. His sister Lisa had meanwhile been calmly reading and had not even bothered to look at the two men.

"Do not be tempted to add stupidity to the list," Lieutenant Larkin advised. "Just accept the fact that you will accompany us to Bovey where you will be put to the question. If you are truly innocent, you will be released unharmed. Resist, and you will be taken by force!"

"Were my father here, you would be cut down!" Lisa at last looked up.

"Were your father here and attempted to harm an official of parliament, I would be forced to shoot him. The same applies to the pair of you – make no mistake on that score!" Larkin said quietly.

"Our lives are of no worth – so do your worst!" Lisa replied.

"That just about confirms my suspicions," Kent was as quiet as Larkin. "That damnable sect advocates the ending of lives deemed worthless. But you *will* come with us, whether you require a quick death or not."

Larkin drew his pistol and aimed it at Francis' head. "Let us put that desire to the test, shall we? Master Kent will take you and bind you for the walk back. If you resist, I shall shoot you. It is now time for you to consider your desire for death very seriously!"

He was relieved to see the Adam's Apple in Francis' throat wobble up and down, sure signs of indecision and real consternation. He gave an almost imperceptible nod to Kent, who reached for the young man and bound his hands behind his back with a short length or rope that he had brought with him specifically for that purpose.

"May you be damned for all eternity!" Lisa spat at them both. Neither responded in any way at all, although Larkin was tempted to laugh.

"You, mistress, will walk beside your brother. Make one false move and you will also be bound."

"Then you shall learn that I have more courage than he has. You threatened him with death. Do you also threaten me with the same? For if you do, then I welcome it!"

So saying, she turned on her heel and made as if to run off. Larkin simply extended one long leg and tripped her so that she fell in a heap by the bench. In moments, she was trussed like her brother.

"And now, we shall proceed as stated," Kent said, leading the pair out to the horses. He produced another small piece of rope from his saddlebag and joined their bound wrists together.

"You now have ensured a far more uncomfortable walk."

* * *

There being no school that day, Mary took the rolled map to James and Avril to show them what Lady Violette's money had purchased. The map was spread out on the parlour table, this time held down at its four corners by heavy glass vials from the shop.

Nell, left to her own devices in the shop, was busily engaged in crushing dried feverfew in the large pestle and mortar. With winter not that far ahead of them, the apothecary shop was fully engaged in preparing for the worst – though heaven forbid another outbreak of the deadly winter fever. The last bout had carried off many of the small town's inhabitants. Now and again, Nell looked back into the parlour and wished she could see that precious map.

"Before I came to open this business," James reminisced, "I travelled to Spain to learn from the very best – those from the Mahommedan countries who had remained, or who had been allowed to remain because of their wide knowledge. It was from them that I learned the workings of the muscles, how an open wound may be closed safely, how a bone may be set back into its proper position. Seeing that country spread out before me brings back all those memories. I travelled to Granada and to Seville and it was there I encountered the wisest man I have ever come across. He was called Ali ben Tewfik, and he was born in what the crusaders came to call Outremer. His knowledge of the human body, its ailments, and how to counteract those ailments, has remained with me ever since."

"And yet we still refer to hm and his kind as infidels," Mary muttered.

"Not to forget that he and his kind apply the same epithet to us!" Avril grinned.

Mary had just thought of an idea. "Uncle James, would you trace your journey for me, and the journey you took back again."

"I suspect a far deeper motive behind that request," James laughed aloud.

"Aye – you always could see beneath the surface of my speech," Mary gave him a smile of resignation. "If you could attend the school and trace that journey and tell of the countries and people you encountered on the way, it would serve to open eyes to a world larger than South Devon."

"I should be happy indeed to do so. But there are aspects of my travel that should be kept from young ears."

"Oh? And what should also be kept from mine?" Avril snorted. "Your diversions into houses best left unmentioned?"

James gave a big guffaw of laughter. "Nay – not that sort of aspects. I witnessed starvation, death, religious practices that would certainly raise more than an eyebrow. I also witnessed an execution and a maiming of a thief. No, those I shall certainly not mention."

By then, Nell could stand no more. She had listened avidly to the conversation going on not ten feet from her. She emptied the crushed feverfew into a jar and stoppered it. Then, wiping her hands on a piece of clean linen, she marched into the parlour. She was still short of her tenth birthday but hated to be kept away from accessing new knowledge. Avril regarded her as she would regard the banks of little drawers in which they stored their many ingredients – a store of knowledge that was forever being added to.

James, Avril, and Mary exchanged a knowing look as Nell perched up on a stool to peer at the map. They also noted that Nell kept her fingers well away from the parchment, knowing deep within her brain that it was special and needed preservation.

"Where is Granada?" she asked, thereby revealing that she had not missed one word.

James took a wooden pointer that he had been using and, being careful not to touch the surface, pointed at a small dot far down in the south of Spain.

"There is Granada – and it is very hot. It was for many years the centre of Arabic knowledge and custom. I visited the Alhambra Palace, and that is a wonder to behold, full of gardens and fountains, and so much stored knowledge it would take many lifetimes to assimilate."

"I should like to visit there one day," Nell muttered wistfully. "Do they know about the movement of blood as you all talk about?"

"Aye – they most certainly do. I suspect that they knew of it well before our own Master Harvey who wrote of it only some few years back," Avril nodded.

"Why do we not have their writings to guide us? They sound as if they know far more than we have yet discovered."

"A few of us do follow their teaching," James nodded in his turn. "But to all the Christian folk of Europe, they are damned by their beliefs – and thus should not be acknowledged."

"Like the Jews?" Nell persisted.

"Aye – just like the Jews. Damned in the eyes of Christian folk because of their betrayal of the Saviour."

"But the Jews that live today did not betray anyone!" Nell looked up and challenged everyone.

"Read the Good Book, young Nell. The sins of the father shall be visited upon the son until the third or fourth generation. That is according to the Book of Exodus. But – and it is a very large but – the Book of Ezekiel states that the son shall not bear the iniquities of the father, nor shall the father bear the iniquities of the son" Mary stated. "Should the third King Henry carry the responsibility for the sins of his father, King John? Nay – this is utter stupidity! And our own Good Book is not much help either!"

"That sentiment would best be kept within these walls," Avril advised with a shake of her head towards Mary. "Heaven alone knows what these Puritans in Parliament would make of such an utterance – although I agree wholeheartedly with it."

"Have no fear, Aunt Avril – I know exactly to whom I can speak my mind. I have yet to experience any of my pupils ask me a question where I would have to prevaricate. Believe me, I would most certainly err on the side of caution!"

"This is all very confusing!" Nell groaned. "And all because I asked where Granada was!"

"We have done little but muddy the waters for you," James gave Nell's curly head a pat of sympathy. "But you already have a mind well in advance of your years – so you will know exactly who to speak to and who not to."

"I shall never speak of any like matter other than to my family," Nell assured them. James, Avril and Mary exchanged a look – Nell was a very large part of the family, despite not having one drop of their blood in her veins. Since taking the little four-year-old under her protection, Avril had regarded the girl as a daughter, the daughter she had never been blessed with. James regarded her as his daughter as well, but knowing she would never be able to call him dada – that was reserved for the young man in his grave up at the church where Nell visited every week without fail.

Mary rolled the map back into its case and went to the school room where she very carefully pinned it flat to the wall. Underneath it, she pinned a notice in very bold letters. 'DO NOT TOUCH OR MARK THIS MAP!'

* * *

Having brought the two Axelbys back to Bovey Tracey, Kent was not at all sure what he should do with them. It seemed to him to be wrong to impose them upon either the steward or the bailiff. Larkin, who had the authority of his uniform, had nowhere that he could use, being resident at the tavern. The two of them had discussed the matter as they had ridden back to the town.

"I have my warrant and you have your commission – and between the two of us we are like dandelion seeds blowing in the wind!" Kent had grumbled. "I know full well that I can have them taken to a secure place in Newton Abbot, but I need to start interrogating them as soon as possible."

As a last resort, they took the two prisoners to the tavern and begged the use of a back room. Dick and Sal had looked rather bemused but agreed to let them use the small room off the main taproom that some travellers used who needed privacy.

Lisa and Francis were sat in chairs and their ropes were removed. Kent drew up a chair facing them, whilst Larkin stood at the door.

"First of all, I need to know whether or not you are members of a sect that calls itself the Vale of Sorrow. Are you, or are you not members?" Kent opened his questioning.

"We both refuse to answer any question that you put to us. We do not recognise your authority," Lisa said quietly, looking down at the floor and not at Kent.

"Then let me put it this way," Kent pursued his line. "If I were to assume by your refusal that you were indeed members, hoping to conceal the fact by your silence, I would have no option to take you under arrest to the Sheriff in Exeter and have you put to much harder questioning. Is that what you are prepared for me to do?"

"You will do whatever you see fit!" Lisa almost spat back.

Kent decided to gamble, sensing that Lisa was the far stronger willed of the two. He turned to Larkin.

"Would you ask your soldiers to take this woman away and keep her safe and secure?"

Larkin immediately cottoned onto that line of thought. "Aye – no trouble at all." He poked his head through the door and asked young Zachary to find his sergeant.

Everything went quiet until Sergeant Tamplin and Trooper Dellow knocked at the door.

"I want the pair of you to take this young woman and keep her safe and secure for a while. She is not to speak to anyone, she is not to be spoken to, she is not to be harmed in any way."

After the two had removed Lisa, Kent again faced Francis, Larkin again leaning against the door.

"Right – let us start again. I am going to assume that you are indeed a member and stick by its principles. Therefore, you are prepared to end your life at any time, preferably by your own hand. I am not going to allow you that luxury. I am going to offer you a choice. Tell me what I want to know, or I shall end your life for you."

Both he and Larkin knew this to be a gamble, but seeing the sweat break out on the young man's brow, maybe it was one worth taking. Kent pulled his pistol from its holster on his belt, cocked the hammer and pointed it firmly at the head of the now quaking man.

"That would be murder!" he gasped.

"But not if you were to attempt to escape arrest – which both of us here would swear you did!"

"Only course left open to us!" Larkin nodded.

"So, let us start again. Is your father also a member of this sect?"

Francis slumped in his chair and dumbly nodded. Kent breathed a sigh of relief. One gamble had paid off.

"Ann and Lucas Dodds – were they also members?"

The result was the same – a nod.

"And where do the members meet?"

"That I shall not reveal!" the head raised to stare defiantly back at Kent.

"Oh, indeed you most certainly will!" Kent stated. "Let me relate to you exactly how that shall come about. You shall be taken to Exeter and arraigned before the sheriff. You will then be given a choice – and your sister shall not be there to curb your tongue. If you again refuse, you will be condemned as a member of a proscribed and heretical sect. The penalty for that will be immediate death by hanging. However, should you choose another path, you will be offered an additional chance – to renounce forever your heretical inclinations and released to freedom. Do not ask me how this will come about, just accept the fact that it will. Alternatively, you could answer all my questions fully and truthfully so that I may report your willingness to the sheriff – who will then release you. So, Master Francis Axelby, what is it to be? Your immediate cooperation or face the sheriff?"

Tears were now falling uncontrolled down the haggard face. Kent simply knew that his gamble was about to pay off.

"I shall answer your questions," Francis gulped.

"And I shall fetch someone to take down all that is said," Larkin almost smiled as he slid out of the door. He thought carefully before making his choice. He needed someone of integrity and who could be relied upon for absolute silence. He went in search of Mary Cove.

Finding her where he first suspected she would be – in the school – he explained what was being requested, and the need for absolute discretion. Mary blanched at the prospect but agreed to act as scribe. She fetched paper, ink and pen, placed them in her small satchel and went back to the tavern with Larkin.

CHAPTER XII

May had made arrangements with Ella that she could finish her work with the hens an hour before her usual time. Therefore, she bustled about after a very rushed dinner so as to be ready on time. Then, promptly at four o'clock in the afternoon, there came a knock at the front door. Gil and Ella gave May a solemn bow that had her giggling as she went to answer the summons.

On the front step of the cottage stood Hob, resplendent in brushed tunic and shiny shoes, hair for once plastered down so as to curb the usual unruly mess. In his hand was a bunch of late autumn flowers which he shyly presented to May. Gil and Ella, who had both known Hob all his life, could hardly contain their laughter at this complete change in the young lad. Hob was usually to be seen with tears in his clothes, hair awry, rushing like a thing possessed as he delivered messages for either the bailiff or the steward. Recently, he had been entrusted with far more fitting work, helping out on the large estate and shadowing Harry. Now, here he was, a shy suitor, not at all sure of himself.

"Thank you, Hob – they are lovely. Come inside for a moment whilst I set them in water," May seemed the far more self-assured of the young pair. She took her shawl from the peg by the front door and wrapped it around her shoulders, having set the flowers in a jug of water.

"When will somebody bring me flowers?" came a demanding little voice from the fireside where Rosie was tickling Jamie's toes.

"When you are at least ten years older!" Ella told her.

"But I shall be too old by then!" Rosie objected. "I shall be nearly as old as Hob – and he's very old!"

Hob obliged her by bending over and pretending to shuffle with the aid of an imaginary stick. "I'm in my dotage," he quavered.

"You're a silly bugger!" Rosie snorted.

"And where did you discover that word?" Gil wanted to know. "It is not a nice thing to call anyone!"

"Your dada said it to a man who brought his horse to be re-shod, mama!" Rosie retorted.

Ella, who had heard her father use far more pungent epithets in her life, could well believe it. However, she had to back Gil in his remonstration.

"I do not want to hear you use the word again – it is *not* nice!" she wagged a finger at her truculent daughter.

"I shall escort May back to her home in time for her supper," Hob announced, offering his arm to May. May tucked her hand under the proffered arm and the two young people set off looking for all the world like a middle-aged couple.

That state of affairs lasted all the way up the main street and past the church – and around the corner away from prying eyes. Then, beneath a hawthorn tree slowly turning its leaves from green to yellow, May could contain the pretence no longer. She faced Hob and put her arms around his neck. Hob obliged with a soft kiss that turned out to the first of many. They were so deeply absorbed in this pastime that they failed to hear a set of footsteps approaching.

"Well bless my soul – tis Hob and May. I assume this is not your first meeting!"

They broke apart guiltily to see Lou Crowley grinning at them. In front of her was a sheet fashioned as a sling inside which was cradled the little boy known as Felix. He had been found as a tiny, wailing babe by Hob just over two years previously, seemingly abandoned in a tumbledown hut up by the bank of the River Bovey. A search had then revealed the badly battered body of a young woman in the nearby vicinity. Despite searches and enquiries, no identity for the young woman had ever been discovered. Having very recently lost her husband to the winter fever, and her son Matt to heaven alone knew where, Lou Crowley had eagerly taken the young chap into her care. Because he had favoured everyone with a cat-like grin, Mary had immediately said that he had to be called Felix. The name had stuck, and little Felix now knew no other mother than Lou.

"Er, good day, Mistress Crowley," Hob stuttered, for the first time ever in his life embarrassed by a situation in which he found himself. May on the other hand, gave Lou a big smile, not at all put out by the circumstances.

"And a very good day to you Hob and May. I was taking Felix for a walk – well, I'm doing the walking as you can see. When we get a bit further along the lane, I shall set Felix down and he can demonstrate his abilities by walking back by my side."

"Walk," Felix gave his usual happy grin from the sling. "Eelix walk!"

Lou gave them another good day and walked on, happy to see the way things were progressing between two of her very favourite young people.

"I wonder if we shall ever find out his real name, where he came from, and whether that young girl was actually his mother," May mused, staring after the 'mother' and child.

"The bailiff and I spent hours trying to find out what we could – and we ended up with nothing at all," Hob remembered the time spent ferreting about up by the river. "If nothing else, little Felix has found a loving home. Does Mary see much of them as they live above the school?"

"I doubt that she does as Mary lives with us at the bailiff's house and is at the school little other than when she is teaching. Also, as she is now with child, she will be spending less time there herself."

"I wonder who will take on the teaching when Mary is forced to take leave," May asked of nobody in particular.

"I heard tell that the Lady Violette will take over some of the teaching."

"And she will stand for no nonsense from the children!" May laughed, then turned serious.

"And now, Hob – where were we?"

* * *

Mary, complete with her writing materials, sat down at a small table in the back room of the tavern. Francis Axelby, now a very subdued young man, sat in a chair by the window facing Matthew Kent. Lieutenant Larkin resumed his pose against the door.

"Mary," Kent began, "would you start by writing the following at the very top of your page? This statement is given by me Francis Axelby on the fifteenth day of September in the year sixteen fifty-one. I make this statement of my own free will."

Mary looked up and nodded. "And now, will you write my questions and the answers given in the exact words used by both of us?"

Again, Mary nodded and sat pen poised.

"Francis – are you now a member of the sect that calls itself The Vale of Sorrow?"

"Yes, I have already said that I am."

"And are your father, Thomas Axelby, and your sister, Lisa Axelby also members of that sect?"

"Yes, both are."

"Is one of the teachings of that sect that a member must take his or her own life when that person has reached a point where they realise that they are no longer worthy of that life?"

"Yes, it is."

Mary started to look up as the free admission came. She was horrified.

"And are you, your father and sister aware of two people by the names of Ann and Lucas Dodds?"

"Yes – they are from a large house beyond Teigngrace – or I should say that they *were* from that place as they are now dead."

"Do you know how they came to meet their deaths?"

"They will have agreed between them that they would end their lives together."

"In other words, they agreed upon a pact of self-murder!"

"Yes – they had been contemplating it for some weeks past."

"And how do you know that?"

"Because they were the leaders of the group in this part of Devon. We used regularly to meet at their house for prayers and conversation. We had been attending meetings there for two years past and were all well aware of the desperation that they both felt."

"So, you have absolutely no doubt that their deaths were self-inflicted?"

"Nay – none whatsoever."

"And did they ever disclose the means that they would use to effect this ending?"

"They said that they had decided upon the use of aconite in a drink."

So, Kent thought. Avril and James Ramsey were absolutely right. And young Nell was also a part of that determination, he remembered.

"Who else attended those meetings – apart from you, your sister, your father, and the Dodds?"

A look of rebellion was his answer. "That, I shall never reveal."

"But you are ready to admit the other members of your own family were complicit! Why then not the others? Have they some hold over you? Have they positions of power and influence that keep you from accusing them?"

That was met with a stony silence. Kent felt that he had gone as far as he could.

"Finally, are you now willing to renounce the teaching of this evil sect? To present evidence to the courts as you have presented here today?"

"Aye – I am willing to renounce and give evidence – but *never* about anyone I have not mentioned here!"

Kent turned to Mary. "Would you please then add the following? I sign that this is a true record of my interview with Matthew Kent, witnessed by Lieutenant Larkin and Mistress Mary Ramsey."

Having obtained Francis' signature, plus those of Mary, Larkin and himself, Kent folded the document and sealed it. Francis was taken away to be held pending removal to Exeter.

"Thank you for your help," Kent said to Mary. "Not one word must you reveal to anyone until the trial before the court is completed – the trial could well be compromised if any evidence presented has been made public prior to the hearing."

"Believe me, my lips are sealed!" Mary stated. "Such wickedness! How can any rational being be so misguided? I sometimes despair of the lack of logic displayed by some people."

"And you are a person of logic, are you not?!" Kent gave her a big grin.

"The only way to succeed in any task is to persevere. If you fail, then your method was at fault. Logic will tell you where to amend the method – and you try again. If your own logic is unable to fathom it, then you seek someone whose logic is better suited to the problem!"

"I have an uncanny belief that the child you are now bearing will become one of the greatest thinkers of this or any age. With a teacher such as his or her mother, how could he or she fail?" Larkin observed.

"The fact that you include the possibility of a female child in your predictions does you immense credit," Mary gave him a small curtsey.

* * *

The seventeenth day of September turned out to be a lot warmer than anyone had expected it to be. Certainly, Matt and Herb were sweating inside their layers of clothing when they eventually arrived at the shoreline to the west of Cardiff. They had been told that their best chance of getting a lift across the channel was down at a small fishing village called Barry. They arrived there as the church clock struck eleven o'clock. They scanned the beach expecting to find fleets of fishing boats. What they found were three – and they were all devoid of any fishermen.

"And now what?" Matt asked in exasperation. Their journey had not been that easy since they had left the edges of Chepstow. All except for one old chap sucking on a clay pipe as he sat on the pebbles in the shade of one of the boats.

Herb went over to the man who looked up and, removing the pipe from his mouth, regaled Herb with a set of toothless gums. "A allaf eich helpu?" he spluttered.

Herb latched onto the last word and assumed it meant 'help'.

"We want to cross the channel," he said slowly, gesturing out to sea.

The old chap certainly understood the gesture and pointed across the water in his turn. "Bristol?" he said.

"Nay – Burnham," Herb replied.

The old chap slowly got to his feet, looked into the bowl of his pipe and filled it from a pouch taken from his pocket. He burst into musical Welsh again.

"Rydym yn gadael am dri y prynhawm yma. Rydym yn pysgota ger Burnham."

Herb looked blank, except for again latching onto the last word.

"Burnham?" he repeated.

"Oes – Burnham. Dri." He pointed to the church, held three fingers up and added, "bong, bong, bong."

Herb related all this to a somewhat bemused Matt. "Says he leaves for fishing off Burnham at three this afternoon," he explained.

"Didn't know you spoke Welsh," he grumbled.

Herb again faced the old fisherman. "You take us?" he asked, pointing at first himself and Matt, then at the boat, and across the sea.

The old chap gave another toothless grin and simply nodded.

"Thank you very much," Herb gave the old fellow a broad grin, took Matt by the elbow and walked him back off the beach to what he believed to be a tavern. There, using sign language again, he obtained ale and dishes of fish stew. The two sat quietly by the window and waited patiently for the hours to pass. Eventually, they saw two more men join the old fellow. He gathered them into a huddle and was obviously explaining that they would have two passengers when they set off. Both other men looked back at the tavern and grinned.

At about two-thirty, the boat was slowly manoeuvred on rollers to the small breaking waves. All three clambered aboard and started sorting nets, laughing uproariously as they toiled. One of them looked back at the tavern and waved, beckoning the two to come and join them. Matt and Herb scuttled down the beach and clambered aboard. Even they could see that the tide was coming in and would soon float the craft off the pebbles.

The old man gestured to the foot of the only mast – obviously, Matt and Herb were expected to sit there patiently out of the way. The tide in the Bristol Channel is one of the highest and fastest in the world, so it was only minutes before they were properly afloat, the sail hauled up, and they were off, scudding across the incoming current at a good rate of knots. The old chap manned the wooden tiller at the stern whilst the two other men busied themselves in the prow with ropes and nets. Matt and Herb simply sat in the belly of the boat and nodded off.

Seeing that the passengers were asleep, the old chap silently beckoned the other two crew members to join him. They crept past the two slumbering men and listened as the old chap whispered.

"They do not speak Welsh – and they do not know that we speak English. When we get just off the Burnham shore, we take money from them and cast them overboard. They will be waist-deep and will be able to wade ashore. Then we turn back a little and start fishing."

The sun was still above the horizon when Matt and Herb were woken up. One of the crew, a short, barrel-chested man of forty or so, nudged them with his foot. They looked up as the man pointed just off the port bow.

"Burnham!" he grinned. Matt and Herb were immediately on their feet. They were still about a hundred yards off the beach, which was flat and sandy. The fisherman was joined by his mate – another squat fellow who looked as if he had been hewn from the trunk of an oak tree. The two of them pulled out their gutting knives, wicked looking things with long, thin blades.

"Arian!" the first one growled, rubbing thumb across two fingers in the universal sign.

"They want money," Herb said. Matt, who had that day's allowance in his pocket, took out the remaining coins and offered them to the man, who looked at them, did a rough calculation, then grabbed all of them. He cast his eyes to Herb who simply shrugged and held out his empty hands in the accepted sign of 'I am skint!'

"Jump over the side. The water here is about three feet. You can wade ashore!" the fisherman grinned at the pair.

Matt glanced over the side and doubted it. They had taken his money and would probably leave them to drown. The other man gestured to the old chap, who left the tiller and grabbed a long-handled boat hook. He thrust it over the side, then drew it up so that they could see that it went no further down than about the three feet promised.

Matt was the first to jump into the water and to start wading for the shore. Herb, seeing that he was not going to drown, joined him. By the time they had taken ten steps, the boat had turned around and was heading back out into the channel to begin fishing.

Some minutes later, two very wet young men plumped down on the sand. Herb looked at Matt.

"Back in dear old England," he grinned, fishing the purse out from its place of safety. "And we've still more than enough to see us for months."

"Assuming I even still have a home!" Matt muttered.

* * *

That evening, Mary sat alone by the fire in the Bailiff's house. She could not get out of her mind the words she had written down during that interrogation. What astounded her most was the fact that any thinking individual could be so weak-minded as to be persuaded to subscribe to such utter nonsense. The fact that it was both heretical and unlawful seemed to her to be of almost secondary importance. It was utterly illogical.

The brother and sister had been escorted, along with the written testimony, to Exeter. The father had somehow miraculously disappeared. She hoped against hope that the young man could escape dire punishment. In time, surely he would come to his senses? Mary was nowhere near as sanguine about Lisa Axelby. That young woman would see her execution as the culmination of her wishes!

CHAPTER XIII

Sir Horace Drew, deputy sheriff, fixed Francis Axelby with a gimlet eye. The man stood before the sheriff's desk in Exeter looking down at his shoes – anywhere but at that glare. Matthew Kent and Lieutenant Larkin stood behind Francis, not that they had any suspicion that the chap was likely to make a run for it.

"You stand by this?" Drew grated, waving the statement at him.

"Yes, sir," Axelby muttered.

"You do realise the jeopardy in which this places you?"

"Yes, sir," another mumbled nod.

"And whilst implicating your father and your sister – not to mention those two wretches who ended their own miserable lives – you still decline to name any others of like mind?"

"Yes, sir," a third mumble.

"Why?"

Francis at last raised his eyes to look directly at the sheriff.

"Sir, I cannot, I dare not!"

"Then that leads us all to the conclusion that those who remain unnamed are people of substance, people of rank and power – or just perhaps, people of evil intent – maybe both evil intent *and* rank! I am willing to indulge this farce a while longer. Now, answer 'no' if that is the true answer, or remain silent if the answer is 'yes' Are these unnamed people of rank?"

Absolute silence greeted that question. The deputy sheriff glanced at the two people standing behind Francis and gave a nod of satisfaction. "Next question – same rules. Are these unnamed people living within a five-mile radius of your home?"

"No, sir."

"Ten miles?"

Silence again. Another significant glance towards Kent and Larkin. The deputy sheriff gave a bellow.

"Hoskins!"

The door opened immediately to admit one of the sheriff's men – a massive figure in uniform.

"Sir Horace?"

"Put this fellow back where he came from. No visitors. No contact whatsoever!"

When Francis had been led away, Drew motioned to two chairs for his other 'visitors' to sit.

"Well, gentlemen. You seem to have kicked over a hornet's nest. The search for the father continues?" he received assurance that it most assuredly was.

"Then, your task seems clear enough. Scour the countryside within that ten-mile radius, and beyond five miles. Find me the people of power and influence that this wretched man seems to regard in some terror. You have the necessary authority? Or do you need my written warrant?"

"I have sufficient authority in my own warrant, Sir Horace," Kent said.

"I, on the other hand, have only my commission and my rank – so a written warrant from you sir, would be welcome," Larkin admitted.

"Have you enough men at your disposal?"

"I have my sergeant and one other trooper. The four of us should cope."

Drew again bellowed for someone named Norris. He was rewarded by the appearance of a small, wizened clerk.

"Supply these gentlemen with a list of all persons of rank that reside within a ten-mile radius of Bovey Tracey – and say not one word to anyone or I shall remove your balls in a most painful manner."

Larkin and Kent sat at a table in a tavern close to the castle. They ate their way through fish pie and surveyed the list.

"Only five names – and I know of nearly all of them from my previous stay in the town," Larkin observed. "I have to say that all of them seem most unlikely candidates!"

"I recognise only three of those names," Kent stated. "I agree with you that those three would never appear on my list of suspects. One of them is close to eighty years of age!"

"Stupidity does not diminish with age," Larkin grinned. "Some would say that it increases!"

"Then there is little hope for any of us. I suppose we had better start back and plan how we intend to carry out this investigation."

By supper, both were back at the tavern in Bovey Tracey, again occupying the back room. Sergeant Tamplin and Trooper Dellow were briefed on the mission that they would begin the next morning.

The first call was to the bailiff and steward as their combined knowledge of the neighbourhood could prove invaluable. Tamplin and Dellow prepared the horses as Larkin and Kent called upon Peter Cove. As luck would have it, the bailiff was not only at home, but had the steward with him, as well as two visitors.

Ethan and Ellen Dodds sat side by side in hard chairs, looking both apprehensive and distinctly uncomfortable. Cove, normally noted for his hospitality, was at somewhat of a loss as to how to treat these two. They were, first and foremost, the children of two suicides, suicides who were proven members of an heretical and proscribed sect. On the other hand, they were now deprived of their parents and therefore demanded some measure of sympathy. Cove introduced the two to Larkin and Kent.

"They have travelled together from Exeter to take possession of the house and the two jewels that were discovered," Cove explained. He had already retrieved the brooch and cross from the strong box and had laid them on the small side table.

"Legal stuff first," Cove faced the two. "Are you able to identify these two pieces?"

"Indeed, we are so able," Ellen replied. "If you turn the brooch over, you will see there are initials etched into the surround – plus a year. The initials are A.L.D. and stand for Anne Lauren Dodds – our mother. The year is MDCXXIX – standing for 1629, the year of their marriage."

"And," added Ethan, "the cross is unadorned and thus not a crucifix. On its reverse you will find two very small indentations in the gold. Those are the result of a small boy – me – biting it when a mere three years old. My father was chastising me for some act of defiance, and I did not take kindly to it."

Cove examined both pieces, then handed them to Barton. "Exactly as you describe. They are undoubtedly a part of your inheritance. I shall ask you to sign receipt of them. Now, gentlemen – have you questions for them?"

"Thank you, Master Bailiff, we do." Kent faced the two young people. "My name is Matthew Kent and I hold a general warrant from Parliament. Lieutenant Larkin is, as you see, a commissioned officer. We are jointly pursuing enquiries into a sect that calls itself The Vale of Sorrow. So first, what knowledge have you of this sect?"

"Knowledge?" Ethan blurted. "None whatsoever into its workings. Ellen and I escaped from that nonsense at the first available opportunity. Our parents some five or more years ago started displaying what were to us very worrying habits – moaning and beating their breasts, going out for long walks and returning looking for all the world as if that same world was about to end."

"Not to mention the strange people who now and again descended upon our home where they all congregated in the furthest parts of the garden to writhe and moan aloud," Ellen was close to tears as the memories flooded back. "As Ethan said, when I was eighteen and he twenty, we both moved to Exeter to find work and to live as separate from this madness as we could manage."

"And did either of your parents ever speak of their beliefs, their behaviour, what it was all about?"

"Only once, and to me alone as I demanded to know," Ellen replied. "I cornered our mother one day and said that we were worried almost sick with their behaviour. I can recite her answer word for word. It is not for any of us to question the mind of the Lord, she said. It is our bounden duty to spend our entire lives seeking forgiveness for the manifold sins of His creation and to end those lives when we reach the point of utter hopelessness. Now, is that not the mantra of these misguided fools?"

"As far as we can ascertain, yes, it is," Kent replied. "Now, we have obtained a list of names, and we would ask that you listen to them as, one by one, I speak them aloud. Please feel free to interrupt at any time."

Kent took out the list and read out the first name. "Aurelius Bentley."

"Good Lord, is he still alive?" Ethan raised eyebrows. "An eccentric and nearing eighty summers or more. We would sneak away when we were much younger and walk along the lanes to peer into the garden of his old house. He was invariably occupied in constructing various things from wood and iron, muttering to himself and shouting at a servant whenever he needed a special tool or something. To this day, we still do not know what he was making!"

"Sir Baldwin and Lady Hermione Walker?"

Those two names were met with blank faces and shrugs.

"Lady Agnes Villiers?"

"Oh – she was married to Sir Carter Villiers – he was killed at Torrington supporting the old king. Lady Agnes always greeted us with cakes and drinks whenever we visited her as children."

"Torrington. That was five years past. I know plenty who were there on the Parliamentary side," Larkin remarked.

"Bertrand Salter?" Kent read the penultimate name.

More shrugs and blank faces.

"Sir Walter and Lady Penelope Fredericks?"

Ellen looked as blank as before, but Ethan looked up. "The name Fredericks is somehow familiar. Do you have the address for them?"

"Yes – a place called Upway House."

"Aye – one time, some years past now, I overheard the name Fredericks when people were arriving at the house. Usually, Ellen and I were ushered away but that one time I was half-way down the staircase when I heard the name as two people arrived. I hurried back upstairs again and thought no more about it."

"Then we have at least a starting point," Larkin muttered to Kent. "Where is Upway House, do you know, Master Bailiff?"

"Aye – I believe it is way beyond Chudleigh Knighton, east through Gappah and Olchard. If you ride beyond there and into the village of Ideford, the tavern there will know of it. I am sure you will have to travel back the way you came, but I can think of no other way to discover its exact whereabouts."

"One final thing," Kent faced the two young people again. "This will sound like an imposition, but we need urgently to come with you to your old home where we will need to search it for evidence of their doings and possible fellow-members."

"Believe me, we have absolutely no objection whatsoever," Ellen stated, her mouth in a thin line of determination. "We have consulted a lawyer and have been advised that the house and property reverts to us jointly – in the absence of any testament being found. We both wish as speedy an end to this horrible business as may be achieved!"

* * *

Hob, chancing his arm, went to call on May at the Ramsey's chicken run – hoping to snatch a few minutes with her during the break for dinner. May was dusting seed and straw from her pinafore as Hob poked his unruly head over the back fence.

"My morning tasks are all done," May said, responding to Hob's cheerful greeting. "I have perhaps a half hour until dinner, but I must tell Ella where I am going."

A few minutes later, the two were walking side by side up the town's main street, May's hand tucked under Hob's arm. They had gone no more than a hundred yards when they were stopped by a somewhat abrupt summons.

"Stop right where you are," came a voice from just ahead. Up to his waist in the roadside ditch was Will Fletcher, the town's hedger and ditcher – and May's father. He clambered out and put his shovel down.

"Good day to you, Master Fletcher," Hob got in first. "May and I are just taking a quiet walk together before her dinner."

"Then I need have no fear for the safety of my daughter? She is in safe and honourable hands?"

"Indeed, Master Fletcher. There be no safer nor more honourable hands. I give you my solemn word!"

"Disappoint me on any score and I shall attend to parts of your carcase with one of my more savage implements!"

"I take due note, Master Fletcher!"

"And you, young May, preserve your modesty and remain the virtuous person I know you to be!"

"I, father, am the very soul of modesty and chasteness. How could you doubt it for even one second?"

"Because I was once your age and know what temptations lie in wait!"

"Temptations that you, as a virtuous man, would never have yielded to," May gave her father a broad smile.

"Er, well, that is somewhat beside the point," Will grunted. He gave Hob a piercing stare. "Treat her properly, young Hob – she is very special to us."

"May I assure you, Master Fletcher, she is as precious to me. I respect your daughter and shall treat her with the utmost care."

The two walked on, leaving Will Fletcher standing in the middle of the road, scratching his head.

"Bloody 'ell," he muttered. "One day a rapscallion messenger, the next a blossoming gentleman! Who would ever have thought it."

* * *

The large house was in darkness and totally unoccupied. Each room, and there were many, had furniture under covers; each window shuttered. Ellen and Ethan busied themselves with removing the shutters from the large parlour windows and removing dust covers from table and chairs.

"It would seem that we can offer you no hospitality," Ellen announced, returning empty handed from the kitchen and larders. "What items of food that remain are mouldered beyond recovery; the ale remaining in the barrels is sour; and there has never been even a drop of wine in the house."

"It would appear that the servants, at least those who remained, closed the house and went their separate ways," Ethan remarked, bidding the visitors take their places around the table. "The first call will have to be our father's study. If there be any paperwork, deeds or testaments, they will be there somewhere."

"To start with, would you write the names and addresses – if you know them – of the principal servants? They might well have valuable information." Kent went straight to business.

"The steward, cook, housekeeper, maids – they all lived in. Where they would be now, I have no idea. Clearly, they are not here. This house, and it is with some reluctance that I am here at all, holds no pleasant memories for me!" Ellen grimaced.

"Not even when you were a young child?" Kent asked.

"No, not really. Both Ethan and I were transferred to the care of an elderly nursemaid. Contact with our parents was minimal – and that was by their choice, not ours!"

The search of the house proved absolutely fruitless – not one scrap of paper gave any hint as to the beliefs or practises of the dead couple; no clue as to the disposition of the property. All that was relevant was a rolled parchment that showed the transfer of the house and adjoining lands to one Lucas Dodds. It was dated in the March of 1630.

"The lawyer told us that we need to show him this document – as it proves ownership. But there is no testament, and the lawyer could find no trace of one anywhere. It would seem that both Ellen and I now own this mausoleum. Believe me, should that prove true, we shall dispose of it as soon as we may. Neither of us would ever dream of returning to live here!"

Kent thought it about time he made a statement.

"Whatever the rights and wrongs of the manner of your parents' conduct, I have no doubt whatsoever in declaring that I harbour no suspicions of you both. Your obvious detestation of their beliefs, your willingness to help our investigation, plus your obvious repugnance of this darkened house – well, they all speak for themselves. That will be the first paragraph of my eventual report."

"Is it not strange," Ellen mused aloud, "that we have found no bills from suppliers, no accounts of household spending, no itinerary of the contents of the house, no detailed account of the income from the land – indeed, not one mention of what was produced, by whom, and for what purpose!"

"It is almost as if the house has been scoured and sanitised, pending a visit from someone such as ourselves!" Larkin observed. Up until then, he had maintained a discreet silence.

"That is a very sound observation!" Kent nodded. "Unless Lucas and Ann Dodds did it themselves prior to their final act, then someone else must be responsible. Perhaps at the behest of the owners; perhaps by the servants, obeying instruction. Even perhaps, by some third party following the deaths – and for reasons of secrecy."

"Then the sooner we are able to interrogate those on our list – and especially this steward, should we be able to trace him – the better," Larkin declared.

The house was again locked tight before the four rode back to Bovey Tracey. The amount of questions and the people needed to be questioned was now larger and more urgent.

A messenger was awaiting Kent and Larkin when they entered the large taproom.

"Sir Horace's compliments, Master Kent. He is arriving here in the morning with men at arms. He wishes to be present at any interrogation – especially that with Sir Walter Fredericks."

"Then he obviously has some inkling as to that man's involvement – or he would not stir from Exeter!" Larkin observed. "His duties there keep him extremely busy."

* * *

It was late in the afternoon when two rather weary travellers settled themselves into a corner of the tavern in Chagford. They ordered ale and whatever had been left over from the earlier dinner. They were very pleased to hear that they could each have a large bowl of mutton stew.

"Come from afar?" the potboy asked, plonking two mugs of ale on the table between Matt and Herb.

"On our way to Bovey Tracey," Herb answered; he was becoming a master in the art of obfuscation.

"Then you will not get there today!" the potboy sniffed a penny for himself if he were to convince the two travellers to take a room.

"That is a fact," Matt agreed. "Have you room for two tired travellers?"

"Let me go and enquire," the potboy shuffled off, knowing full well that there was room aplenty. Always make the customer feel obliged to you, his master the tavernkeeper had instructed him a year ago when he had first started.

He left it a few moments before reappearing at the table beaming. "I have managed to secure you a room," he said, looking smug. "We had reserved rooms for a group of travellers who have yet to appear. Perhaps they are delayed." Therefore, when the place seemed empty the following morning, the potboy's seeming favour would be readily explained.

Some while later, Matt put his spoon back into his empty bowl and sat back with a sigh of contentment. Herb, always quicker at his meals, had finished some time before and was sitting back sipping an excellent ale.

"You are the local lad – do we have much further to travel?" he asked quietly.

"Nay – the next town is Moretonhampstead, then the village called Lustleigh, then we are as good as home. We shall be there by mid-afternoon. But what we shall find there, I have no idea."

"Have you really no idea?"

"Not the slightest notion. As I have told you, my father passed during the winter fever many months past, and my mother would have been left a widow with no real means of support. But she would have been able to sell the cottage and perhaps set herself up in lodgings somewhere. Whether or not she be still in the town I have no notion at all."

Herbert Grindley was silent for a few moments, debating whether or not to ask the next question – but decided it had to be asked.

"Did you feel no remorse abandoning your widowed mother?"

"At first, no I did not. But of recent months, remorse has crept up on me. To begin with, all I could think of was travelling anywhere to join the king's forces. But the ease with which we were beaten every time taught me a lesson – that the cause was hopeless, and I should not have left. So, aye – I feel remorse and now hope to make what amends I may. And speaking of amends, what riches remain so that I may even make a start on it?"

Herb turned a grinning face to his friend. "Far more than you may imagine," he winked. "When we found that bulging purse, I emptied a goodly quantity into my own which I have never showed to anyone. The coins I have been giving you on our journey is what remained in the purloined purse. There are five shillings left in the latter and over three pounds in the former. And that is not to be broadcast or we shall make ourselves vulnerable to theft!"

"Then I am very grateful for your thrift but dislike the secrecy. Cannot you have trusted me?"

"Aye, I certainly trust you. But I am thrifty by nature, whilst you are spendthrift – and that was a chance I could not take. When we get to your home, I am happy to halve the coin and go on my way."

"But what of our plans for the business we intended to start? Have you already dismissed the possibility?"

"Nay – not for a moment have I dismissed it. But think carefully – what do we both really know of the art of coopering? How long will it take us to learn and, more to the point, have we enough funds left to support ourselves whilst we learn?"

"How far removed can it be from the trade I once studied? Carpentry is at the heart of coopering – and there is a blacksmith for the hoops!"

"And what of accommodation, the timber, the tools, the oven where we have to steam the staves for bending? They all have to be bought somehow."

"My mother will never have parted with the tools – and all I need will be there. That will save that expense. If we do not attempt it, what else may we do?"

"You have the skill to start as a carpenter. I have no such skills, so I will travel on and seek my fortune elsewhere."

Matt was quiet for a while, then faced his friend.

"I ran away when I should have stayed. I ran away from a battle when my conscience should have told me to see it through. I shall not run away again. My heart is set on this enterprise, so I shall do it whether or not you stay to be my partner."

"Then, how can I possibly desert my friend when he so obviously needs me by his side?" Herb laughed.

The two went up to their small room and slept soundly until the cocks crowed to wake them to a sunny day.

* * *

By the time May had finished work, the cart had been loaded with vegetables, eggs and pullets for sale – ready for an early start the next morning. This market would be held in Ashburton – further away than Newton Abbot, so necessitating the start almost before daybreak.

"Stay for some supper – you have well earned it," Ella prompted, setting an extra place at the parlour table.

Ella and Gill had both expected it, a spat from Rosie. They were not disappointed.

"Why cannot I go to market with Dada and May? I spend all my days with Jamie and I'm very bored!"

"You cannot go to market for one very good reason," Gil replied, looking sternly at his daughter. "You would not stay quietly with May and with me; you would go wandering off and we would have to spend valuable time searching for you to see you came to no harm. May and I go because we have things to sell, people to talk to. You cannot be trusted to stay with us and to do as you were told."

"But I *promise* to be a good girl and to stay quietly with you and with May. I *promise* not to go wandering off by my own!"

"Exactly the same promise you gave me the other day," Ella snorted. "You promised to stay with Jamie in the parlour whilst your dada and I hoed the carrots. And where did we find you? Playing all by yourself upstairs and Jamie all alone in the kitchen reaching for the knives!"

"But I was gone but a few minutes!"

"And now you add a lie to your disobedience!" Ella was fast losing patience. "May came through and saw Jamie all alone in the kitchen. She was concerned and stayed with him for at least one half hour before you came back downstairs to resume doing what you had faithfully promised to do. No, Rosie – you are not to be trusted!"

Little Rosie was never one to resort to tears. Instead, she stormed up the stairs and sat sulking on her bed. Ella and Gil shared a look, whilst Jamie sat quietly on May's lap being fed his supper. He was the only one in that house who was in a state of permanent calm; nothing ever seemed to upset his equilibrium. He faced the entire world with a cherubic smile of contentment. Gil wondered just how much longer that idyllic state would last.

"Can we afford the coin to send Rosie to Mary's school – at least two days per week?" Ella wondered aloud. "It would perhaps do her a power of good to be amongst a properly disciplined environment."

Gil thought about it. "You are our financial guardian," he replied. "If you can find the coin from somewhere, then I think it a very good idea."

CHAPTER XIV

It was past ten o'clock on the following morning when Sir Horace Drew, deputy sheriff, arrived on horseback together with four mounted soldiers. Wasting no time, he bustled into the tavern to speak with Larkin and Kent.

"Found out where this sod lives?" he demanded.

"Aye, Sir Horace. We have got the precise location," Kent answered. "May we assume from your presence that you have information concerning the two people?"

"You may so assume. Their names have been bandied about for some months – and nothing to their good. Strange, clandestine meetings reported. Stinks to high heaven – and I will have some answers!"

"It will take us about one hour to ride there," Larkin observed.

"Then time for a sup of the excellent ale that this tavern is noted for. You bringing your two with you?"

"Aye, Sir Horace. My sergeant and trooper would sulk for days were I to leave them behind."

"I shall leave the questioning to you, Master Kent, as you are more acquainted with the circumstances. But I shall most certainly interpose should I feel the need!"

"I could not perhaps dissuade you, should I even dream of doing so!" Kent grinned.

"No – you bloody well could not!" the Deputy Sheriff returned the broad grin with a bellow of laughter.

Upway House proved to be a large, rambling mansion situated about one and a half miles north of the village of Ideford. The nine mounted men rode at a sedate trot through the open gates and through an avenue of beech trees to see the brick house nestling against a wood of mixed oak, ash and birch. It had grass areas to the front and both sides. Sir Horace stopped at the large old oak front door and looked around for grooms to hurry out to see to the horses. His face mirrored the others of his colleagues as a silence greeted their arrival.

"Either everyone's dead, or this is the poorest served house I have ever encountered," he grunted, dismounting and striding to the door. He hammered loudly and stood back. After a minute or two, the door creaked open and an old face peered around.

"Sir Walter is not accepting visitors," the old face creased into a frown.

"I care not a rat's arse whether he is accepting or not! Inform your master that Sir Horace Drew, Deputy Sheriff of the county, demands immediate entry. Now, bugger off!"

"Sir Walter does not respond to peremptory demands!"

"Listen to me, you old fart! Either we are admitted immediately, your master and mistress summoned, or my men and those of the good Lieutenant will kick the bloody door in and rouse the sod from wherever he lurks. Now – what is it to be? An open door of welcome or a horrible mess made of this house?"

The old man took a further look at the irate face, opened the door wide and shuffled off down a corridor. Drew signalled to his party. "Goodhew, care for the horses. Everyone else, follow me."

He marched inside, turned left to where he knew that the main hall would be situated. He was right, but stopped abruptly at the sight that greeted them. Arranged around the walls were wooden benches. The large fireplace was empty, spotlessly clean, but devoid of kindling, logs, or any sign of the makings of a fire. At the far end, in front of large windows, was a table with three chairs ranged at the back. Looking around the walls, he could see no sign of sconces for candles or torches. The place looked for all the world as if nobody had ever been in there – despite being spotlessly clean.

"Looks like a mausoleum," Larkin muttered.

"Then his bloody lordship had better not antagonise me further or I shall turn it into a working mausoleum," Drew grunted.

The eight men were grouped in the centre of the floor when they became aware of rapid footsteps approaching the main door of the hall. The person who then confronted them was a strange sight indeed. Well over six feet tall, he was dressed from head to toe in a black robe that buttoned all down its length. No ruff, collar or belt adorned then garment. The head that arouse from the neck of the robe was thin, almost emaciated. A long nose separated two piercing blue eyes. The mouth was merely a slash, set down at its corners into a snarl.

"And what is the meaning of this intrusion?" a voice grated. "You should be aware of who I am and the influence I wield!"

"Aye – we are so aware – you are distantly related to a couple of the members of the Council of Stare. Means not a pile of shit to me! We are here to put questions to you – and those questions you will answer fully and truthfully – or I shall take you back to Rougemont and have other methods employed. Now, sit down on one of those benches, shut your mouth until an answer is demanded."

"Sir Gavin shall hear of this outrage!" Sir Walter snarled, making to leave the way he had come. Drew nodded to his men. They grabbed an arm each and marched the man to a bench, sat him down and stood either side, grinning like idiots. They were enjoying this.

"Sir Gavin will distance himself from you in a heartbeat – unless, of course, he is as deeply immersed in this disgusting business as I am sure you are! Master Kent?"

Kent went to stand facing the glowering knight. He had rehearsed his opening statement quietly to himself on his ride from Bovey Tracey.

"Lucas and Ann Dodds. Two people who were found dead some while ago in a field in Bovey Tracey. Two people who were known to be members of a sect that goes by the name of The Vale of Sorrow. Two people who committed self-murder, an act that is encouraged by this sect. You and your wife, Lady Penelope, were known to have visited the Dodds house on several occasions and were seen to participate in their strange, disgusting rituals. So – first question. Are you now, or have you ever been a participating member of the sect?"

"I shall not dignify that with an answer!" came the grating reply. "As you all know, I am well connected with the Council of State. You would do well to remember that if you have any expectation of furthering your miserable career."

"Then I shall start again from the beginning," Kent was not in the least put out by the truculent man. "Were you acquainted with Lucas and Ann Dodds?"

"I have heard of them, naturally. I make it my business to be acquainted with all landowners in the vicinity. Not that my social cognisance is any of your business!"

"Oh, it most certainly is," Kent replied, fishing out his warrant and dangling it before the lean face. He could see at once that the signature above the seal registered with Sir Walter. He was also pleased to see an Adam's apple bobbing up and down in some consternation. "You will see that I am entitled to enquire into whatever matter that interests me. You will also note that everyone, irrespective of status, is obliged to assist me in those enquiries. I have only to say to Sir Horace that I am being thwarted in my enquiries and he is likewise obliged to act in the manner he sees fit to ensure that my enquiries are properly fulfilled. So, I ask again, and this for the last time in the comfort of your home. Sir Walter Fredericks, have you Ever participated in the rituals carried out at the home of Lucas and Ann Dodds?"

Everyone else could see the wheels turning in that domed cranium as Sir Walter strove to find some way out of what was turning out to be a dire predicament.

"Then, I have to admit that on one occasion my lady wife and I did attend such rituals. We had heard of them and were curious as to their nature. So, we attended just the once, saw what we suspected were irreligious carryings-on, and left immediately afterwards."

Is that the best you can come up with? Kent almost smiled.

"So, Sir Walter. You and Lady Penelope attended what you had good reason to suspect were both unlawful and irreligious happenings. Yet you, a knight of the realm and a prominent member of society – not to mention a relation of members of the Council of State – chose not to disclose these happenings to the authorities, to turn a blind eye to what you knew to be serious and damaging infringements of the law. Is that what you are telling me?"

"Well?" boomed Sir Horace. "Either you are a fool or a knave. Which is it to be?"

The man drew himself up as upright as his sitting position would allow him. He turned an eye full of hatred to the deputy sheriff.

"I demand that you allow me a moment alone so that I may question my own conscience!" So saying, he shrugged off the restraining hands and stood up to stalk to the large window. He stood motionless, looking out at the distant woods, until he suddenly dived a hand into his robe and came up with a pistol which he put to his head. There came a loud click, then nothing.

"Couldn't even get that right, could you?!" Drew snorted as his men removed the misfired pistol. "We now have to assume that you were attempting the same self-murder that your erstwhile colleagues attempted – with a far greater degree of success, I might add!"

The man slumped between the restraining hands and was again led back to the bench, two soldiers at either side of him, holding tight to his arms. There was no way they would allow him another chance.

The meeting was interrupted at that point by the appearance of another emaciated figure. Lady Penelope Fredericks stood in the doorway, dressed almost identically to her husband – a long, black robe with no adornment. Also, like her husband, her mouth was turned down into a permanent snarl of disapproval.

"This is an outrage!" she spat at Sir Horace. "How dare you invade the house of perfectly respectable people!"

"Perfectly respectable people do not cavort around in black robes and seek to end their miserable lives. Nor do they encourage others to do the same!" Sir Horace retorted.

"And who says that we do such things? Whoever they are, they lie – and therefore condemn themselves to everlasting damnation!"

"Who says?" Sir Horace roared back. "This miserable specimen of a husband of yours says! He has just attempted self-murder, thereby admitting to it, you daft cow!"

The look that Lady Penelope directed at her husband would have turned ale sour at fifty paces. "Pathetic!" she hissed.

"No, madam – what *is* pathetic is your belief in this farrago of stupidity!" Kent said quietly. "Your husband has as good as admitted by his actions that the so-called beliefs of this damnable sect are so important to him that he willingly obeyed their most cherished demand – that a member *must* end his or her own life by his or her own hand. Lucas and Ann Dodds so obeyed the demand; your husband attempted to do so. You will now answer questions. If you fail to answer truthfully – or fail to answer at all – I shall ask Sir Horace to arrest you and to hold you in a safe and secure place until such time as Parliament sends down a respected judge to question you. So, Lady Penelope Fredericks, my first question is this. Are you willing to answer questions that I shall put to you?"

"Damn you to hell, sir! I answer to no one but to my God and Creator."

"Then you leave me with no alternative. Sir Horace, my warrant from Parliament is quite specific. These two persons have failed to render me the help and assistance that is demanded. I now ask you to take them into custody to await further action."

"Willingly, my dear fellow. Willingly!"

The two were unceremoniously bundled outside, horses were fetched from the stables and Sir Horace, his men and two captives trotted off. Kent then turned to Larkin.

"We now turn this house upside down. We all know what to look for."

"In the absence of the master, I must protest, sir!" the old steward stood in the doorway.

"You, master steward, may protest to the heavens. It will avail you nothing. I urge you to read this warrant and to instruct all the staff that I shall be questioning them – and you – most thoroughly."

The bent old man peered at the warrant long enough to realise that any further protest was futile. He gave a resigned shrug. "It shall be as you demand, sir," he muttered.

"But before you go on that errand, I need you to list for me all the staff of this house – so that I may know if anyone decides to sidle off before we get around to them."

The old man needed nothing to jog his memory and listed fifteen members of the staff, their names and positions. Then he was allowed to go and inform everyone.

"Bugger all in here to discover!" Sergeant Tamplin grunted, waving his arm around the scantly furnished hall.

"Might be some secret places behind the panelling," Trooper Dellow observed.

"Then you stay in here and find it," Larkin ordered. "I would suggest that the rest of us repair to the study – or wherever this miserable man keeps his papers. I would also suggest that we do *not* ask help from the servants, or they may well misdirect us."

Larkin, Tamplin and Kent left Dellow, who had started at one corner of the large hall and was systematically tapping the panels with the hilt of his dagger. They found themselves in a long passage with two doors further along on the right and a final, large door at the very end. They opened the first of the doors and found themselves in a small room that boasted a desk, some cupboards, an old, oaken commode at one side, and three chairs. Kent immediately went to the window and threw wide the shutters, thereby letting in shafts of sunlight that illuminated dust motes and a layer of the stuff over nearly every surface – except for the desk.

"From the state of this place, I would hazard a guess that the staff are prohibited from entering this room. It's filthy!" Kent grunted. "I wonder if that means that there are secrets in here that are kept from the prying eyes of the maids?"

"You are the man of learning," Larkin observed. "Why do you not take the desk whilst the good sergeant and I rifle the commode and the cupboards?"

Kent needed no second bidding, sat himself at the desk and opened the topmost, middle drawer. He withdrew a bundle of papers and spread them over the desktop. And then he gave a quiet whistle.

"Ye Gods!" he said. "I would never have believed it!"

* * *

Ella called Gil and May in for their dinner. Unusually, Rosie had helped prepare it without the slightest murmur of dissent. Little Jamie, happy playing with wooden blocks under the parlour table, let out a shrill cry of delight.

"Din-dins!"

"Aye, my sweet – dinner, and your favourite afterwards. Apple custard."

"Yummy, yummy!"

Gil had decided that it was time he and Ella broke the news to Rosie so, when they were all seated and digging into bowls of stew, he broached the subject not having the slightest clue how it would be received.

"Your mama and I, Rosie, have decided that it would do you good to attend Mary's school – at least for two or three days every week."

Expecting a thunderstorm of protest, he was utterly amazed at the reaction. Rosie looked at him and her pretty little face broke into a cherubic smile.

"Really, papa? That would be so scrumptious!" Scrumptious being her favourite word. "What will I learn? Shall I learn all about numbers? I love numbers!"

Ella had been quite prepared to offer the bribe of a visit to market. She was astounded that this was not then necessary.

"Aye – numbers, letters, history, all about the world. Mary is so clever that you will learn a lot from her."

"But I already know my letters! I write and I read all my stories!"

"But think on this, Rosie," Gil prodded. "Let us say that Mary takes you children for a walk into the woods, then asks you to write about what you have seen, what you think of it all. That's not just writing your letters – it's writing your own thoughts."

"I would love to do that! Thank you, mama and papa. I will learn so much I shall be the cleverest in the town."

"Aye - you probably will, at that," Ella muttered.

* * *

"What have you discovered?" Larkin asked as both he and Tamplin abandoned their searches to cluster around the desk.

"Just this," Kent said, almost in wonder as he displayed a piece of paper that contained a list of names. Larkin cast his eye down the list and found immediately what had aroused the excitement.

"Dodds, L and A." he read aloud. "And this seems to be in alphabetical order. Surely the man has not been stupid enough to list everyone in this damned coven?"

"It would appear that he is and that he has," Kent sat back and again read through the list. "There are six surnames on this list, including his own and Dodds. We have Axelby, Dodds and

Fredericks – and those we already know about. But we then have Goodhew, Parsons and Wendover. Goodhew and Parsons could be anybody, but Wendover is a name very well known to Westminster – Sir Percival Wendover is some sort of financial advisor to the Council of State, if indeed this is the same Wendover."

"Perhaps we need to consult the bailiff and the steward – or others in Bovey Tracey. They might be able to identify these Goodhews and Parsons," Larkin thought aloud.

"Then I suggest we leave your good sergeant and trooper here overnight to ensure that nobody goes missing and that nothing is disturbed. You and I should immediately get back to Bovey Tracey and start enquiries there."

"I agree," Larkin nodded. "Sergeant, I am sure you and young Dellow can find sustenance here."

"Aye, sir, I am sure we may!" Tamplin grinned.

* * *

Before Kent and Larkin arrived back at Bovey Tracey, the town witnessed the arrival of two other travellers. Matt and Herb plodded the remaining few yards down to the crossroads, turned left and then crossed the bridge over the river and started plodding up the main street. Matt looked around him and noted that almost nothing had changed since he had left. In some ways he found that very reassuring, but in other ways he found it rather boring. About half-way up the street, he stopped and knocked at a cottage on the right. It was almost too much to hope that his mother would answer the knock. He was not in the least surprised when a little curly head peered around the door.

"I'm Clara. Who are you?"

"I'm Matt Crowley and I used to live here. Is your mama at home?"

"Mama – someone asking for you."

A very young woman appeared behind her daughter and peered short-sightedly at Matt.

"Please excuse the intrusion," he began. "My name is Matt Crowley and I used to live here with my mother, Lou Crowley – and with my father, until he was taken with the fever."

"Then you will be received with a great fuss," the young woman beamed at him. "Indeed, Lou lived here until she moved with the little one to rooms above the school."

"School? Little one? I certainly have no little brother or sister! But I thank you. Perhaps you would point out this school so that I may find my mother."

The young woman pointed at a very large cottage across the street, about twenty yards further up. Matt again thanked her and, with Herb trailing in his wake, plodded to the main door of the large cottage. Seeing the door ajar, and noting the silence within, he knocked on the upper panels. Footsteps approached the door, and it was opened wide. Mary gaped at Matt and Matt gaped at Mary.

"Matt – is it really you after all this time?"

"Aye, Mary – tis me. And what be you doing here. I heard tell it is a school now."

"That it is, and I am the schoolteacher. Much has happened here since you left. I suppose you went first to your old home and they directed you here."

"Aye – they said my mama lived above the school with a little one. I do not remember any sibling!"

"Oh! That is no blood relation to you, but I had better leave the explanation to your mother. Come in and I will take you up to her."

Herb had been standing on foot and then the other whilst this had been going on. "I shall find the tavern and meet you later, Matt. You have a lot of personal things to catch up on."

"Tavern be at the top of the street on the left. I shall meet you there later," Matt was ushered inside the large room with its rows of desks and stools.

"So, Mary Ramsey is a schoolteacher," Matt gave her a grin.

"Wrong! Mary Cove is a schoolteacher. I am married to Harry and, unless your powers of sight have failed you, I am carrying our first child."

"Then may the Heavens bring blessings on all three of you. I have been the biggest fool in Christendom, leaving my mother when she needed me most. I hope that she can forgive me as I shall not be leaving again! But if this be a school, where be all the children?"

"They are all with Lady Violette. She is the school's benefactor, and she sometimes takes the children onto the heath to collect wild flowers and to learn about the trees and bushes. It gives me the time to prepare lessons. But you are no doubt eager to see your dear mother."

Mary led him to the door at the side of the classroom and pointed up the stairs.

"She is probably at work. She spins and works at her small loom. She also looks after the schoolroom for me. She will be overjoyed to see you."

I just hope that be the case, Matt thought as he climbed the stairs and knocked at the door at the top. He heard various noises from within, footsteps, then the door opening.

"Hello, mama," he said, then had to make a grab as the woman swayed and almost fell.

"Can it really be you Matthew, after all this time?" she gasped, being led into the larger of the three rooms where there was a comfortable settle. Matt lowered his mother onto the seat and clasped her hands.

"Aye, mother, it is me. I have returned and swear I shall never leave again. I know that what I did was wrong and can only beg your forgiveness."

"I was so desperately lonely, what with your father dying and you heaven alone knew where. When Mary, bless her, suggested I move here with little Felix, it was as if a new beginning beckoned. I work some of the time and look after the school for her. In return, I live up here free of rent, thanks again to Mary and to that lovely Lady Violette."

Matt knelt down before his mother and took her hands in his. "What or who is this little Felix?" he asked.

"Some time after you left, Hob – you must remember Hob – well, he was walking up along the river and heard a little babe wailing in misery. He found the babe in a tumbledown shed and no sign of any mother or father anywhere. Being a sensible lad, he brought the babe to the bailiff where he was cared for properly. A large search was made, and the body of a young woman was found some distance from the hut. To this day, nobody knows whether or not this poor soul was the mother. Anyway, it was suggested that, as I was completely on my own and desperate for company, I take the babe and raise it as best I might. Mary gave him the name Felix because she said he had the smile of a cat. The wee thing never has known any better and firmly believes I am his mother. Come and meet your little brother – he should be waking soon from his nap."

Matt followed his mother as she went to the smallest of the three rooms. Opening the door, Matt saw a mass of blonde curls peeping out from a warm blanket. The small bed was against the far wall. Small, wooden toys were scattered over the floor. The little lad opened his eyes and gave a huge yawn.

"Cake time, mama?" he asked.

"Aye, my little angel, tis cake time. Up you get and come and meet your big brother. He is called Matt."

Felix sat up and regarded Matt with a round-eyed stare.

"Why is you mat? Mat is on the floor!"

"My name is really Matthew, but everyone calls me Matt. I am very pleased to meet you, Felix." Matt went across and stretched out his hand, somewhat formally.

Felix burst out laughing and grasped Matt's index finger with his little, chubby hand. "I got a bruvver!" he chortled. "Can you make me wooden soldiers?"

"Believe it or not, I most certainly can – and shall, as soon as I get tools and a small workshop."

"So, you really do intend staying?" Lou asked, almost desperate to hear an affirmative answer.

"Aye, mother. I am staying. After my adventure – which was really no adventure at all – I want nothing more than to settle back where I'm known and know everybody. I have a new mate called Herb who has been with me almost ever since I left Bristol. He and I travelled all the way back here together and we have plans to start making barrels. I have the carpentry knowledge and Master Smith can make the hoops for us. Whether or not it will work, where we might find space to do it, how we might even afford to start – well, these matters have yet to be thought through. But fail or succeed, I shall not be leaving again."

"Then my big, grown-up son is still not too grown for a big hug from his mother!"

* * *

Herb had managed to get a small room at the tavern which was bursting at the seams as travellers stopped on their way to the big fair and market soon to be held further west in Tavistock. Dick and Sal Allen were just about rushed off their feet, with Zachary running between tables fetching and carrying platters heaped high with food and jugs brimming with ale. Now and again, a slightly wealthier traveller would want a jug of wine.

Herb sensed an opportunity and, knowing that this tavern and its locals would soon be his neighbours, went to stand at the doorway between the taproom and the vast kitchen. Sal was supervising her two kitchen maids as the food orders were relayed from Dick, who then supervised the ale and wine. All were drenched in sweat both from the heat of the grills and ovens and from the frantic pace of the orders. As Zachary came tearing back for a refill of ale, he made his approach.

"I can do the fetching and carrying for you," he offered. "You all look fair frazzled, and I have nothing else to occupy my time until my friend puts in his appearance."

"And who might this friend be?" Zachary was immediately suspicious. No guest in his young experience ever offered help for no reward.

"He be called Matt Crowley – and he and I are here to start a business."

"Do you mean to tell me that Matt is back at last? His poor mother will be overjoyed!" Sal had overheard what Herb had said.

"He is with her now. We arrived earlier today having walked back over many weeks from Worcester."

"That is a tale you must relate when we have finished the supper!" Dick stated. "We are starved of information down here. But if you were sincere, we could do with whatever help you might supply."

For the next hour or more, Herb ran between the tables, doing half the work for Zachary. He readily donned an apron and fetched and carried with a will. Zachary was overjoyed as he had been pleading for help for many a day. And then, just as the supper service was slowly dying down, in came Matt with Lou. Matt had little Felix in his arms and was tickling the lad's chin and making him squeal with laughter.

Sal Allen sat slumped at a vacant table and mopped her brow, then took a large gulp of her own-brewed ale. She in her turn gave a loud squeal of delight and rushed over to Lou Crowley.

"So, tis fact then? Matt be returned like the prodigal!"

"Aye, Mistress Allen – I am returned. But not as a prodigal I fear – more like a whipped dog."

"No matter how you are! You are here and Lou is happy as a pig in clover, as I observe. Your friend Herb has been a Godsend and has helped Zachary as we have been almost overwhelmed. Now, sit you all down and, when our guests have departed, you must tell us all of your adventure."

Zachary, meanwhile, freed at last from his labours, sidled out of the door and went to the Ramseys and the Smiths to tell them the news. By the time those families had all arrived, Sal had organised a late supper in the smaller, back room, jugs of ale ready. As each of the newcomers arrived, Matt was welcomed back. He was made welcome but castigated for having left his mother at such a dreadful time. Matt hung his head and admitted the fault – and was forgiven by one and all.

"And now, your story!" Dick Allen demanded as Matt and Herb dug into their supper.

Matt told them in detail all that he had experienced, meeting up with the others outside Bristol travelling north until eventually being a part of the king's forces at Worcester.

"All we have ever heard of that battle is that it was a defeat for the king. We know of no details!" Abel Smith growled.

"Defeat? Aye, it were that and more!" Matt replied quietly. "Herb and I were in the rear ranks of a large force under that useless Scot, David Leslie. We were in place called Pitchcroft Meadow, just to the north of the city. During the day, the king, at the centre of things, ordered an attack on a couple of the bridges. For a while, this was successful – that is, until Cromwell sent a mass of troops and artillery to retake them. After that, we expected to be moved south to help the main body of the king's army. Whether or not such an order came, I know not. But Leslie kept us where we were. That is until the main thrust came towards us. Believe me, it were nothing short of murder. Our fellows fell like hay under the scythe. And then Leslie's force simply turned tail and ran. They were mostly Scots and feared that they would simply be massacred – either by Cromwell's lot of by the locals who regarded us all as invaders. Rumour said that we lost some thousands. If Parliament lost more than two hundred I would be surprised. Enough to say that Herb and I ran north to escape – and we ran like hares in March."

"No blame there!" John Ramsey muttered. "Run to fight another day!"

"Believe me, Master Ramsey, there will *be* no other day. The King is fled abroad, the Scots either lay dead or fled back across their border. Whether we like it or not, Parliament is now totally secure. But I have nowhere near finished our tale. Herb and I kept to the woods as we trudged north. We had thrown away our weapons and had the appearance of mere working men seeking employment. We had coin enough as we had found a large purse on a fallen knight. He had no further use for it, but we did. Two days after Worcester, we had arrived at a dense wood surrounding a very large house. Herb scouted about and said it were a place called Boscobel. During that night, two important looking riders came and were admitted. The following day, Parliamentary troops arrived and made a search. We melted away and started our long journey south. Into Wales seemed the safest. So, after some many days, found ourselves at Chepstow and seeking a crossing to the southern shore. We were eventually ferried across for a fee and landed at Burnham. It was then just a long walk south, down the side of the moor. And here we both are. No more military adventures for us! We now intend to start as coopers – if we can find a place to work and a brilliant smith to fashion the hoops!"

"Hah!" Bellowed Abel. "And how may these hoops be paid for?"

"With coin and a share of the profits from selling the barrels – or that is our fondest hope!"

"You must first see the steward. Luke Barton may be able to put a large hut your way," John Ramsey nodded. "But you also need to know that there is a Parliamentary agent here, plus soldiers who were here before. If I were you, I would keep your royalist sympathies and adventures to yourselves. No need putting your heads into another noose – not that they would hang you for it. But it would be better all round if you simply reappeared having been seeking work elsewhere."

"That, Master Ramsey, is good advice for which we both thank you."

CHAPTER XV

Gil awoke early the next morning. His first thought was to leap from his bed and hop across to the window. With a sigh of relief, he saw the beginnings of sunlight in a clear sky. Market day in Ashburton would hardly be improved with a downpour of rain. Ella raised one eyelid and peered across at him.

"Rain?"

"Nay – it has the look of a fine day. That will be a huge relief to our little hurricane of a daughter."

"Need I remind you to spell out to her the need to stay close?"

"If necessary, I shall chain the little devil to the cart! And now, I shall go and rouse her. If she is to go to market, then she can help prepare the breakfast."

He need not have worried – Rosie, four and a half years old – bounded from her bed and shot downstairs. "I shall make the porridge, dada," she announced, saving Gil from the necessity of making it an order. May arrived a few minutes after. She had collected the old horse and had coupled it to the shafts and left it with a well-stuffed hay bag.

"Do everything that your dada and May tell you – or that will be the very last time you are taken to market – and we may think again about you attending school!" Ella gave this as a very stern reminder.

From her look, Ella was sure that going to school was Rosie's dearest wish – and would do anything at all to see that that wish came true. Ella, holding little Jamie, waved the cart off and went inside to their own, leisurely breakfast.

The road to Ashburton was fairly flat. First almost due south past Bovey Heath on their left, then a turn to the right and south-west through Bickington to Ashburton itself. That road skirted the south-east corner of Dartmoor and would take them almost three hours at the slow pace of the horse pulling a laden cart and three passengers. Gil and May took it in turns to drive from the raised driving seat, whilst Rosie, perched high atop a pile of potatoes, waved at everyone they passed. Leaving just after six, they planned to arrive at nine. The clock on the church in the stannary town was showing ten minutes to nine when they at last arrived at the little square, having negotiated the humped bridge over the river that fed into the Dart some miles further west at Buckfastleigh. Gil chocked the wagon wheels and set up the trestle so that May could start piling the vegetables for sale. A smaller table was erected so that the eggs could also be sold. May had an idea and drew Gil aside to whisper. Gil grinned and said it was an excellent idea.

"Rosie," he beckoned his little daughter who was staring around with wonder at the other stalls being set up. "Why do you not sell the eggs whilst May and I sell all the rest?"

He had jumped at the idea. First, it would make Rosie feel important; second, it would keep her tethered to the cart.

"I can do that, papa," the little girl swelled with pride at being given so important a job. Another reason that had occurred to May was that a very pretty little girl would attract customers like bees to honey. She was proved to be absolutely right.

* * *

Following on from the advice they had been given, Matt and Herb made their way to the Parke estate after they had finished eating breakfast in the tavern. Matt renewed many old acquaintances as they walked down the street, so many that they were quite late arriving at the house of Luke Barton, the estate steward.

"So, the rumours are true – you really are back!" Barton greeted Matt and ushered the two into his office after Matt had said they wished to discuss business. Having listened carefully to the outline plan, he sat and thought for a while.

"Abel Smith is willing to undertake some of the work?" he asked.

"We have proposed that we share a percentage of the profits with him, as he is supplying a major component of each barrel," Matt replied.

"Then that answers that question. But here is another. Where, and to whom, do you propose selling your finished barrels?

There are coopers in Newton Abbot, Ashburton, Torquay, Teignmouth – to my certain knowledge. I have never heard that there is a shortage of barrels."

"Aye, that we do know," Matt answered. "But Herb has a plan."

"Master Steward," Herb began at his most formal. "Most barrels hereabouts are used for storing ale. Some are indeed used for cider. But I happen to know that cider is produced in great quantities not far away in Somerset. And it is there that we intend to sell our barrels. I know that we would have to transport them many miles – Taunton being our goal some forty-five miles away. So, we intend to visit that town and find for ourselves whether I am right and there is a need for our products. In the meantime, it would be madness to find that there *is* this need if we have no means of satisfying it. Therefore, we first need to know if there is a shed or yard that we could rent where we might start production."

"Very sensible. Next question. Why, if there be this need, do you not locate your business where the need is greatest? Why here in Bovey?"

"That is easily answered," Matt bowed his head. "I foolishly deserted my mother when she had the greatest need for me. I vowed never to do so again. I know what you say makes the greatest sense, but I have given my word and will not break it!"

"Then I respect your word, Matt. However, I cannot but feel you are incurring considerable costs to your enterprise by adding this long journey every time you have barrels to sell. Are you not dangerously reducing your profits?"

"We believe not," Herb replied. "We would only ever undertake the journey when we had considerable numbers to sell. We would never add the cost of the journey to a small consignment."

"Hm – I will think on it," Barton steepled his fingers. "You have obviously set your hearts on this enterprise, I have two or three possibilities in mind, but my first duty is to ensure that you will have the necessary coin to pay the rent on a regular basis. However, this much I can promise you. Come to me again when you have determined the need in Taunton; present a detailed plan, then if I find it to hold water, I shall produce a yard and a shed for you."

"That, Master Steward, is all we could ask at this time. We thank you for hearing us and we shall report back with the plan that you seek," Herb rose and gave a graceful bow.

"Off to Taunton, then," Matt grinned as they made their way back to the tavern.

* * *

Mary was collected from the school by Harry. She always looked forward to those times when he was able to call for her as he was on his own horse and brought Mary's own horse with him; they would go riding across the Heath, around to Chudleigh Knighton, then back to the Cove's house. Harry, when he had first been courting Mary, had always lifted her onto her horse, then lifted her down again. Now, with Mary's pregnancy already starting to show, he recommenced the practise knowing that Mary disliked intensely having to accept the help.

However, half-way across the Heath, Mary's mood improved considerably. The leaves were starting to turn slightly yellow, heralding the autumn when they would turn various shades of russet before falling to the ground. She sat and allowed her mount to a slow trot, knowing that walking was better, but a full trot would not suit her burgeoning waistline. The air was warm, a slight breeze bringing to their nostrils the aromas of the open Heath – gorse, grasses, yellow hawkbit and teasel. To Mary, it seemed that this was the best way to clear her mind of the day's worries, blown away as the scents took their places.

By the time they had returned to the Bailiff's house and had handed their horses to the waiting groom, Mary was fully relaxed and looking forward to her supper alongside her husband and his parents. Laura Cove had always insisted on doing the bulk of the cooking, despite being fully entitled to cook, scullery maids and bottler. Scullery maids and bottler were in place – had been for some years – but no cook lasted very long as Laura's standards were the equal of those of the palace, and no cook measured up!

However, instead of a cosy settle, a mug of ale and a pre-supper chat, other matters had insinuated themselves. For a start,

152

Matthew Kent and Lieutenant Larkin were present, along with a tall and burly man in his middle years. This chap sat on a stool in the corner of the hall and glared defiantly at the world in general.

"Ah, Mary – just the person we need," her father-in-law greeted her with a big grin. "We need you to take down notes. This individual is Thomas Axelby. You will remember taking notes when his two children were interviewed."

"Oh Lord," Mary groaned. "Is he yet another of these Vale of Sorrow people?"

"Aye – that he most certainly is – and seemingly proud and totally unrepentant."

"We have been searching for him and found him just this afternoon returning to his cottage in Lustleigh," Kent explained, facing Mary and directly away from Axelby. He gave her a mouthed version of 'shush' and a broad wink. Mary correctly interpreted this as a warning not to divulge any word of those previous examinations, especially that part concerning the son's recantation. She gave a slight nod of understanding, went to the Bailiff's study and came back with paper, pen and ink. She sat herself down at a side table and waited.

Kent approached the crouching Axelby and started the questioning.

"Simple stuff to begin with," he said. "First of all, are you Thomas Axelby of Lustleigh, father of Francis and Lisa Axelby?"

"You know full well that I am!" came the surly reply.

"Your offspring have already confessed to being members of an heretical sect that calls itself The Vale of Sorrow. Are you yet another member of that sect?"

"Aye – and I do not *confess* it. I declare it with pride!"

"Were you acquainted with Master and Mistress Dodds, also members of the sect?"

"Aye, and proud of that acquaintance! They carried out the injunction to the letter!"

"And what injunction might that be?"

"Why, simply to end life when all else seems hopeless. They did so and are now reaping their full reward."

"And how is this command justified by your sect?"

"That, whoever you may be, demonstrates the depth of your ignorance! It is written in scripture that 'if thy right eye offends thee, pluck it out!'. It is therefore a simple step to say that, if your whole life offends, then pluck that out as well!"

Mary could hardly restrain herself.

"That is utter and complete nonsense!" she almost shouted. "If you had digested scripture properly, you would have read the next part. I will put it in plain English. It is far better to discard one part than to endanger one's whole life. What you have added is sheer blasphemy. It is also utter balderdash!"

"And there is no one to my knowledge who could have put it better!" Kent gave her a broad grin. "So, Thomas Axelby, you will now be taken to Exeter to be lodged with the sheriff until it is determined what to do with you and those others already apprehended."

"What others?" demanded the man.

"Oh, nobody of any importance," Kent grinned. "Sir Walter and Lady Penelope Fredericks, your two children – and others yet to be arrested!"

He did not mention the fact that the son Francis, had been released and was now actively helping the investigation.

"I will detail my sergeant and trooper to escort this idiot, along with the report, to Sir Horace in Exeter," Larkin offered.

"But that cannot be today," Cove remonstrated. "Tis not far from nightfall!"

"Oh, indeed, Master Bailiff. This oaf shall occupy the cellar until the morning!" Larkin laughed.

Needless to say, supper at the Cove's that evening was taken over with talk of the sect and its strange teachings. Harry, who had been a mute witness to the interview, was yet again taken aback by the depth of his young wife's knowledge.

"I learned my Bible when I was young," he said. "Indeed, it was impressed upon all of us. But I have to admit that your reply would not have occurred to me."

"It only did so because I had heard mention of the passage when young Francis muttered something like it when he was first questioned. Being very inquisitive, I looked it up."

* * *

Late supper at the smallholding was also a time for talk. Gil, May and Rosie had returned in the late afternoon from market. Rosie had spent the entire return journey fast asleep in the back of the cart, wrapped in an old blanket. However, when she was again back in the parlour, she was absolutely full of herself.

"I sold all the eggs, mama. I sold them all by myself!"

"Indeed, she did – and made a very good job of it," Gil nodded. "She shall be our egg seller at every market in the future."

Ella was wondering, if Rosie sold the eggs, what did May do?

"Believe me," Gil carried on. "It was just as well that we had Rosie to undertake that job because May and I were rushed off our feet, weighing and selling all the other produce. It was so successful that we brought back only one sack of potatoes. Everything else sold out. The money pouch is fit to burst!"

"Then I am very proud of all three of you," Ella served a dish of apples and raisins in cream and cinnamon. Jamie had almost to be hosed down before being fit for bed.

After May had gone home and Rosie had also been tucked into her bed, Ella and Gil sat side by side on their settle.

"So, a successful experiment," Ella observed.

"Believe me, having a very pretty little girl selling eggs is the best idea yet!" Gil grinned.

"And our little Rosie is regarded as a pretty little girl?" Ella smiled.

Gil turned to his young wife, cupped her face between his hands, gave her his broadest grin, and looked straight into her eyes.

"And how could she not be?" he asked.

CHAPTER XVI

There had been a change of plan; Kent and Larkin both accompanied the group to Exeter. It had been Larkin's idea for, as he had said, they needed someone with considerable authority even to approach Wendover, Luckily, it was yet another dry day, getting a mite colder but cloudy.

"And I suppose this is another of the buggers," Sir Horace viewed Thomas Axelby with a scowl.

"Indeed, Sir Horace, it is. This is Thomas Axelby, the father of Lisa who you have in custody." Kent proffered the written account of the preliminary interview. The deputy sheriff read through it, grunted and turned to a couple of his soldiers.

"Chuck this blighter in a cell – but nowhere near his daughter and certainly nowhere near those Fredericks. Can't have them chatting and making up excuses, can we?"

Axelby was hustled away, his head drooping as he heard the name Fredericks mentioned. It seemed that he realised that the investigation was proceeding apace – and sounded comprehensive.

Tamplin and Dellow sloped off to grab ale and pies from the soldiers' canteen whilst Kent and Larkin accompanied Drew to his office. The deputy sheriff plonked himself down in his office chair and bellowed for ale.

"Well," he grunted, wiping froth from his moustache. "And how many more do you have to bring me?"

"That, Sir Horace, is something with which we urgently need your help and advice. We discovered a list as you know. The names Goodhew and Parsons would seem to present no problems – once we have located them. But the name Wendover smacks of power and influence. Despite my warrant, I am sure that Sir Percival Wendover would find it totally inadequate – beneath his notice!"

"You are probably right – from all I hear, he's a cocky sod. So, what do you want me to do about it? Add my weight as a provincial deputy sheriff? I sincerely doubt he would take more cognisance of my position than he would of your warrant!"

"Would Sir John Northcote have the necessary power?" Kent asked.

"Our redoubtable county administrator? I doubt even he would get past the Wendover front door. And before you ask, neither would Sir Thomas Reynell, our member of parliament. Doesn't have the necessary clout. And bear this in mind – the sheriff and I as the deputy are appointed for just one year, and that year ends this November. No – what we need is someone who the bugger would recognise and who has the backing of the council – from the very top. Master Bradshaw needs to issue the warrant himself – and that warrant must name Wendover in person! I first need to write a full report and in that I shall rely heavily on your assistance, Master Kent. It must stress the heinous nature of this bloody sect, its heresy, and its threat to good order. Naming Wendover as someone of particular interest will probably do the trick. So, let us get my wretched scribe in here and start the report. Then, off you go to Westminster!"

Kent viewed a long journey at the start of winter with some misgivings. But he knew that was the correct way to proceed – always smother people with warrants and high-blown signatures. He shrugged his shoulders and accepted the need for a long and cold ride.

Larkin gave his friend a look of commiseration, then went to find his own dinner and his two soldiers. The three of them trotted back to Bovey Tracey into a westerly breeze that slowly strengthened as they rode on. Not only stronger but getting colder. Kent would not have the easiest ride that afternoon, albeit with that wind at his back.

* * *

"Hoops!" Abel Smith announced.

His son Simon, hammering a piece of iron into shape on the anvil, looked at his father who was poking another piece of iron into the middle of the forge.

"Hoops?" he enquired, wondering whether his immense father was suffering from a bout of hiccups.

"Hoops!" Abel repeated. "You know what hoops are – bloody round things."

"Aye, father – I know well what a hoop is. What about them?"

"Remember young Matt Crowley? Well, he's back now as you know and he's wanting to start up coopering with his new mate. That means wooden staves and ends, and metal hoops. We make the hoops and charge for each piece made, plus take a share in the profit on the sale of each barrel."

"What's to go in the barrels? Makes a difference surely! If ale or cider, hoops should be of copper or brass."

"Aye, son – I know that full well. Brass is far too costly, so must be cut out and bent in copper. Even that's a fair price – and the damned stuff stretches – so has to be fairly thick."

"Has Matt even given thought to the expense? Seems to me to be little more than a pipe dream. Coopers make them by the hundreds to make sufficient profit!"

"Aye," Abel stretched up to his full height to ease the cricks from his spine. "Job for you, son – make an estimate of costs, five hoops per barrel, material and our time and labour. Start with the cost for one barrel and then see if we could do cheaper in quantity."

"Aye, father – I shall do that after supper. But I'm willing to wager that Matt's eyeballs will fall out of his head when he sees our cost."

"And I shall have to see where we might get thick copper sheet for cutting and shaping. I agree with you, my boy. This plan has all the marks of dismal failure!"

* * *

Matt Crowley and Herb Grindley arrived at Cullompton just as the sun was setting that evening. They had walked about half the distance to Taunton and were pleasantly tired and satisfied with progress – especially as they were both still dry.

Being very used to walking, as were most ordinary people, they reckoned on a maximum of between twenty-five and thirty miles in a day of nine hours. That gave them a good hour for a meal and another quarter of an hour for a rest in the afternoon.

Sitting in a wayside tavern supping cool ale and munching bread and cheese, Matt started planning ahead.

"We sleep here tonight – straw pallets will suffice – and then start after an early breakfast. Our first job when we arrive in Taunton will be to seek out the first cooper we can find. Taunton is quite a large town, so it will probably hold at least two coopers. And then we start to make enquiries."

"And that will have to be done slowly and with tact," Herb warned. "We must first of all say that we hope to start making our barrels many miles from them. Perhaps we could even stretch the truth and say we are from Bodmin or somewhere very far distant from them. Even Bovey might seem to them to be too close for comfort!"

"But Bodmin is just as large as Taunton, or so I believe," Matt objected. "By all means let us stretch the distance, but we should choose somewhere just as far but much smaller where there is little likelihood of there being a cooper."

"Then that also rules out Plymouth and Tavistock, possibly Barnstaple and Bude as well. I suggest Ilfracombe. It's a small town, probably a little smaller than Bovey – and it's quite remote!"

"Right – Ilfracombe it shall be."

* * *

The Bovey Tracey tavern was packed that evening. Word (inevitably) had got around about the capture of Thomas Axelby. That, and the rumours about the Dodds family, was more than enough to ensure a large gathering. Larkin, Dellow and Tamplin were the centre of attention, and they bought not one single mug of ale that night!

James Ramsey, the town's apothecary, put down his own half-emptied mug and summed up what had been gleaned. He, and his wife Avril, were always listened to as being recognised as 'clever' people.

"So, we have the two older Dodds, three Axelbys from Lustleigh, The Fredericks from further afield – and now people named Goodhew and Parsons – plus suspected involvement by

159

Sir Percival Wendover – and we have all heard of him. Does anyone here know of Goodhew or Parsons?"

"Goodhews live at farm just beyond Teigngrace," Simon Dingle the butcher spoke up. "Bought pigs from him some years back."

Larkin made a note of that and looked pointedly at Luke Barton and Peter Cove.

"No good looking at us," Barton grunted. "Our authority does not stretch that far!"

"Oh well, then I shall have to do that myself," Larkin stated. "My authority extends wherever I need it to. We three shall go and visit these Goodhews tomorrow. How about Parsons?"

That met with blank stares from at least sixty faces. Nobody had any knowledge of such a family. Talk then turned to the strange beliefs of the sect; the crowd split into groups, mainly around the tables at which they were sitting. However, one voice was heard above all others – that of Reverend James Forbes. He had been the priest at Bovey Tracey – and chaplain to Prince Charles – until parliament ordered his removal from office. That had never stopped him ministering to what he had always regarded as his flock.

"To take one's own life is, and always has been, considered the most terrible of sins. Now it would appear, we have people not only undertaking self-murder, but encouraging others to do the same. It is almost beyond belief. I care not who sits, or who does not sit, upon the throne. It is the most dreadful crime no matter who governs the land. It has to be eradicated!"

His words were greeted at first with a silent nodding of heads, then with a bout of verbal agreement. Mary, who had been listening attentively to all that had been said around her, suddenly raised a hand and looked at Matthew Kent.

"Correct me if I'm wrong," she said, "but you have so far discovered five groups of people who subscribe to this appalling nonsense. But – and I almost hesitate to mention the fact – only two members of one group have actually gone to the extreme of ending their own lives. Neither Lisa nor Thomas Axelby have; neither of the Fredericks have, although one did attempt it. As far as we know, the Wendovers, Goodhews and Parsons have not attempted it. So, why just the two deaths?"

"That is an extremely good point," Kent quietly nodded. "It is something that I had not considered before. Maybe, it is of no significance at all; on the other hand, maybe it is of great importance. Have you thought any further along those lines?"

"Yes, I have – and again, it may be of no significance as you say. We know that meetings were held at the Dodds' house. The two children have said so and have very sensibly distanced themselves from the taint. Were all the other named people present at those meetings and, if so, which of these others encouraged the Dodds to take that final step? Did anyone? Were the Dodds and Sir Walter the only ones to find the courage to attempt self-murder? I have thought about the state of mind that would allow such an action. I cannot conceive being able to do it - nor could I ever envisage encouraging anyone else to do it! Have the others faced that state of mind and turned away from it?"

"Your mind has been far busier than mine," Kent gave her a grin. "Perhaps I should recommend that you lead this investigation!"

"I would not know where to start," Mary acknowledged. "And not one of those people would deign to answer questions put to them by a young woman!"

"That is sadly true," Kent acknowledged. "But I would certainly appreciate your assistance. Perhaps you would be willing to attend preliminary meetings with them and then list the questions that should be put to them at subsequent meetings."

"But that would mean me travelling repeatedly to Exeter. I have a school to run and would not be able to spare so much time. My little ones must always come first."

"I have another suggestion, and I think that this one might be of benefit," Reverend Forbes offered. "If I attended these first meetings with the purpose of pouring scorn on their beliefs, that might well cause them to divulge more than they ever intended, to defend these absurd beliefs. That just might open the way for Mary to formulate the necessary questions that then could be put to them."

"A reversal of Devil's Advocate?" Kent laughed. "That, Reverend, could indeed be of great use. Perhaps, if Mary is able, we could all try this out with the Goodhew family – see if this adversarial approach yields a rich harvest."

Mary reluctantly agreed to attend this first encounter. She would simply sit silently in the background and make mental notes whilst Forbes tore into the suspects with the weight of the church behind him.

"Then, we are agreed that we shall attempt this tomorrow?" Larkin summarised. "I shall be there with my sergeant and trooper to represent the power of parliament. Matthew shall be there to represent the civil law. Reverend Forbes shall be there to goad them into indiscretions. Mary shall be there to worm into their twisted minds. An irresistible force!"

"Well, perhaps," Kent nodded.

CHAPTER XVII

The following morning, with a slight easterly breeze at his back, Kent set off for Westminster. The meeting the previous evening had arrived at one further conclusion – it was absolutely necessary that Kent sought and obtained the necessary warrant for when they bearded Wendover in his home. The Goodhews were going to be left to Larkin, his soldiers, Forbes and Mary. It was hoped that Larkin's commission would be sufficient to force compliance.

Matt and Herb also set out early on the final leg of their journey to Taunton. Luck immediately sprang into action as a light cart passed them as they trudged along the road north. The cart was empty and was being pulled by a rather large horse that seemed in a hurry to get home. Sitting on the small driving seat was a young man of impressive size. Just past the two travellers, he pulled up and glanced back.

"Are you wanting a lift?" he asked politely.

"If you be bound for Taunton, then we would be very grateful," Matt answered.

"Then hop aboard. Old Silvester here will hardly notice the added weight. Used to be my father's mount when he rode with the old king's army. He's as strong as an ox and as fast as a good rouncey!"

Perched inside the cart, Matt and Herb were full of praise for the speed the cart immediately attained.

"At this rate, we shall be in Taunton well before time for an early dinner," Herb grinned. "Have you come from far?"

"Nay – left Cullompton after my breakfast. Delivered a load of hurdles to a farm yesterday. I was hoping for a load to take back, but no luck. Have you business in Taunton?"

"Aye – we are seeking a cooper there. We plan to start our own business coopering and need to ensure we are not trespassing on another's bailiwick!"

"And where would you plan to start?" the young man asked.

"Oh, Ilfracombe," Herb answered quickly, just in case Matt put both feet in his mouth.

"And you have travelled all this way? Seems excessive!"

"Ah – but we have stopped on the way to enquire – Tavistock, Totnes, Newton Abbot, Cullompton. We need to make doubly sure. We do not wish to start a coopering war!"

"Then we are very well met!" the young man laughed. "My uncle – my mother's brother – is the cooper in Taunton and I can drop you right at his yard."

"Then today may well turn out to be our lucky day," Herb grinned.

* * *

Before starting work for the day, Abel Smith asked his son Simon whether he had been able to set costs for the making of barrel hoops. Simon grunted and pulled a piece of grubby paper from his pocket.

"Aye, father, that I have – and it makes sorrowful reading!"

"Sorrowful enough to make Matt and his friend abandon their plans?"

"That I cannot tell for I have no idea how much they intend to charge for a barrel once made. I know that it seems an awful lot to me!"

"Why do you not go and ask Sal up at the tavern how much it costs to buy a barrel?" Imelda asked, feeding the last of little Jack's porridge into his ever-open mouth.

"Because Sal and Dick do not buy barrels," Abel grinned. "They buy barrels filled with wines and have had their own barrels for ale for many a long year. I doubt they would even know how much they originally cost."

"But they cannot keep on for ever filling the same barrels!" Imelda persisted.

"Then why do you not take Jack for a walk across to the tavern and ask. Perhaps you are right, and they have bought barrels more recently. Now Simon – what are the costs you have worked out?"

"I have thought five hoops per barrel, seven pence for the copper and ten pence for our work. One shilling and five pennies per barrel. I have no notion what their costs would be – the oak, cutting, shaping and final fitting. But I would doubt that their costs would be less than twice ours. That would come to over four shillings for a barrel – and that ignores any profit they hope to make."

"Then they would have to charge well over five shillings for a completed barrel. That sounds a hell of a lot to me! But again, I have no idea what a barrel really costs to buy!" Abel grunted. "It is like I thought – it is not the start of a profitable business!"

* * *

Mary arrived at the school cottage early that morning. She needed to make sure everything was in order before setting out to play her part when the Goodhew family was questioned. Lady Violette had been only too willing to sit 'in loco parentis' for the rest of the day.

By eight o'clock, and the dark of a rainy night still not completely cleared, all of the children had arrived and had shed coats and cloaks ready for a morning of reading aloud. But Mary had a job to do first.

"Children, you all know Rosie Ramsey. It is her first day here amongst us and I would like you all to stand up and say a big welcome."

Most of the children did exactly as asked, but one small boy at the back of the room made a subtle alteration to his welcome. 'Welcome Rosie Turnip', he shouted. Tommy Lester, five-year-old son of a farmer from further down on the heath, sat down giggling to himself. Rosie turned towards him and gave him one of her menacing scowls. Anyone who had known Rosie since she had started to walk would have recognised that scowl. It boded ill for Master Tommy.

"That was not a nice thing to say, Tommy," Mary said as everyone sat down again. "Why on earth did you call her that?"

"Please, Miss Mary, everyone knows her mam and dada grow turnips – and her head is the same shape!"

"Tis not!" Rosie exploded.

Mary knew children very well and was certain that this nickname would persist for the rest of Rosie's school life. She

165

also knew Rosie well and was just as certain that some form of retribution would be meted out as soon as an opportunity presented itself. However, she had limited time and promised herself that she would deal with the matter the very next day.

"Lady Violette has very kindly offered to run the school today as I have a mission to accomplish. I do not need to remind you that Lady Violette does not tolerate bad behaviour! This morning, you will be taking it in turns to read aloud. Then, after dinner, she has brought paper and inks so that you can do some drawing. I expect to see some very good pictures!"

So saying, she gave a little bow to the formidable old lady who was seated behind the desk, ready with the nominal roll to call on the first reader. She picked up her small valise within which were paper, pens and ink, put on her thick riding cloak and walked up to the tavern where she was to meet the soldiers and the reverend. Her own horse, saddled, was waiting patiently for her.

"I expect this ride will take us no more than one hour," Larkin announced, heading down to the crossroads. He, like his sergeant and trooper, was dressed in full uniform, with pistols and broadsword. Reverend Forbes rode behind them at Mary's side.

"I sincerely hope that these Goodhews are home – and that they do not cause us any trouble," he muttered.

"I'm sure that our soldiers can handle any trouble," Mary said confidently. "They seem very competent and professional. In any case, my job is simply to write a concise account and to make notes that may be useful for any further questioning. I still find it difficult to believe that any sane person could subscribe to this nonsense. Not only is it heretical, it simply makes no sense at all. If one has a burning desire to do something, then the only way to achieve it is to remain alive!"

"You, my dear, are speaking as a reasonable and thinking individual. I'm not so sure that these people *are* sane and thinking! I have lived a long life so far and have seen all manners of beliefs and customs. There are people far off to the east that believe that, when an important man dies and is ceremonially burned, his concubines must throw themselves upon the fire to be consumed as well. There are also people who *still* believe in the value of human sacrifice to whatever strange gods they revere. Nothing on this earth surprises me any longer. To my certain knowledge, there are people around the area we know as Outremer who offer sacrifices to their god – sheep or goats are the usual victims.”

“What utter nonsense!” Mary grunted. “We are taught that God made all things in heaven and on earth. Some animals kill other animals to sustain their own lives – and have always done so. We kill animals so that we may eat and sustain our own lives. But wantonly to offer to God what is God’s own property anyway, seems to me to be sheer stupidity!”

“But Mary, there you go again, attributing logic and right-thinking to all and sundry. Believe me my dear, you are in a small minority. I agree with every word you say, but many, many others would disagree most vehemently. However, let us see what utter tripe and nonsense these Goodhews spew forth.”

Larkin had done his homework and led them unerringly to a large house set before a small wood about a mile beyond the hamlet of Teigngrace. As the small cavalcade approached, they were able to see quite a bustle of activity going on. To one side of the house was a stable block where a couple of grooms were leading horses to where a farrier had set up his travelling workshop. One liveried servant was carrying buckets of water into the back of the house, whilst another was emptying pots onto a compost heap. This was obviously a busy and well run establishment.

As the five drew up, a couple of small lads rushed out from the stables to take the horses. A tall and very distinguished man in his later years appeared at the front door and performed a stately walk across to them.

“Reverend, Lieutenant, Mistress, what may we do for you?” he asked in deep and ponderous tones, making him the obvious steward of the household.

“We are come to seek audience with Master Goodhew,” Forbes replied. “Would he be available?”

“I am certain the master will be available, reverend. If you would be so good as to follow me.”

He led at a stately pace in through the wide front door, along a passage and into the main hall where a fire was blazing in a massive hearth. A man dressed in very good quality clothes that were muted as if the wearer wanted to be anonymous, turned and stared hard at the procession that faced him. He picked out Larkin immediately.

"Lieutenant, this seems to be a formal visit. Am I to assume you are here not for idle chatter but for serious talk?"

"Aye, sir. You may assume so," Larkin gave a slight and formal bow,. "I assume I am addressing Master Goodhew?"

"I am he," came the very formal and elegantly grammatical reply. "May I enquire as to the nature of your visit?"

"Certainly, sir. It concerns the matter of The Vale of Sorrow."

The man gave a sigh and shrugged his shoulders. "This day was bound to dawn," he said quietly. "Let me say immediately that I know more about that sect than I would care to admit to anyone other than one in authority. I, my wife and children were swept into that damnable sect some two years past. Having learned all that we could of them, we all of one accord left and have had nothing to do with them ever since. We came to abhor everything they stood for!"

"Then, what you have to tell us will be of immense help, sir. We found your name on a list at the home of Sir Walter Fredericks. He and his lady wife are at present in Exeter under arrest."

"Aye, our names would well be on such a list. That wretched man seemed to believe himself the amanuensis of the group. But I am being woefully inhospitable. Carruthers, wine, ale and cakes if you please. Reverend, Lieutenant and you Mistress – please make yourselves comfortable whilst I summon the rest of my family. Between the five of us, we should be able to furnish you with much valuable information."

Four others duly trooped into the large hall and were introduced. First came a very aristocratic lady, Ann Goodhew. Then their three children; Charles, a youth of fifteen or thereabouts; Grace, a girl of thirteen; Susan, a younger girl of about ten. All three children ranged themselves with their mother on a long settle.

"First, let me reiterate for the benefit of your family, sir," Larkin gave a short bow to the lady. "We are here because the name Goodhew appears on a list found at the home of Sir Walter

Fredericks. He and his wife are at present in Exeter being questioned concerning a sect called the Vale of Tears."

Ann looked across at her husband and shrugged.

"Then, at long last, the authorities have caught up with that evil lot. It is long past time that they were stopped!"

"That immediately poses a question, madam," Larkin interrupted. "If you were so concerned about them, why did you sit here in silence?"

"Oh, that is very easily explained," came the unladylike, snorted reply. "We were threatened with dire retribution when we announced we wanted nothing further to do with them. Should we approach anyone in authority, they would immediately know about it and this family would be executed. Hence our silence!"

Mary, sitting quietly at her small table and writing furiously, appended the word 'who?' in large letters at the mention of the immediate knowledge.

James Forbes, who had been listening intently, almost nodded in unison with Mary's appended word.

"Master Goodhew, Mistress Goodhew," he spoke for the first time. "You say that they claimed they would know immediately if you informed on them. That automatically suggests that someone, or indeed some people, in positions of authority would be privy to that information. Have you any idea who they may be?"

Father and mother exchanged glances, then shook their heads. However, Charles gave a defiant glare at his parents.

"I can name one person in authority who would know immediately," he almost shouted. "Sir Percival Wendover – he would know as he, certainly not damned Fredericks, was the leading light in the group. He attended every meeting and was about the most vehement in his lectures!"

Forbes and Larkin also exchanged a glance. "That name we also know. It was the last on the list as that list was in alphabetical surname order," Larkin acknowledged. "We are also fully aware of the position Sir Percival holds – as a close adviser to the Council of State. Therefore, I can fully appreciate your reluctance to name him. But a colleague of ours is at present on his way to Westminster. He already holds a signed warrant but is seeking a further warrant naming Wendover. He will approach John Bradshaw himself."

Goodhew gave a sigh and spread his hands out in an attitude of almost surrender.

"Then, if that be the case, we shall tell you all we know of this damnable sect. We had heard that a group met each week at the home of the Dodds. At first, it all sounded very innocuous – prayer meetings seeking forgiveness of sin and a betterment of life. We were not privy to the follow-up meetings for at least the first six months – presumably we were being observed and judged. And then, slowly over a period of months, the full implications were made clear to us. According to their doctrine, every man and woman on this earth is a hotbed of sin and corruption. The members recognised this in themselves and inflicted pain and suffering on themselves. Finally, we were informed, that when a member found that prayers were not enough, self-punishment was not enough, the member was encouraged to take his or her own life. It was at that point that we fully recognised the group for what it was – a dangerous and violently heretical sect. Instead of quietly sliding away, I was fool enough to express my disgust to them, plus our intention to sever all contact. It was at that point that the threat was made."

Mary motioned that she needed a little time to get all this down, so a period of quiet ensued. Eventually, she laid down her pen and massaged her right hand.

Forbes then took up the questioning. "At what point did they seek to justify this nonsense? Did they ever use scripture?"

"Oh, indeed they did," Ann declared with a derisive laugh. "Remember what scripture tells us, Wendover repeatedly shouted at everyone. If thy right eye offends thee, pluck it out and throw it from thee. He then went on to expand this to life itself!"

"What they never said was the corollary to that quotation," Goodhew growled. "Tis better to cast off one part than to suffer eternal damnation of the whole – or words to that effect."

Mary gave a silent chuckle as she wrote this down, remembering her own riposte some time before. Forbes simply nodded his agreement. Larkin was intent on more earthly matters.

"Having been so open and frank with us, the very least we can do in return is to make sure you are safeguarded until this whole group is under lock and key. I shall leave my soldiers with you until such time as you are no longer in any danger."

"Believe me, Lieutenant, we would be eternally grateful. Rest assured that they will be treated to the very best we can offer," Ann Goodhew was close to tears.

Tamplin and Dellow were very happy with the news – billeted with this family would be a real pleasure. They would guard them and train some of the servants to do the same.

Forbes, Larkin and Mary rode back together in almost complete silence. They now needed Kent back with the necessary authority.

* * *

Rosie arrived home later that afternoon with a large piece of paper, carefully rolled, in her hand. She waited until Gil and Ella came in from their work before very carefully unrolling the paper on the parlour table.

"Mama, papa – look what I drawed at school today," she said proudly. "Lady Violette said it was very good and that I must bring it home to show you."

Her young parents peered over Rosie's shoulder. "Ye gods and little fishes!" Gil breathed. "You drew this yourself from memory?"

"Yes, papa. Why? Is it not good?"

"Good? It's wonderful!" Gil exclaimed. Rosie had drawn in black ink a picture of May sitting on a bench with one of her chickens on her lap – something she often did. There was absolutely no mistaking that it was May, even down to the slightly crooked smile she made.

Ella picked up her little daughter and gave her a kiss and a hug. "You, my little rascal, have an exceptional talent. We shall show this to everyone. I'm sure you will be asked to make pictures of many of them. How did you ever learn to draw like this?"

"I dunno," Rosie shrugged. "I just can."

"One day, you will be a famous artist," Gil grabbed little Rosie and hoisted her aloft. "This is just marvellous, and we are very proud of you."

"But I only drawed May!" Rosie was somewhat at a loss to understand what all the fuss was about.

CHAPTER XVIII

Three days later, Matthew Kent arrived at the offices of the Council of State. He had spent the previous night in a good tavern, thinking through his approach on what he knew would be a very sensitive topic. He knew that he needed to have a very senior signature on any warrant he was able to acquire. He needed to proceed with care.

His first port of call was to the large administrative office. What he saw resembled an ant hill that had been suddenly disturbed. Men, mostly young and clothed in sombre black, were scurrying between desks. The young men carried armfuls of paper; the older men at the desks wielded pens. What was also evident was the air of frantic activity that was accomplished in almost funereal silence. There was an air of quiet but frenetic and organised professionalism. Kent stood and was resolutely ignored. People scurried past him both into and out of the huge office space.

He had been standing, dithering for about fifteen minutes when he received a tap on his shoulder. Turning, he recognised a thin and ascetic face.

"What brings you to this hive of activity?" the face split into a smile.

"Master Ireton?" Kent queried. "I am here from Devon where I have uncovered something that is of the utmost concern."

"What? You mean this coven of stupidity – the vale of something or other?"

Kent was staggered but knew almost at the same instance that the reach of Parliament extended much further than Devon.

"The Vale of Sorrow sect is known to you, sir?"

"Oh, yes indeed. We have heard about it, but the finer details remain a closed book to us. Come with me to a more convivial spot and you can tell me all about it – and, probably more important, what you need – as I'm sure that is why you are here!"

Henry Ireton was as close to the seat of power as it was possible to get – he was Cromwell's son in law, reputedly a firebrand but also someone who knew how to get things done.

Ireton led the way through a maze of corridors and ended up in a small room where it was possible for two men to sit in comfort and discuss matters in private.

Kent began his tale, all the way from the discovery of the two dead bodies in the field to the discovery of the list in the Fredericks' house.

"Wendover," Ireton mused quietly. "I can certainly see why you found it necessary to travel the distance to get some clarification and authority. The man advises on financial matters. From all I hear, his advice is normally sound enough. But you have confirmation that he is the leading light in Devon concerning this abominable sect?"

"Aye, sir. Confirmation from both the list, word of mouth, and the sworn testimony of others."

"Then, at the very least, he needs to be brought to question. Come with me and I shall endeavour to get you an audience with those who wield far more clout than do I."

By the time Kent was again in his comfortable room at the tavern – having taken supper in very exalted company – he felt that his head was swimming. He had presented all his evidence to no less a person than John Bradshaw. Along with two other members of the Council, Bradshaw was appalled at the tale. He was also extremely decisive. Kent had in his possession a warrant that named Wendover specifically, along with reference to anyone else associated with the man. Not only that, but he would travel back to Devon with a large contingent of parliamentary troops commanded by a Colonel Fisher.

Kent read the warrant for the fourth time. His power of arrest was almost frightening in its scope. Wendover, the Wendover family, retainers, associates, in fact, anyone and everyone who Kent believed may have even the merest connection with the sect. He had met Colonel Fisher and had been impressed by the air of quiet menace that was displayed on those craggy features. But he wondered at the inclusion of fifty soldiers – fifty? Enough to start a minor war!

* * *

Kent was not the only one to go to bed that night in a mood of quiet satisfaction. Back in Bovey Tracey, Matt and Herb also settled down in an upstairs room of the tavern with smiles of pleasure. Their tale of starting a cooperage in Ilfracombe had yielded the result they had wanted. It was seen as being no threat to the Taunton enterprise. They had also learned a lot about the business, watching the steaming process and the final construction. They had even learned much of the financial implications. They had pretended far more knowledge on that subject than they in fact possessed. They were more convinced than ever that they could make a fair living.

Matt knew that he would have to convince Abel Smith that the figures stood up to scrutiny. Without the input from the smith, the business would not get off the ground. Matt and Herb spent the evening going over their calculations until they were both word perfect. And then, hopefully having acquired Abel's blessing and cooperation, they would need to go and see the estate steward for available premises. Once again, this would need the presentation of their business plan. And again, this would have to stand up to further scrutiny.

* * *

Mary was yet another to go to bed in a state of enlightenment. She had responded to a call from Gil, her brother, and had in her turn marvelled at the drawing that Rosie had produced.

"That is something that none of us could have foreseen," she said, examining the drawing for the umpteenth time. "Where on earth did she acquire this remarkable talent. You and I do not have it; neither do either of our parents. How about your family, Ella?"

"My abilities end at drawing water from the well!" Ella grinned. "My father and Simon *do* make drawings when there is something complicated to make from iron – but absolutely nothing like this. Mother has never displayed any talent either. So, where Rosie got this from, only the Good Lord above knows."

"But she drew this in school – where May was not available for reference. Therefore, she had only her own memory to guide her. I can understand the chicken – after all, she sees them every day of her life, and they all look roughly the same. But May is here on the paper as large as life and unmistakable. This is indeed extremely rare – and something I have never come across. She must be encouraged to continue. You must be very proud of your little girl!"

"Aye, we are," Gil nodded.

Hidden at the top of the stairs, Rosie could hardly stop herself from screaming her delight. She was special and her mama and papa were proud of her. One other small person went to sleep that night in a state of happiness.

* * *

At their first stop on the way back to Devon, the garrison in Reading proved to be a very useful resting place. The soldiers – five sergeants and forty-five troopers – were happy to bed down for the night in the company of fellow soldiers. Not only were the horses properly stabled, groomed and fed, but they themselves slept on palliasses rather than on straw or simply under the stars.

Colonel Fisher had with him a young officer, a Lieutenant Carstairs. The two of them plus Matthew Kent repaired to a small dining room where they partook of a hearty supper. Young Carstairs looked as if this was his very first foray as a very junior officer. He was obviously in awe of his colonel. Kent was sure he would be equally in awe of Larkin when they eventually arrived in Bovey Tracey.

"Colonel, excuse my ignorance, but why as many as fifty soldiers?" Kent asked, sipping at a glass of medium quality wine.

"Force majeure, my dear chap, force majeure!" came the reply. "The first law of warfare - intimidate the buggers. It's something we all never grow out of. Remember your days as a scruffy young boy? Being set upon by the local bully, probably no more than a year older than your five years? Well, this is no different! Turn up with more soldiers, more weapons, much better training and discipline – and that's stage one of your victory. Works every time!"

"It certainly did at the battles with the old king," Kent nodded.

"And why, you ask? Let me tell you why. The idiot trusted family and effete fools and thought that a ceremony where he was anointed with oils would be more than enough to see him through. Wasn't, was it! He lost because he was a fool, listening to no one other than the supposed voice of God. No training, no leadership, simply a twisted faith in himself and his own righteousness."

"You will pardon me for saying this, colonel – but you do not sound and act as I would have expected a senior commander in the New Model Army."

"What? You think that my shouting and bluster makes me less of a committed puritan? Suppose it does, really!" he gave a loud guffaw. "However, I am a soldier through and through. I despised that wretched Charles, hiding behind his wife's Romanism most of the time; refusing to hear any opinion but his own; refusing to call a parliament in case he heard opinions that opposed his own. No – this country of ours needed strong leadership – where opinions were voiced aloud, and a sense or order and discipline imposed upon it."

Kent could only nod his agreement. He would not have voiced his thought in so forthright a manner, but he agreed with every word.

"And how do you see the future, colonel? Will there be any part in it for the younger Charles?"

"What? That philandering oaf? Heaven help this country if ever he comes into a position of power and influence. The man is an effete scoundrel. He is reputed already to have sired numerous bastards dotted about Europe. One in particular – born of a Lucy Walter and named James – presumably after his grandfather or after Charles' brother. That little boy is now two years old and residing in The Netherlands. Wonder what he will make of all this when he grows up. For some reason, he is called James Crofts or James Fitzroy – bastardized form of the Norman-French 'son of the king'. Bloody insolence!"

"Is there any truth in the rumour that Charles, after Worcester, climbed into a tree and was smuggled out of England dressed as a washerwoman?"

"Not sure. Wouldn't surprise me if it were all true. Fits the oaf's personality. Lose and run away. Let us hope that it is the last England ever sees of him!"

"But he has already been declared king of Scotland. In fact, the Scots did that immediately his father was executed two years past!"

"And that wild country is welcome to him. And how will he be able to stick to his vow to uphold their damned Covenant? That will soon come to bite him in the arse – that and the fact that he's hundreds of miles away!"

"I wonder if England will ever see again a Stuart on their throne?" Kent mused, turning to young Carstairs, trying to bring him into the conversation.

"Young, newly appointed officers are not allowed opinions!" the colonel grinned at the young chap. "But do not make the mistake of confusing him with the officers Charles Stuart relied upon. Gone are the days when you father, being the Earl of Snuffleborough, was enough to guarantee you a commission. This young chap, like all his contemporaries, has been selected for his ability to think, to understand strategy, and to construct the necessary tactics. He is part of a truly professional army."

Carstairs had the good grace to blush at this fulsome appraisal of his worth.

Kent slept well on a feather mattress and awoke refreshed and ready for the next leg of the journey back to Devon, a place that he was starting to like more and more. He especially liked the company of the steward, Luke Barton, and the bailiff, Peter Cove. He also had a very great respect for Lady Violette, who he saw as embodying the very best qualities of a Lady of the Manor – caring deeply for the countryside, kind and courteous to her staff and, most of all, doing whatever she could to safeguard the community in which she lived. At the same time, standing absolutely no nonsense from anyone.

* * *

It was with some trepidation that Matt and Herb approached the smithy the next morning. Abel, stripped to the waist, was hammering at a piece of iron rod that he held on the anvil. Simon, similarly stripped, was working the bellows at the forge and easing out another length of iron, this one glowing a fiery yellow.

"Aha!" roared Abel, seeing the two approaching. "Come to tell us that you cannot start a business that is going to lead you into deep debt?"

"On the contrary, Master Smith! We come to inform you of our success in Taunton, of our plan for the future of our business, and to convince you that you should join us in the enterprise."

"Oh, do you, now? And what magnificently positioned argument are you going to use to persuade me?"

"Just the one, Master Smith," Herb answered. "Profit!"

"That is a magical word, young man. What profit? How engendered? What magnitude of profit?"

"We are envisaging a minimum of seventy percent!"

"Envisaging, are you? And seen through the eyes of reason – or through a crystal ball?"

"Reason and good arithmetic!"

Abel looked at his massive son and gave a broad grin. "Then we must certainly give it our deepest consideration, must we not?"

"Aye, father – as deep as the ocean."

"Come back after dinner when we shall have finished this latest commission. And be prepared to be questioned very closely. A warning – if either Simon or I believe for the merest second that you are trying to pull a trick – or to mislead us in any way – I shall personally hold you across this anvil whilst Simon hammers your manhood to pulp with the largest of our hammers."

Matt Crowley and Herbert Grindley shared a look of apprehension. They were in no doubt that they would be severely mistreated if they were to try anything underhand. That would not entail the hammering of their most private parts, but it would be painful in the extreme.

"Master Smith – how long have I known you and your strength. Do you believe for one minute that either of us would dare incur your wrath?" Matt asked quietly.

"No, I suppose not," Abel granted with a nod. "However, we shall be ruthless in our examination!"

"Then we are content to present you with our plan."

* * *

Rosie was very happy to forego her own dinner. Mary had provided her with bread and cheese and had asked her to stay whilst the other children went to their homes for their midday meal.

"If I were to ask you who you would like to draw next, who would it be?" Mary asked the little girl who sat at the desk with paper, pen and ink.

Rosie screwed up her face and gave it serious thought. "Reverend Forbes," she said after some minutes.

"Why the reverend?"

"Oh, he has an old face with many lines – and I can see him in my head. Also, he has no moustache or beard – and that shows his whole face."

"Would you do a drawing for me whilst you eat your meal?"

"Yes, Miss Mary. I love drawing."

About thirty minutes later, Rosie put down her pen and took a mighty bite of fresh bread. "Finished, Miss Mary," she announced.

Mary had not interrupted or looked over a shoulder. She had sat patiently at some distance. She looked at the drawing and was hardly able to contain her amazement. There on the paper was the head and shoulders of Reverend James Forbes, surrounded by the lychgate that led to the church.

"That is indeed an excellent likeness, Rosie. I shall take you to see the Reverend after school so that he may see for himself that we have an artist of rare talent."

Rosie again glowed with pride. She also knew enough at her young age not to show undue pride in her achievement. That would be classed as 'showing off' – and that was not acceptable. However, she knew that she had a talent that none of her classmates possessed – not even those many years her senior. She galloped down the street and burst into the parlour.

179

"Done another drawing," she announced. "Miss Mary is going to take me to Reverend Forbes to show him – and she thinks I am very clever!"

"And so you are," Gil said, grabbing her and hoisting his daughter aloft. "But do not start getting a swelled head or you will make all the other children cross and dislike you."

"No, papa. I promise I shall not tell them I am better than they are!"

"At drawing, you most certainly are," Ella replied. "But at writing, reading and sums, you are probably a lot worse. Remember that everyone is good at something."

"Aye, mama. I shall not boast!"

Gil and Ella exchanged a glance. They wondered if that pledge would be maintained.

* * *

Abel and Simon had listened carefully when Herb outlined the entire plan. Faith, who kept all the accounts for the smithy and was considered to be highly competent with the financial affairs of a business, also sat in and said not one word until Herb laid down his small pointer and sat back. Then, she started the questioning.

"To even start this business, you will need many things in place. First is a workshop. Then you will need tools and the means to steam the staves to shape. Then comes the business of transporting your finished barrels to wherever your customer needs them. Finally, you will need the means to support yourselves until at least your first customer pays you. How do you intend to meet these needs?"

"We have already approached the estate steward about a workshop. He assured us that he would make one available when we are ready to start," Matt took it upon himself to supply answers – in case his audience believed this was going to be all Herb's idea. "I already have access to all the tools I shall need as my mother kept back all those that belonged to me when I left. I have devised a steaming cupboard that will be easily constructed. As for transporting the barrels, we will buy a large cart and a dray horse. Believe me, Mistress Smith, we have the necessary funds to cater for all of this, plus sufficient to tide us over until the money starts to come in.”

Faith had not finished. “You will also need stock of oak and the means to pay for the hoops that Abel and Simon will provide. We cannot allow any credit to a starting business. We will require coin upon delivery of the hoops.”

“Believe me when I say that we really *do* have the means to satisfy all of those needs.”

Faith gave a shrug and turned to her husband, who in turn, received a signal from his son.

“Then consider us your partners in this venture – as long as we can agree a fair percentage of the profits.”

“We have worked out that the hoops represent fifteen percent of the value of a finished barrel. Would you be content with that figure?”

“Hoping for twenty!” Abel gave a huge grin and a bellow of laughter. “But fifteen is reasonable. Let us shake hands on it and agree that, should anything go amiss, I shall rip the heads off your shoulders!”

“I have grown quite attached to my head being in its proper place – so, believe me when I say that we shall never do anything to arouse your ire!”

Imelda appeared with little Jack in her arms.

“When you rowdy lot have quite finished, I shall endeavour to get this mite settled for the night. Anyone would think that there were a hundred people in this room, the amount of noise!”

“See what I have to put up with?” Abel gave another massive laugh. “One woman governing the purse and another regulating the noise level!”

“Yours is indeed a life of suffering, Master Smith,” Matt observed.

“Begone, before I remember that I’m supposed to be a lady!” Faith scowled - but ended with a grin of her own.

CHAPTER XIX

The arrival of a troop of soldiers did nothing for the peace and tranquillity of the town of Bovey Tracey. The last time that had happened on any scale was nearly six years before. Then, a large part of the king's army under Baron Wentworth had been billeted in the town and on the heath. That had ended in a complete rout of Wentworth's force by Cromwell himself. The town immediately went into panic mode at the sight of a mere fifty soldiers along with their sumpter horses bearing tents and equipment.

The last day of September had dawned fine, cold and with a light wind. Fifty mounted soldiers plus a colonel, a young subaltern and Matthew Kent, raised speculation immediately they turned up into the town from the crossroads. The first to raise the alarm was Kat Gates, the daughter of Adam and Olivia Gates who ran the mill over the bridge.

"Mama, papa!" she shrieked, rushing back into the mill where the machinery was for once standing silent. "Soldiers are coming!"

Adam, patting his apron amid a cloud of flour, ran outside immediately and failed to notice the one face he would have recognised immediately – Matthew Kent. All he saw was an invading force, armed to the teeth. He shot back, shut and barricaded the door and put his finger to his lips demanding silence.

The immediate destination for the troop was the tavern, at the top of the village where Lieutenant Larkin, Sergeant Tamplin and Trooper Dellow were residing. Kent wanted to know what had been taking place in his absence. To reach the tavern, they had to pass numerous shops and cottages, all containing citizens who gaped in horror at the seeming invasion. Doors were shut and locked tight.

Colonel Fisher had a quiet chuckle as door after door was slammed shut. He turned to Lieutenant Carstairs. "See what effect we have on the good people?" he guffawed. "They seriously believe we are here to harm them. It will come as a huge relief when we inform them our real purpose!"

Arrived at the tavern, a very apprehensive Sal Allen came out to greet them, then heaved a huge sigh of relief when she recognised Kent amongst the first two ranks.

"Mistress – can you manage a hearty meal for all these behind me?" Fisher enquired, dismounting and giving a courteous salute.

"I am sure that, given an hour, we can manage that, sir," Sal replied as Larkin, Tamplin and Dellow appeared behind her. The two had left the Goodhew house having made sure the servants were competent in the defence of the family.

Dick Allen, also hovering in the background, gave Kent as cheery wave of welcome. Kent realised that he needed to stop the spread of alarm and despondency. "Master Allen – would you be so good as to spread the word that we are here *solely* for the purpose of furthering enquiries into the evil sect that is already known about?"

"Indeed, Master Kent – I can do better than that. Hob is here and there is nobody better than he to spread word. Hob!" he yelled.

An hour later, the whole town knew it had nothing to fear, but wondered at the size of the force necessary to further the investigation. By late afternoon, the colonel, Carstairs, Larkin, Kent, Bailiff Cove and Steward Barton were all sat down together in the back room. The soldiers under the sergeants had repaired to the bottom of the Heath where tents were being erected, horses fed and watered, and a cooking fire for the evening meal had been prepared.

Gil, Ella, May, Rosie and Jamie looked over the back fence of the chicken run and watched the activity on the Heath. Gil took Ella's hand in his. "Remember when we last saw such activity?" he asked quietly.

"Aye – that I do. Tis when you asked for my hand in marriage," Ella replied.

"And have you regrets that you said yes?"

"Only when you come into my kitchen with filthy boots!" she replied with a smile.

Back in the tavern's back room, Peter Cove was addressing the matter that had occurred to nearly everyone in the town.

"Colonel – we are all wondering at the size of the force you have brought. Are so many really necessary?"

"Probably not," Fisher admitted. "But this is not just an investigation we are carrying out – it is a show of the measure of importance that is attached to the matter of this bloody sect!"

"That is heartening to hear," Barton nodded. "We all are aware that it is probably only a very small group, but it has to be quashed with whatever degree of force is necessary. Any assistance that is within our power will be given. Of that I can assure you."

"On the morrow, we intend to ride to the home of this chap Wendover. It seems likely that he is the leader of this group. I intend to haul him out of his lair by the scruff of his neck, round up everyone in his household, and watch as Master Kent here exercises his warrant. Any question not answered will incur my displeasure!"

"Then I can supply you with precise directions to his house, Colonel," Cove offered. "It is no part of my bailiwick, but I certainly know where it is, and how to get there."

"Then your guidance will be most welcome. We will leave precisely at eight of the clock."

As Cove and Barton made their way in the gathering gloom of evening back to Parke, Barton was curious.

"Peter – I have obviously heard of this Wendover chap but have no idea where he lives. How do you know this?"

Cove grinned quietly to himself. "Who lives in my house that has knowledge of every living soul for twenty miles around?" he asked aloud.

"Oh – Hob! Yes, of course! That lad seems to be settling down into a more peaceable young man. But he would certainly be the one to know."

"You may thank young May Fletcher for his maturity. He is pursuing his suit with eagerness and very good manners. However, Wendover lives to the north of here in a large house to the east of Tottiford. Apparently, Hob used to take coneys from there some years back."

"I wonder what the wretched man will make of the sudden arrival of that Colonel and his soldiers?"

"Put the fear of Lucifer up him – or so I hope!"

* * *

Luke Barton met Matt and Herb at the church the next morning. The two young men were a mite puzzled why they were asked to meet the steward there, but sat on a low wall waiting, basking in the early morning sun. October had arrived with a smiling face.

Barton rode up and, not bothering to dismount, beckoned the two to follow him across the road and through a gate into the field. There, a few paces to the left, was the remains of an old barn. The steward dismounted and waved his arms expansively at the ruin. Matt and Herb exchanged very glum faces.

"Surely, Master Steward, you do not expect us to start a business in that wreck?" Matt was very put out.

"Of course I do not," Luke Barton gave them a wide grin. "Hear what I have to say first. This old place has been in semi-ruins for some years now. If you remember, it was where that idiot of a nightsoil man was shot, having attempted to assassinate a couple of soldiers. After that, young Gil Ramsey made free with some of the timbers for his cottage. Now, if you two are prepared to repair it, you are welcome to it rent-free for a whole year. A year's rent would be considerably more than you would have to spend on it."

Matt, casting his carpenter's eye over the place, gave a nod of agreement. "Indeed, it would be cheaper for us to make it good. After all, we need only sound walls, a sound roof, and a couple of workhorse benches. I have enough tools already to do all that *and* to make the steaming chest."

"And we could put a couple of straw pallets down to sleep here until we have made enough money to find a cottage of our own," Herb was in a much happier frame of mind. "Master Steward, we accept – and gladly!"

"Then consider it your workshop. I shall go back now to draw up the agreement – and to let it be known that you are legal tenants."

185

After Barton had left, Matt and Herb sat on a pile of old, dusty straw and surveyed their premises.

"Are you certain sure we have enough funds to do all this, buy the cart and horse, buy materials, pay the Smith, *and* support ourselves for some months?" Matt was again getting edgy.

"As long as we deny ourselves any luxuries, yes, we can. And you have my solemn promise on that," Herb replied.

"And by luxuries, you mean what precisely?" Matt probed further.

"We eat simply and drink water with our meals, only going for ale once every day."

"Then it is fortunate indeed that we have John and Evelyn Ramsey to buy our bread; Gil and Ella for our vegetables and eggs. Cheese we can get from the dairy down on the Heath. If that is what it takes, then we should manage nicely. But my first job will be to erect walls and a roof *before* I make two beds for the straw pallets!"

"Then, let us repair just this once for a mug of ale to celebrate!"

* * *

In the church dedicated to Saints Peter, Paul, and Thomas, the Reverend James Forbes surveyed the porch and the main south door. Where, he wondered, could he best put the picture that an excited little Rosie had presented. With a rather proud Ella and Gil, she had handed it to the Reverend and said that 'she hoped he liked it'.

At first, Forbes had found it hard to believe that a child so very young could have produced the likeness. However, he had consulted Mary, who had confirmed that Rosie had indeed produced it – and it could also be verified by consulting Lady Violette.

"She is indeed blessed by God with a very rare talent," Forbes muttered, and not for the first time. He had been further astounded to learn that Rosie had produced it entirely from her memory. How was that even possible, he wondered? It was as if Rosie had a detailed, mental image that she was able to transfer via her hand and a pen onto a piece of paper. Almost miraculous!

Very carefully, he pinned the picture onto a piece of board, then attached the board to the inside of the right-hand door of the south entrance. It would be seen by everyone as they left the church – as only the left-hand door was ever opened to allow entrance and egress. He anticipated a storm of questions from very inquisitive parishioners.

The first of these was already approaching the door. Alice Grubb, wife of Josiah Grubb, the town's shoemaker, had finished her stint at cleaning the church and arranging flowers.

"That be a remarkable likeness, Reverend," she said, stopping to admire the picture. Who did you have to produce it, I wonder?"

"Would you believe it was produced by young Rosie Ramsey?" Forbes answered, expecting the look of utter disbelief.

"What? That wee mite? Never. You be making a joke with me, Reverend!"

"Believe me, Alice, I had just as much difficulty when I first saw it. But it is vouched for by Gil and Ella – plus Mary Ramsey and Lady Violette. They have all witnessed the wee girl making pictures like it!"

"Some would say that be the work of witchcraft!" old Alice grunted. "Tis not natural at all!"

"Then I must order you never to speak such words in public," Forbes wagged an admonitory finger at Alice. "There is no such thing as witchcraft. What we see here is the work of a gifted child – a gift from Almighty God – and something to be marvelled, never condemned."

"Still, tis not natural!" Mistress Grubb insisted.

"There, I have to agree with you. It is a gift bestowed on a very few, and not in the normal order of things. But look around you at the carvings on the beams. Can you or I make something as wonderful? I suspect we would both make a horrible mess if we attempted it. But someone did – and his hand was guided by the same sort of gift that Rosie has been granted. Rather than saying it is not natural, we should say that it is very, very unusual – but a blessed gift nevertheless."

"Aye, I suppose it be that. Well, bugger me. Who ever would have thought it?"

Forbes managed to conceal a broad grin at the profanity.

* * *

Hob had been invited to supper. Invited to attend the supper in May's home. Hob was nervous, and that was totally unlike the normal attitude of this gregarious young man. Hob had been for many years seen as the town's own practical joker, always ready for a laugh and a merry jape. Now, having reached almost to his sixteenth birthday, he had become quiet, thoughtful, and quite serious. And that, he knew full well, was all because of May.

May loved her work with the Ramseys, being a sort of surrogate aunt to Rosie and little Jamie, working with the hens and the eggs. She was honest enough to recognise that she could not have worked for a more kindly pair than Gil and Ella Ramsey. She was also honest enough to know that she was not a raving beauty. Her sister Maud was going to blossom into a real beauty. But she also knew that she was attractive enough to have snared the ever popular Hob. Therefore, May was content with life.

Will and Patience Fletcher were very naturally concerned for the future of their elder daughter. That she had been pursued by no less a rascal than Hob gave rise to some uneasiness. Hence the invitation to supper. Will had spoken briefly to Hob before and had been assured that the young man's intentions were honourable. He had also noted the almost one hundred and eighty degree turn in Hob's behaviour. Now, he actually *walked* everywhere, walked with purpose and treated all and sundry with a respectful greeting or a nod. He grinned to himself, remembering only too well how he had been obliged to act responsibly to win the hand of Patience, a move he had never regretted.

There came a polite knock at the cottage door. May almost ran to answer it – and that told her parents all they needed to know. May was just as serious as Hob was!

They were treated to an unusual sight – Hob was dressed as a young gentleman, hair neatly combed and plastered to his head, face shining with recent washing, clothes brushed, and shoes shined. He was greeted warmly – and that immediately put him more at ease than he had been walking sedately to the cottage.

May would celebrate her fifteenth birthday in the coming January, an age when girls were considered mature enough to marry, or at the very least, become betrothed. Hob, one year older almost to the day, sat down next to May and endeavoured to make the most of the supper of mutton stew and ale. His nerves returned at the thought of what he intended to do and say when the supper was over. Talk over the supper table had been almost exclusively about the latest arrivals – soldiers commanded by no less than a colonel. But at last, the moment he had been both dreading and relishing; talk faded, and he gave a polite cough.

"Master Fletcher, Mistress Fletcher," he stopped again to clear his throat. "It will not be long before both May and I become of age. I seek your permission and your blessing to ask May to become my betrothed on that day." He paused and gazed hopefully at May's parents.

"And what has May to say about all this?" Will looked at his daughter.

"I would be thrilled and honoured to accept and become betrothed to Hob," May answered in a clear voice. Her hand sought Hob's under the table.

Patience and Will exchanged a glance. They had almost been expecting this.

"Before we grant either permission or blessing, we want to know how you would support our daughter when you end the betrothal with marriage," Will put on his stern, parental face.

"As you know, Master Fletcher," Hob began a well-rehearsed speech. "I have since being a small boy been employed by Master Bailiff as his runner and messenger. For a year past, I have been entrusted with other tasks for the estate – supervising moves, inspecting premises, writing reports. I am assured that this is to continue – indeed, to expand into other and more important duties. I receive a living wage and have been also assured that, when the time comes, I shall be given a small cottage in the grounds of Parke. My prospects are therefore assured – and it is my firm intention to progress further with diligence. I will be in a good position to support May and to keep faith with her."

"That was some speech," Patience gave him a broad smile. "Be honest, Hob – how many times have you rehearsed it?"

Hob almost reverted to type by grinning, then managed to stop himself. "Oh, many times indeed. But I mean every word of it, no matter how well rehearsed it may have sounded."

"The fact that you have carefully thought it through, means that you take the matter seriously – as you should. Therefore, you have our permission and also our blessing," Will reached across to shake Hob's hand.

Hob sat back and let his breath go in one long exhalation. It had all come as a huge relief. May squeezed his hand and gave him a kiss on his cheek. Maud, who had been listening avidly to the conversation then added her own comment.

"That means that I shall have a brother-in-law. I have no idea how that makes me feel! I suppose I should be happy, but it means that I shall lose my sister."

"Do not be a silly goose," May gave her sister a poke in the ribs. "I shall be here until we marry, and then not half a mile distant. You will never lose your sister – no more shall I when you marry!"

Hob was so elated that he forgot to knock at the Cove's parlour door when he returned. "They have agreed and granted their blessing!" he blurted out with a massive grin.

"Then you are indeed a lucky young man. May is a lovely girl," Laura Cove said in reply as Hob dashed out again to go up to bed. Laura looked at her husband and gave him a smile, echoing the remark said earlier that day by Alice Grubb.

"Well – who ever would have thought it!"

* * *

Earlier that day, a cavalcade arrived at a very large house near Tottiford.

From the colonel down to the lowliest soldier, the house impressed in size, neatness and the abundance of servants seen scurrying about on various missions. One other thing definitely impressed itself on the visiting parliamentarians – the absence of noise. Everyone seemed to be dashing about in complete silence.

As the large troop came to a stop at the large, double front door, it opened on silent, well-oiled hinges. An ancient servant in the dress of a house steward stood at the top of the steps and raised one enquiring eyebrow.

"Colonel Fisher and Master Kent to see Sir Percival," Fisher barked, making to dismount.

"You may spare yourself the trouble of leaving your horse. Sir Percival is not to be disturbed," came the reply from the steward who stood immoveable with arms folded.

"Then go and tell Sir Percival to move his bloody arse down here this instant. We come with a warrant from Parliament – signed and sealed by Master Bradshaw himself."

That shook the old retainer. "Master Bradshaw?" he faltered.

"Indeed!" boomed Fisher, dismounting and signalling his soldiers to do the same. "So, two jobs for you. Go and rouse bloody Wendover and tell him we will await him in his hall. Second job – rouse stable hands to attend to these mounts. Move!"

Kent dismounted, marvelling at the sudden turn of speed the old chap managed as he sped back inside to relay the message. Fisher merely grunted, signalled Kent and five of his soldiers to follow, mounted the steps and marched along a corridor to the main hall on the left. He stood in front of a blazing fire in an enormous grate.

"The moment he appears, seize him and prevent him from doing anything at all," he ordered quietly. "If what we hear about this lot is true, he will attempt to end his miserable life. That I shall not allow. He will answer questions and do absolutely nothing else!"

Two soldiers nearest the large door immediately took station to right and left and waited. So did everyone else – they waited – and waited.

"Bastard probably ending his life as we wait," Fisher growled. "All five of you, scour this house and find the sod! Master Kent, with me!"

Just as they were about to leave the hall, there came a commotion from the passageway. Lieutenant Carstairs and one of the sergeants had hold of a tall, aristocratic man who was dressed in one long black garment. Carstairs and his sergeant had tight hold of the man. Behind them were another two soldiers holding tight to a woman as tall as the first, also dressed in the one long black garment.

"After you had entered the house, sir," Carstairs explained with a rather self-satisfied grin, "I thought it prudent to take the rest around the whole building, leaving five at the rear door. Then, as we arrived at the side door, these two were just emerging in one hell of a hurry. Thought we should bring them to you. All entrances and exits are now covered."

"You, young man, will do very nicely," Fisher gave the young man a beaming smile. "Right – I suppose these two are the Wendovers?"

"No idea, sir. They have not uttered a word yet."

"Oh, believe me, they soon will. Now, in view of their disgusting predilection to self-harm, bind their wrists behind their backs, then sit them down well apart. Sergeant, you stay behind the man's chair and you, soldier, behind the woman's. Any slightest move from either and just grab them around the throat. According to their disgusting beliefs, they are obliged to end their own lives – and this is something they really look forward to. So, we shall not allow it! The hardest thing for them to bear is their inability to die. Therefore, we shall withhold that from them!"

Fisher stood at the top of the long table, watching as Wendover was sat in a chair to his left, his wife in a chair to his left. The two soldiers stood behind the chairs, ready to grab if necessary.

"I shall leave you to supervise the outside of the building. No one is to leave!"

Carstairs gave a smart salute and left. Fisher turned to a very interested Kent.

"Master Kent – you hold the warrant, so I shall leave the questioning to you."

Kent sat down at the head of the table whilst the Colonel stood back to observe proceedings. Kent first drew out the warrant and placed it flat on the table between the husband and wife.

"Before either of you starts bleating about how high and mighty you are, cast your eyes on the signatures above the seals. They really *are* high and mighty. The Colonel and I have been given the task of apprehending you and any others we have reason to believe are a part of this abhorrent sect that calls itself The Vale Of Sorrow. So, before we begin, let me first tell you of the progress we have made so far. The two older Dodds are, as you know, dead by their own hands. Their children, now both living in Exeter, distanced themselves from something they saw as disgusting. They have been very helpful since then. In Lustleigh, we found the Axelby family. The father is now in custody, as is the daughter. The son has very sensibly renounced all belief in the sect and is again being very helpful. Sir Walter and Lady Penelope Fredericks are also in custody. The Goodhew family has also been apprehended. Your name is prominent among the papers we have uncovered. It has been suggested, very forcibly, that you, Sir Percival, are the leader of this group here in South Devon. So, bearing all this in mind, have you anything to say as a sort of opening statement?"

As Kent looked at the two in turn, he was unsurprised to be met with looks of defiance and absolute silence. Kent gave a shrug of utter indifference.

"It may then come as no surprise to you that your entire household will be arrested and taken in for very close questioning. So, to spare any you know to be innocent of membership of this vile sect, tell me who they are, and you will save them a deal of unpleasantness."

Again, those same looks of defiance and silence. Kent tried another tack.

"Arriving here, I saw two very young girls and a young lad working outside what I presume to be the kitchens. Are they to be taken as well? Because, if they are, it will take just moments to get them talking like chattering jays!"

Receiving no response, Kent turned to the Colonel and asked if one of the young girls could be brought in. Fisher bellowed a command that could probably have been heard in the furthest field. A few minutes later, a young maid was brought in by a young soldier.

"What is your name?" Kent asked in not too officious a tone.

"Tis Bess, Master," the poor young girl was trembling.

"Bess – what can you tell me about a group calling itself The Vale of Sorrow?"

Lady Wendover made the mistake of straightening her back preparatory to shouting an instruction. The soldier behind her immediately grabbed the woman and placed a meaty hand over her mouth.

"There – see – your mistress is not able to give you instruction," Kent looked at young Bess. "All you have to do is to tell me the absolute truth and you have nothing at all to fear!"

Young Bess, seeing her mistress thus rendered helpless, squared her small shoulders and started speaking, as if a tap had been suddenly turned on.

"T'were horrible, Master! Master and Mistress made us all go to the meetings and to fall on our knees to beg forgiveness – and I hadn't done nuffing wrong! Then we were told that, if we weren't sorry enough, we would have to kill ourselves. Well – that is a wicked sin! Why should I want to kill myself when I've only just really started living?"

"And how many others feel about it as you do, Bess?"

"Carrie and young Walt do! Walt were always scheming how we could all run away and find somewhere proper to live. Cook always said nothing, but we all knew she hated it. Two of the stable lads were planning on running away too! Is you sure, Master, that I won't get beat for speaking like this?"

"Bess, I give you my solemn promise that your troubles are over. Whether or not we can find you better places to live and serve, I do not yet know. But I shall certainly try!"

"Then I hopes Master and Mistress burns in Hell for their wickedness!"

"Oh, I'm sure that they will, Bess. But here's the thing – they both *want* to die in their great sorrow. But we are not going to let them! We are going to make sure they stay alive in misery for many a long year!"

"Well done, young Bess," Fisher added. "Now – go with the soldier who brought you in and help him find your friends, the stable lads and the cook. They and you will be kept separate and safe."

After Bess had disappeared, Kent sat back with a grunt. "Out of the mouths of babes," he said aloud. "Colonel, I feel that we need no more from anyone here. Please will you round up all but those kept safe, tie their hands safely and we shall take the lot to Exeter for proper imprisonment."

"You may not put us with the common herd!" Wendover at last found his voice.

"Oh, indeed, you will be kept separate," Kent grinned. "Separate in cells deep underground without any means to harm yourselves. When it is deemed the right time, you will be interrogated by those far senior to me. Until then, you will have all the time in the world to wallow in your sorrow!"

CHAPTER XX

Matt stood back and cast a critical eye over the barn. It had taken him, with Herb's help, just on a whole week to get it into a state where both work and habitation were feasible. It had quickly dawned on him that the barn needed be nowhere near as large for what they needed. He had used every inch of timber that he was able to salvage. The repaired roof had already proved itself weatherproof, the floor swept, and a large door hung. To cut down costs, Matt had even forgone glass in the window, using a fold-away shutter in its place. At the far end were two bed frames. Down one side was a large and a small sawhorse; down the other side was the steaming cabinet. In the centre was a paved area, levelled off for barrel construction. Matt's tools were hung on hooks. He was satisfied, as was Herb at the minimum expenditure.

Herb was almost jumping for joy. "That has cost us just a little less than two months of rent – so, we have another ten months rent free!"

"Not a bad start, then," Matt grinned, taking a bite out of a mutton pie he had just bought from the bakery. "John and Evelyn Ramsey certainly deserve their reputation as the best bakers between Exeter and Plymouth!"

"That is quite some family," Herb replied. "Their daughter Mary is the school teacher and their son owns his own smallholding. That wife of his is rather a peach!"

"Who? Ella? Yes, she is very lovely," Matt agreed, and gave his friend a mocking glance. "You do know who her father is, do you not?"

"No. Who?"

"Abel Smith – and Simon is her brother. So, unless you want to have a fork thrust through your foot by Gil, or a hammering from Abel and Simon, you had far better not try any moves in that direction! In any case, Ella has Rosie and Jamie – and is the most contented wife I have ever seen."

"Abel and Simon? Bloody hell! I will give the lovely Ella a very wide berth from now on."

"That would be for the best," Matt laughed. "Now – we need enough good oak to try to make our first barrel. No good buying horse and cart until we know we are going to need them. I shall cut, steam and shape the staves, then make the bottom and top ends. We can use rope to start with until we receive the hoops from Master Smith."

"And how will we know if it is successful?"

"By filling it with water to get the staves to swell. We keep topping up the water until none escapes. Then we shall know if it works."

"That will need many a trip to the river!"

"For a sensible fellow, you are sometimes as thick as pig dung! We roll the barrel to the river with a bucket to fill it with water!"

Herb looked suitably chastened. But then quickly cheered up again at the prospect of a (possibly) successful business. He set about his pie and poured two mugs of Sal Allen's excellent ale.

* * *

Avril was busy pounding mint leaves into a paste when the door to the apothecary's shop burst open to reveal a rather disturbed youngish man, his horse wandering up the street to find something to nibble.

"Luke – what brings you here like the fabled winged messenger?" Avril asked – Luke Farmer, steward to Lady Violette at Brimley was not noted for being in this agitated state.

"Pardon my haste, but Lady Violette is sick, and it is not like her to take to her bed for any reason!"

"No, it is certainly not," Avril agreed. "If there is an example of an indomitable lady, then she fits the bill nicely. What ails her – do you know?"

"My Meg is with her, sitting at her bedside. The good Lady is in some very obvious pain but does not moan or complain. Meg says that she is feverish and keeps feeding her sips of water."

Avril felt a shiver of apprehension. Not that too long in the past, the winter sweating fever had carried off far too many and had reduced her and Mary (who had been her helper at the time) almost to the point of despair. Somehow or other, the two of them had managed to bring far more to recovery than they had lost. She did not want a repeat performance!

"Tis far too early for the winter fever," she muttered almost to herself. "That almost always happens into the new year when things are at their bleakest."

"James," she called out to her husband who was in the small office, "I have to go to Brimley to attend Lady Violette. She is sick and feverish!"

"Far too early for that!" James called back, confirming what she had already thought. "Is Nell back yet?"

"Aye, I am here," came a younger voice from the back door. Nell had been delivering packages of medicinal herbs to some of the residents who were exhibiting signs of a minor flux of the bowels.

"I shall tend the shop," James came bustling in. "Why do you not take Nell with you – it would be valuable experience."

"Then I shall ride back and get Kit to bring the pony and cart for you both," Farmer was out of the door, whistling to his horse, then mounting and galloping away.

"So, Nell – one old lady lying in bed, hot and in pain, needing sips of water. What should we bring with us?" Avril asked.

As was usual, Nell furrowed her young brow before answering. One thing that made James and Avril treasure the young girl so much was her ability to think long and hard before opening her mouth.

"Feverfew certainly, perhaps comfrey as well for the fever. But it would depend on the site of the pain to know which others to bring," she answered. "If the pain is in the head or the neck and throat, then crushed willow bark. If the pain is elsewhere lower down, then it would again depend. Is the pain a cramp that comes and goes – or is it a persistent pain."

Avril regarded her adopted daughter with pride. Not yet ten years old and already able to think slowly and clearly. Would she be as dispassionate when confronted with a patient in pain? Probably!

"Then we take feverfew, comfrey and willow to begin with. Whatever else is needed will depend upon what we find when we see her. In the meantime, we wait until Kit brings the cart for us."

* * *

Gil, May and Rosie were amongst the first to arrive at the market in Newton Abbot. It was situated close to the church of St. Lawrence and was usually very busy and bustling. However, somewhat to their surprise, it seemed not to be as well populated as on previous occasions. According to a man setting up the next stall, it was because there would be a fair that afternoon around the church on the hill in Wolborough, not half a mile from where the market was situated.

"Fair?" Gil queried. "I thought that such things were not allowed!"

"Well – we be a goodly mile from anyone to stop us, are we not?" the man grinned. Gil, who knew that Rosie had picked up on this piece of information, also knew that he would have no peace that morning.

"Dada," came a voice to his left. "Dada, may we go to the fair, please?"

Gil thought rapidly. He would get absolutely no peace unless he allowed a short visit. But he was determined not to simply give in immediately.

"When you have sold all your eggs, then have helped us to sell all our vegetables, then we could perhaps spend a half hour there."

Rosie set her face into a determined scowl. She would sell the eggs in record time and then badger everyone who passed into buying vegetables, whether they wanted them or not. After all, she had heard her parents and various others say that the best seller of anything was a very pretty little girl – as who could resist a plea from such a child? Rosie already knew that she was regarded as a pretty little girl, so now was the time to start trading on that fact!

Gil had spotted another stall on his right where writing materials were being sold – not that many people knew *how* to write! The stallholder was also selling his time by offering to write letters for those who could not do it for themselves – what had for years past had been called a scrivener. Leaving May in charge, Gil wandered over to the man's stall and viewed the goods for sale – quills, pen knives, ink bottles, paper rolls, sticks of graphite and a few of very thin charcoal.

Making sure he was not seen by his daughter he purchased a roll of paper and three of the strange graphite sticks. He went back to his stall and secreted his purchases under the seat, well out of the sight of prying eyes. He was determined, as was Ella, to encourage Rosie in her drawing as both knew she had a very rare talent.

* * *

Kit Warden, long-time friend of his soldier-mate Luke Farmer, drove the small cart through the gates of Brimley and let down his passengers at the front door.

Luke, promoted to steward on the death of the long-time previous incumbent, met Avril and Nell and took them up the broad staircase to a rather magnificent bedroom. The curtains were drawn back allowing sunlight to stream into the room where they found Lady Violette sitting up in the huge bed, surrounded by pillows and swathed in blankets. Sitting at the side of the bed was Meg, Luke's redheaded wife and Brimley's cook.

"Thank you for coming so promptly," the old lady croaked. "Meg has been attending to me all night long with cooling towels and sips of water."

"May I examine you?" Avril approached the bed. "When did this start and what are your symptoms?"

"Of course, you may. I started to feel unwell yesterday afternoon soon after my dinner – which was as excellent as usual." Meg blushed with pride. "My symptoms? Let me start at the top and work downwards. First, I have a throbbing headache; my face and neck feel burning hot and I have difficulty swallowing anything solid. My arms ache whenever I try to raise them; I have a dull ache in my chest. I am also shivering now and again – just as if I have an ague. Apart from that, I am the very picture of robust health!"

Avril would have expected nothing else from this formidable lady – the blunt and unvarnished truth without embellishment or exaggeration. She placed a cool hand on the forehead, then signalled Nell to do the same.

"Hot, but not as hot as with a severe fever," Nell said.

"Now, place your hands lightly at each side of Lady Violette's neck and tell me what you find."

Two small hands were placed delicately on either side of the neck, fingertips probed, then moved further back, then up and down.

"There are slight swellings to both sides, almost directly under the ears. The neck is also hot to the touch."

Lady Violette sat back and watched the exchange between the wisest woman she had ever encountered and the small girl who was obviously being trained.

"So – we have a fever, swelling in the neck, trouble swallowing, headache and general lassitude, plus periodic shivering. What does that all amount to?"

Nell had reached a conclusion long before Avril had finished speaking.

"Lady Violette has caught some quite nasty infection that has affected her throat, causing all the symptoms – except for the pain in the chest."

"And how would you go about confirming the infection?"

"Please, Lady Violette, may I see inside your mouth?" Nell knelt up on the bed so that she could see properly. Violette obediently opened her mouth wide and said 'Ah' in the usual manner. Nell gave herself a grin of satisfaction.

"White spots at the back of the mouth and over the tonsils. It is an infection of the throat."

"I could not have done better myself," Avril gave her a big smile. "But we have to acknowledge that this would not in itself answer the pain in the chest. Tell me, Lady Violette, is the pain severe or merely a tightening?"

"Certainly not severe – more a bloody nuisance! But it is definitely a tightening of my chest!"

"Nell?"

"Could the infection have spread into the lungs as well? If so, it could account for the tightening and the shortness of breath."

"You, my little poppet, will one day become a physician of some renown. I completely agree with everything you have said. Lady Violette, we will leave you with a few concoctions that will ease the headache, slowly lower the temperature, and alleviate some of the other symptoms. There is no known cure for an infection such as the one you have contracted. Only time, rest and our concoctions. I will leave plenty of them with Meg, plus instructions how and when they should be administered. Could you also tell me why you have not asked for the attendance of the physician from Newton Abbot?"

"What? That drunken sawbones? He would have bled me to within an inch of my life – and charged me a king's ransom for the privilege! No – what I wanted was the advice of a sensible and knowledgeable woman. What I got was two of them!"

Avril had a quiet chuckle. "Bleeding is, to my mind, the first resort of the incompetent. Blood is given to us for a purpose and is best kept within the body!"

"I wonder when the so-called medical profession will acknowledge that sensible women know more about the workings of the human body than most men will ever know. Not in my lifetime I fear – and not probably in either yours or Nell's."

"Well, given that we have to cope with those workings for most of our adult lives, it is little wonder," Avril laughed.

"And now you must let me know what I owe you and your rather brilliant assistant."

Avril looked a trifle askance. "What you have done for the town and the school leaves us all very much in your debt, Lady Violette. Your recovery is all that we would need by way of payment."

Leaving a copious supply of comfrey, feverfew, and an assortment of other medicinal herbs – plus how and when to give them – Avril and Nell decided to walk back to the apothecary shop. Luckily, the weather was fine and dry, if a bit cold.

"Well – that went very satisfactorily," Avril tucked Nell's hand under her arm. "You did all the right things, thought them through, then pronounced your findings and diagnosis as well as I could ever have wished. Let us hope against hope that we are not visited by the winter shaking fever again this winter – or you and I will be rushed off our feet.

* * *

May had good reason to remember the winter fever of almost two years previously – her mother had been hovering on the brink for days until Avril and Mary had managed to get the shaking under control and gently, over a period of two weeks, May and her sister Maud had nursed her back to health.

And now Mary was teaching the young children at the school, she herself was as good as betrothed to Hob, and her mother was again in very good health. Sadly, she remembered those of the small town who had not been so lucky – especially old William who had been churchwarden for many years. Too many deaths, she thought. Who then needs wars – especially between good English people where families had been torn asunder by the strife between the king and parliament?

Gil, May and Rosie had packed up their cart when the very last turnip had been sold. It had been quite a good day, but they then had to travel up the hill to Wolborough to visit the fair. Gil and May sat on the cart and watched as Rosie scampered from stall to stall. On one, a man was making things simply disappear; on another, two young women were juggling plates and balls. Various other attractions caught the attention of the little girl who nevertheless always looked back at her father before she moved to another stall.

"So, May – how is Hob these days as we see little of him."

"Oh, he is keeping very busy, making sure that Master Bailiff sees him doing his tasks thoroughly and properly."

"I would never have thought to see such a change in a lad," Gil grinned at her. "It must be something to do with the influence of a fine, upstanding young lady!"

May blushed, then grinned back at Gil. "Ella says you were a bit like Hob when you were younger – always up to mischief."

"Aye, I suppose I was. But Ella and I were always destined to be together. For a start, we lived next to one another. Then, when I was about thirteen, I realised that we were much more than good friends. It was then that I started to grow up, I suppose. That and the fact that her father is built like a mountain!"

Rosie came tearing back and begged a coin from her father.

"There is a man down there selling the most beautiful ribbons, papa. Please may I have one? It's blue like the sky on a summer morning and so beautiful!"

Gil dug into his purse and brought out two coins and handed them to May.

"Get one for Rosie and one for Ella – you know her favourite colour. And get one for yourself."

Uttering sincere thanks, May and Rosie ran off hand in hand, appearing together after a few minutes. Rosie had her ribbon tied into her hair. May handed Gil a long ribbon in saffron yellow.

"Ella will just love that," she said as Gil wrapped it in a piece of linen and put it safely into his pocket.

"And what colour have you chosen?" he asked a slightly hesitant and embarrassed May. She opened her hand and revealed a wide ribbon in deepest red.

"Then Hob must be the one to put that into your hair," Rosie announced. "It is red and the colour of love! Why *is* red the colour of love?"

"I have not the slightest idea," Gil replied. "You must ask Mary as she seems to know just about everything about everything!"

"You are so lucky, papa, having a sister who is so clever! I wish I was as clever as auntie Mary. Are you and Hob going to marry soon?" she said with a complete change of topic.

"We will announce our betrothal after Christmas," May replied. "Perhaps we shall marry later in the Spring. It all depends on when Hob can get the little cottage for us to live in. But still one thing constantly worries me – it will all be perfect as long as Master Bailiff stays as Master Bailiff. If he were to leave, then I do not know what would happen to us."

"But surely, Harry will take over the duties," Gil said. "He has trained all his life to become Bailiff whenever his father decides to hand over the office. Harry would never abandon Hob and you!"

"But what if Harry and Mary also decide that their life would be better elsewhere?"

"Then my sister would tell me well in advance! May – you are worrying needlessly. You will always have a job with Ella and me, and Hob will never starve – he is far too competent for that!"

"Aye, I suppose I fret needlessly," May admitted. "But one never knows what might happen. There might be another war if Prince Charles decides to try another attack. There might be a far worse fever to come. Life is so uncertain!"

"All the more reason to make the most of the one we have!" Gil took up the reins and got the horse moving. It was time that they went home.

* * *

Primrose Hoggs, the daughter of Henry and Eleanor Hoggs, had just turned nineteen and had been concerned that she had been 'left on the shelf' – that is, until she had become reacquainted with Lieutenant Paul Larkin. Two years previously, she had been struck by the soldier when he had been a sergeant posted in Bovey Tracey. Primrose had been the May Queen one year when such frivolities had been allowed. Since then, and with the withdrawal of Larkin and his small troop, she had immersed herself in her father's trade.

Henry Hoggs was a saddler and was very well thought of for miles around for the quality of his work. His son, another Henry and one year Primrose's senior, was almost as accomplished as his father. His main task over the last couple of years had been assisting in the manufacture of saddles and delivering them whenever necessary. Primrose was also immersed in the same trade – well, almost the same. She took on the work of what was known as a Loriner – one who made the other accoutrements of horsemanship – bits, bridles, girths, reins, stirrups and the like. She was therefore accomplished with all things leather.

The second day that Larkin had been back in Bovey Tracey, he had made a point of seeking her out as she worked in the front of the shop. The way that her face had lit up at the sight of him told him that his short journey had not been in vain.

Since then, she had spent as much of her spare time in Larkin's company – encouraged by her parents who saw in the young officer a good and secure future for their daughter. Primrose did not have the same rosy picture in her mind. She foresaw a future where she waited at home for the safe return of a husband who might not arrive back at all – or arrive back mutilated. All the time he was away she would sit and worry herself silly. She resolved that, if Larkin attempted to take their relationship to its logical conclusion, she would endeavour to get him to relinquish his commission and take up something a damned sight safer.

That evening, Primrose and Paul Larkin sat at a table in the tavern. Opposite them sat another young couple, Gaston Bessant and Glory Allen – much to the annoyance of Glory's brother Zachary, who had to wait at the tables by himself.

Gaston, son of the Huguenot Bessants who owned and ran the bookshop, had proposed to Glory some weeks previously – and had been gleefully accepted. Glory saw this as her escape from life in the tavern – which was hard and relentless. It also helped that she was very much in love with Gaston.

Dick and Sal Allen, who owned the tavern, had agreed that they would seek live-in help as it was not fair to expect young Zachary to bear the burden all by himself. Sal had help in the kitchen – two young girls from the town came in every day to help cook, scrub, prepare ingredients, clean down at the end of each busy day. Dick also had help from a local lad in the brewing of ale – and the Allen brew was renowned far and wide for its quality. Dick also made the honey mead and saw to the storing of the wines. As yet, the Scottish 'Usquebaugh' had not penetrated as far west – that fiery spirit that had taken quite a hold in London and other major cities. Dick knew of it and that its name translated into 'water of life' but had tasted it once and had spent the next hour swallowing quantities of spring water to ease the fire left in his innards by an injudicious huge swig of the liquid.

"Do you think that Charles *will* make another attempt to retrieve his throne?" Gaston asked, unconsciously echoing a thought of May earlier in the day.

Larkin grinned at him. "I wear the uniform of Parliament," he chuckled, "but I am in no wise privy to their knowledge and intelligence. But I can make as good a guess as anyone, I suppose. Charles is, everybody believes, in France or The Netherlands. What he is doing there – apart from siring numerous bastards – is the subject of wild speculation. My *guess* is that he will simply bide his time, as France certainly will not come to his aid with soldiers. Scotland will not come either – although he has been declared their king ever since his father's death – they have had enough of facing Parliament's army - and have neither the will nor the money to do so again."

"The strange thing is that we all seem to have settled for life under Parliament," Primrose added her thoughts. "Who would ever have believed that we English would settle for rule other than by an anointed king? But we have. Perhaps we here so far from Parliament itself, are more able to carry on much as normal, despite not being allowed dancing, fairs of fetes. I suppose we have become resigned to it."

"That is simply human nature," Gaston nodded. "We Huguenots know all too well how to adapt to changed circumstances. We were brutally persecuted in our native France. Those who could, and thank the Good Lord my family was so able, escaped to other countries where our beliefs were tolerated. And now we Bessants are happily resigned to live free from persecution. We are far from the land we loved, but we are alive and thriving – and far more important – accepted."

"Well, I for one am very happy that one particular Huguenot came to settle here and to find for himself an English bride – although I am yet to become that person!"

"Patience, my sweet chou," Gaston grinned at her. "Not long now before you and I make our vows."

Larkin, who had a smattering of French, was greatly amused that Gaston referred to his betrothed as a cabbage. Any English girl would be highly offended. Apparently in French, it was a term of endearment.

* * *

Avril and Nell borrowed the horse and cart from Gil after he had returned. They drove slowly and carefully the short distance to Brimley to enquire about Lady Violette's progress. They found her distinctly more comfortable than when they had left her.

"I am still in the land of the living," she croaked as the pair were ushered into her bedroom. "I have sent dear Meg away to sleep as she has been with me all last night and most of today as well."

Avril coaxed Nell through a thorough examination. Temperature was lower, although not completely normal; throat was easier and swallowing a bit more comfortable; pains in the chest were not as severe as breathing was easier. All in all, a distinct improvement.

"And all done without shedding a drop of blood!" Avril laughed.

Violette sat up a bit straighter and took a sip of the mixture of herbs that were diluted in water. "That is something that I have meant to question you about," she said quietly. "Why do supposedly learned physicians so insistent on letting blood from their patients?"

Avril thought for a moment before answering, knowing that she would be stepping hard on toes that had been steeped in this practise for many hundreds of years.

"It is all to do with the balance of humours," she started. "Hippocrates devised the idea that a person's health relied upon a proper balance between the four humours – blood, yellow bile, black bile, and phlegm. For example, if a patient had an excess of black bile, then hot and wet foods would redress the balance. But the easiest and simplest way for balancing was to let blood from the body. I personally think this is all far too simple – good health relies upon far more than this. Proper food, proper exercise, proper sleep – those are to me the essentials. But that takes no account of the sicknesses that afflict us – winter fevers, agues, headaches. One should spend time with a patient observing and questioning before taking any rash moves. Simply letting blood as a first resort can, in my view, do far more harm than good. And in saying this, I know I shall bring down the wrath of all physicians on my head!"

Violette regarded her for a moment before replying.

"Sooner or later, let us hope that more will take your slow and methodical approach. Observation and thought – now, there's an innovation for you! Blind acceptance of anything has always been anathema to me."

"Then we shall leave you to get a good night of sleep. We shall return in the morning."

"Bless you – and you too, young Nell. The health of this little town is in the safest of hands."

CHAPTER XXI

Despite being 'unofficial' the Reverend James Forbes had continued to live in his house close by the church – and had also continued to hold services as and when he deemed them necessary. Strict Puritanism relied only on individual and mass prayer. The Church of England relied upon ritual, as had the Catholic Faith for centuries before.

Every now and again, he would invite members of the parish to spend an evening with him, when mead would flow, and special cakes would be on offer. As the mead was prepared for him by Dick Allen and the cakes were baked by Evelyn Ramsey, he was never disappointed by cancellations or excuses for absence.

That evening was no exception. Gathered in his parlour were James and Avril Ramsey, Mary and her husband Harry Cove, and Luke and Grace Barton. Peter Cove and his wife were on a visit to relatives in Dawlish. The fire was piled with seasoned logs, sea coal being regarded as far too smoky and pungent. The mead was excellent, and the small mountain of cakes was being rapidly lowered.

Talk so far had been all about the recent happenings concerning the sect The Vale of Sorrow. Most present had been pestering Forbes for an insight into the strange beliefs.

"Believe me, I have really no more insight into their minds than anyone else," Forbes held up his hands in surrender. "But is it so unusual for a group of folk to veer off at a tangent and seek meanings that are obscure to say the least. Take this dear country of ours before Augustine and others brought Christianity here with them. Many in the far-flung villages still cling to sone of those old beliefs. The Green Man, for example – signifying a oneness with the natural world of the countryside. Is that so hard for us all to envisage?"

"Well, no it is not," Avril nodded. "We take a walk along one of our leafy lanes and we hear the wind in the trees, the birds calling, the grasses making their soft sounds in the breeze. It is very easy to accept that there is a force of nature at work."

"Hang on for a moment," Luke Barton interposed. "There is a wide gulf between a belief in a force of nature and a belief in self-destruction!"

"But is it so hard to contemplate?" Forbes argued. "Cast your minds back to the days of Richard and the Crusades. On the one hand we have a large population of Moslems firmly believing that to kill Christians is their duty – and to lose their lives in so doing will guarantee them a place in Paradise. On the other hand, we have a large body of Christians who wholeheartedly believe that to kill Moslems is their bounden duty – and to lose their lives will guarantee them a place at God's right hand. Are these not examples of a wish for self-destruction?"

"But that was a decree made by various Popes," Mary entered the fray. "Surely, we have dismissed all this nonsense by now? Spain ejected their Moslem overlords and now live peaceably cheek by jowl with them – or so it is said. But I do take your point – it is not about specifics, it is all about the willingness of some people to be influenced by forceful argument into a belief that would *seem* to be unreasonable."

"That is precisely the point," Forbes gave Mary a smile. "If I were to burst into your school tomorrow morning and, using my position as a clergyman, told your little ones that the moon really *was* made of cheese – I guarantee that some would believe me because of who I am and the position I hold. People are gullible!"

"Aha!" James grinned. "Can that not also be levelled at Parliament? They cry with a loud voice that the governance of the country should be in the hands of those who are elected and certainly not in the hands of one man who claims to have been put there by divine power."

"But are they not right?" Mary ventured, and not for the first time. "How can it be that a country – any country – be led and ruled by someone who is not there by the choice of the people who are to be governed? Have they – we – no say?"

"That, my friends, is a damned good point!" came a voice from the doorway. Colonel Fisher had tardily accepted an invitation to join the circle. He waved a cheery greeting to everyone, poured himself a glass of mead and plonked himself down in a vacant chair. "It was Charles' insistence on his divine right that led us all into the state we now find ourselves in. All the idiot had to do was to agree to consult parliament, listen to them, and offer some amelioration, and he would still be on his throne. But no – he had to persist in the belief that he was God's chosen – and that to my mind is simply an exercise in self-justification. Utter stupidity!"

Reverend Forbes, who had been Chaplain to Prince Charles, simply could not let that pass.

"Whilst I can agree that the old king would have been better advised to listen and consult, I simply cannot agree that there is no such thing as God's anointed sovereign. After all, there has been such right back to Edgar and beyond. Nobody has ever questioned it!"

"Not until now, no," Fisher nodded. "But consider the proposition put by the Council of State – that the position of king is an office that is filled by someone who is accountable for the proper management and conduct of that office. If you can grant that such an office exists, surely you can also grant that Charles Stuart fell woefully short in such management and conduct."

"But I can grant no such thing," Forbes shook his head vehemently. "The creation of this so-called office of king was to my mind a handy creation that some clever person came up with. If such a notion has any merit, and I would strongly deny that it has, then it was used for one purpose – to get rid of the king."

"With respect, Reverend," Mary gave a slight nod of her head to Forbes, "why is the notion of the office of king so unacceptable? After all, we have the office of sheriff – that is for one year and carries with it certain duties and responsibilities. It also is accountable – therefore, so is the office holder. The office of mayor is a similar case in point. Why cannot this be applied to a king as well?"

"Exactly!" Fisher gave Mary a respectful glance. Avril and James also gave her a nod of approval. Luke and Grace Barton looked a trifle uncomfortable with the notion, whilst Harry simply gave his young wife a look of admiration.

"Because a king, unlike all others, is anointed in the presence of Almighty God!" Forbes declared.

"That simply cannot follow," Mary was not going to let go. "King Charles was the son of James, who was king of Scotland, and the grandson of Henry the Eight's sister. She was the daughter of Henry the Seventh – and he snatched the crown from the House of York – who in turn snatched it from the House of Lancaster. Can Almighty God simply go along with all this snatching and bestow His blessing upon whoever manages to grasp the crown? To me, this makes absolutely no sense."

"I have no answer to that, other than to restate my belief in the power of God to guide us."

James felt that this had gone as far as was acceptable - and changed the subject.

"Colonel – you are a servant of Parliament and know far more than any of us here about the way I which the future may pan out. What are your feelings as to the next moves of Parliament?"

Fisher gave a loud guffaw at this. "My dear sir, you bestow upon me a far deeper knowledge than I possess. I am a simple soldier. I fought in battles at Edgehill, Marston, Naseby, Preston and latterly, at Worcester. I heard snippets of conversation between the major generals; I have since heard snippets in and around Westminster. But that is all they are – mere snippets. There are very determined people at the helm – Cromwell, Brahshaw, Ireton, Ingoldsby – but I am in no way privy to their thoughts. However, I am quite prepared to let you into my own thoughts – thoughts that I shall vehemently deny should the necessity arise! I *suspect* that the Commonwealth will run its course for as long as its most vehement proponents remain alive. When they are no longer steering the ship of state, I *suspect* that the people of this England will return to what they know best – rule by a king. But a king severely overseen and accountable. As I said, these are my private thoughts and will be wholly refuted should the need arise!"

A long and thoughtful silence followed that outburst. None had anticipated such an outpouring. Eventually, young Harry decided to lighten the mood.

"If only Parliament were not so damnably *miserable!*" he sighed. "I share Mary's view that rule by an elected parliament is better than rule by a king who listens to nobody. But it would be a lot easier to accept if they allowed us to be happy – to dance and make music; to watch plays and enjoy masques. We cannot all be dedicating every breath we take to God. We are mere humans and have the need to laugh once in a while!"

"And I have married a very sensible man!" Mary bestowed a kiss on Harry's cheek.

Fisher also recognised that a lightening of the mood would be welcome.

"I'm sure that the people of the cities would wholeheartedly agree with that. In every city I visited during the years of war and strife, the citizens came near to starving in some instances."

"Yet one more advantage we have over them," James grinned. "We in the countryside, grow the food – weather permitting. Show me a country butcher, baker or farmer who did not supply food to his family during the strife. The only real hardship we suffered during the recent years was the visitation of the winter sickness two years past. Thanks to my clever wife and her assistant at the time – Mary – many more would have been lost to us!"

Avril added her own tribute. "And now we have a new helper – young Nell. She is not yet ten years of age but is packing her young brain with as much knowledge as she can manage. To think that she was a desperate little mite of four when she lost her papa – and was cruelly abandoned by her grandfather. It was God's will, I am sure, that led her to us. James and I cherish her as our own daughter. She is our future, just as much as is Mary with her school, Harry is with his time eventually as Bailiff. We are somewhat blessed here in our small town."

"There is something to be said to be far removed from Parliament," Fisher admitted with a wry smile. "To be able to concentrate on your own families, your little town – yes, indeed, something to be said for it! When my time comes to hang up sword and pistols, I shall seek a town or village like this and know that the hurly-burly of power and intrigue is at least two hundred miles away from me."

"Then make your retreat to Devon," James advised. "Whatever you do, go no further west. The people of Cornwall are a separate race. Many speak their old language, and some have the audacity to say they have invented a pasty – whereas we in Devon have been making them for many years. No, Devon should be your home."

"Hm," Fisher grunted. "And what if my thoughts actually come to pass? What if Charles is returned? What if General Monck works to bring him back – as well he might? What of me then? Shall I be hunted down? Perhaps it should be as you say – if all these things come to pass. Shed my past and weapons and hide in comfortable anonymity in the depths of Devon – perhaps, even up on that fearsome Moor of yours."

"Come here in peace and you will be made welcome," James spoke for all of them.

AUTHOR'S NOTE

That is the end of the third in the series. We have got as far as late 1651 with the Commonwealth firmly established. Fairs, Fetes, music, dancing – all strictly prohibited, unless one lived in the depths of the English countryside. Things remained much as they were for a few years more.

The fourth offering – **A TIME FOR CHANGE** – takes us forward, to the end of 1659 and into 1660 – when things did indeed change radically. It is almost as if I have created a minor prophet in Colonel Fisher.

However, the small town during the intervening years did not escape entirely from the vagaries of fate. There was yet another, and more vicious, attack of what they still called the winter fever, taking more lives in the process. Some small businesses flourished whilst a few ended. More children were born to swell the families; harvests were on the whole ample to sustain life.

In the volume just ended I have created a character that would have been viewed with suspicion during the period in question. Young Rosie, daughter of Gil and Ella, showed signs of having been blessed with a wonderful gift. This is certainly not impossible – my own young brother at four years of age was drawing steam locomotives that were accurate in detail and were attributed by some as being the work of someone much older. Unfortunately, there were still many people in the 1650's who would happily have attributed Rosie's talent to a visitation by the Devil – or to witchcraft. Deep in the English countryside, witchcraft was still believed to be a clear and present danger. Sir Peter Lely, the famous portrait artist of the period, was also a child prodigy. Perhaps he and his family suffered similar accusations when he was a young lad in the early 1620's.

Once again, I have to stress that this has been a work of fiction. Some things certainly did happen; some people certainly did exist. Worcester happened, as did the desperate escape of Charles via Boscobel House and a priest's hole. Other things did not happen – the Vale of Sorrow did not exist. But other, and not dissimilar, sects certainly did exist – and were ruthlessly put down. Please, always bear in mind that, unlike today, the vast majority of the population believed firmly in the Creator God, His Son, and the absolute right of the established church. The fact that Puritanism severely restricted the ceremonial associated with The Church, in no way diminished the hold basic belief had upon nearly all of the country. Unfortunately for them, Roman Catholics were regarded as anathema and Catholicism and Popery were abhorred – the reign of Bloody Mary had ended only ninety-three years earlier! This state of affairs was to continue for another few centuries. In some small way, it still exists.

Despite all this, I sincerely hope that you have enjoyed my latest offering and can see it in your mercy to continue with the next instalment. Thank you for staying with me so far.

Jim Marshall
July 2023